I0822906

Born of the Mountain

CHES ALLEN

Clearview Press

Franklin, Tennessee

ISBN: 979-8-9893496-0-9

Library of Congress Control Number: 2023919466

1

A few years ago, I decided to get away from where I'd been living and from what I'd been doing. I ended up enrolling in a small college in the middle of nowhere. Or as local people called it, northwest Iowa. After a couple of semesters, I only had one requirement left to get my master's degree in film. I had to submit a documentary. The documentary was my thesis, but I was still looking for a story I cared about.

One night my hedonistic friend, Laura, showed up at my apartment. She'd been smoking hashish. She was pretty high, which meant she was also pretty annoying. Another thing it meant was that she was feeling somewhat *amorous*.

Conveniently enough for Laura, the college wrestling team had a match that night at the athletic center. From time to time she would go over and pretend to be a wrestling fan. She liked to sit as close to the mat as she could. She said there were usually two or three combatants who made her want to run outside and howl at the moon. But she didn't like going by herself. It was a good way to get rid of her, and I told her I'd go.

After a couple of matches, her intentions had gotten a little too obvious. I was ready to leave, and I went over and stood beside the bleachers. But before I left, I noticed a couple of wrestlers on the college team. They were both nice-looking guys, and *yes*, I stuck around and watched them win their matches. *God knows* I didn't care anything about wrestling. I went back and asked Laura who they were. I should've known from the way they cheered for each other, and from how they laughed and joked around afterward, that they were brothers.

I kept thinking about how close they were and all the energy they had. A few days later, I went to watch the brothers wrestle again. The more I saw, the more curious I was about the chemistry they had with each other. I finally asked Laura what else she knew about them. She'd heard that they were really intelligent and they loved to laugh, but when it came to wrestling, they were completely focused.

It took longer than it should have, but I finally figured out what was right in front of me. My film could be about the relationship between two brothers on an obscure college wrestling team in Nowhere, Iowa. What could *possibly* be more compelling than that? The answer turned out to be, not much.

I introduced myself when they were leaving the athletic center after one of their practices. I was able to repress my inner eighth-grade girl, and tell them who I was and what I wanted. I thought they might turn me down right then. Or say that they had to think about it. I was prepared for some awkward response, but they just started smiling. They looked at each other, and then they said they'd do it.

That was my first encounter with the Armstrong brothers. Sam Armstrong was the reigning conference champion, and John – who was a year younger – had made it all the way to the finals the year before. They were only one weight class apart, and they wrestled against each other all the time.

When they were at wrestling practice, and during their matches, they were quiet and focused. But the rest of the time, like Laura had mentioned, they were totally different. The first time I interviewed them, they started going back and forth at each other about politics. I was talking to Sam, and John cleared his throat. Loudly.

Sam grinned and shook his head. "I think my brother has something to say. Okay, let's hear it."

"I think we should pick up some chicken on the way home. There's a Hilary Clinton Special over at the diner. For $5.99 you get fries and a drink, two withered breasts, two large thighs, and a couple of left wings."

It was a few seconds before Sam said anything. "But it's been so long since we had any seafood. There's a place just down the road that has a new specialty dish. It's called *Lobster ala Trump*."

John went ahead and asked the question. "What does Trump have in common with a lobster?"

"Well, they're both primitive grasping creatures with small brains, and most of their weight is in their butts. *And* the meal comes with a gallon of orange Kool-Aid."

The last thing I'd expected to hear was a comedy act.

John was trying not to laugh. "I can't believe you're *ridiculing* an American hero.

Sam didn't miss a beat. "You mean the *hero* who said that his bone spurs were so bad that he couldn't serve in the military? The *hero* who said John McCain – who spent five years as a North Vietnamese prisoner of war – *wasn't* a hero because he got captured after his jet was shot down? You mean *that* hero?

John shook his head. "No, I'm talking about the *man* who went into public service to protect the country from politically correct, abortion-loving liberals. The *man* trying to keep communist homosexuals from drowning America in debt. The *man* who's protecting the country from atheists and immigrants on welfare."

I got the feeling that they'd been picking at each other since they were kids. It wasn't long before they were arm wrestling. They made a bet. If Sam lost, he had to say that Donald Trump was the greatest president in American history. If John lost, he had to admit that Trump was just a lying con man who didn't care about anybody but himself. They taunted each other the whole time. The blood vessels in their forearms were bulging. They were breathing hard and sweating, but they kept talking.

"Hey John, you know why Melania Trump won't ever get a colostomy? She'll never find shoes to match her bag."

"Oh yeah? You know what Bill Clinton says to Hillary after sex? I'll be home in twenty minutes."

They were even brighter than Laura said they were. If I'd been four or five years younger, I might've considered unleashing my *feminine wiles* on Sam. Or on John. But I was thirty years old. I'd convinced myself that meaningless hookups had kept me from having deeper relationships. I was making a conscious effort to behave myself.

2

Before I decided to get my film degree, I taught for three years in a girl's school. If I was sane, I would've probably stuck around. I loved teaching, but in the end I had a decision to make. I could either stop telling my students the truth, or I could leave. I'm not real big on holding back on the truth, which is one of the reasons I qualify as crazy. It's a trait that I shared with my mother.

I taught English to ninth and tenth graders. They were mostly from affluent families. They did *a lot* of writing, and for the first two or three months, just about everything they turned in was superficial, mind-numbing drivel. Otherwise known as crap. I called the girls by their names when we were in class, but when I was talking to my mother, I called them Suzies.

A lot of the Suzies had mothers, or fathers, who went over their papers before they were turned in. The thinking was that if little Suzie made good grades, she would get into the *right* school, and somewhere down the line she'd end up with the *right sort* of young man. That tended to mean a young man from a family with *lots* of money.

But some Suzies were on the other end of the spectrum. Along with several party animals I had in class, a few of the Suzies seemed to be a bit slow. All they wanted was to keep from failing so they'd have one less class to take in summer school. And in the middle were the B and C students. The average Suzies. That's the way I thought of my students at first, but after a while, I just saw fifteen and sixteen-year-olds trying to survive their adolescence.

They seemed to like being in my class, but they didn't start opening up until the first semester was almost over. By the time we were a few weeks into the second semester, I'd gotten to know them pretty well. One of the party girls finally took a chance and wrote an essay about a friend who had been killed in a wreck. A few weeks later I got a major dose of humility. A girl who I'd assumed was a dullard wrote a beautiful paper about how isolated she felt.

Then one of the smartest Suzies came to see me between classes. She handed me a paper after I promised that one else would see it. It was about the terror of finding out she was pregnant. And the ordeal of her abortion. And the deep guilt she continued to feel. Before long I decided to go ahead and tell her the nickname I'd given her at the beginning of the year. As soon as I said, "Grade Whore," she started laughing. And a few minutes later we were on the floor, holding each other and crying.

When I told my mother about the connection I'd made with Suzie, the former grade whore, she was watering a rose bush in her garden. "Well Ches, as I'm *sure* you know, I'm proud of you for helping that girl. But there's something you need to understand. When you're that open with a student, when you're that *intimate*, you're taking a risk. All it takes is for one parent to charge into the school and complain. If you stay on the road you're on, at some point you'll end up sitting in a room across from a *glowering* administrator who will see you as a problem."

The next year I had breakthroughs with a few more students. As soon as I thought they knew me well enough, I let them know that if there was something they'd written – something private – I would be honored to read it. A couple of weeks later, I got five handwritten pages folded inside of an assignment. A quiet, pudgy freshman handed it to me without making eye contact.

It wasn't just that she was bulimic and that she'd been cutting herself. She wasn't sure about her gender. She was from a devout religious family. If I'd told my department head, I would've had to turn over what she wrote to the school guidance counselor.

We ended up getting together in my classroom eight or nine different times after school. Sometimes she was open, and other times she was guarded and passive. It seemed pretty clear that her bulimia and cutting came from her struggles with her sexuality. I was trying to build her up to the point where she could go to her parents, or the guidance counselor, and say she needed help.

But if she ended up going to a therapist, at least some of what I said to her would come out. I started being more cautious when we talked. And every time I hit the brakes, she sensed it. She started holding back, and then she stopped coming to see me. She had a breakdown right before final exams. I could've helped her a lot more than I did, but I protected myself instead.

I had all summer to think about how much I'd failed her. When I went back for my third year, I did some of what I'd done the year before. I let my students know they could show me anything they wanted me to read. Eleven different girls eventually responded, and four of them – three sophomores and a freshman – wrote about being sexually assaulted during summer vacation. One had been raped, and the other three had been hit or groped. I was through playing it safe.

All of the girls took the sex education class the school required.

It was lame. Some parts might've been useful, but it seemed like it was designed to insulate the administration from parental complaints. I talked one-on-one with each girl who had been assaulted. Some knew schoolmates who were dealing with the same experience. A couple of girls started showing up together, and within a few weeks, they had a suggestion. They thought it would be a good idea to meet as a group.

The girls understood that I needed to be discrete. And they wanted to keep what had happened to them as quiet as possible. Being teenagers, they came up with a pretty devious plan. They got the school to approve an ornithology club, and I became the faculty sponsor. We started taking Saturday morning field trips to various local parks. By the Thanksgiving holidays, two sophomore girls, both of whom had been exploited by boys online, also joined the group. I wanted things to be as informal as possible. I told them they didn't have to call me Miss or Ms. Thompson – they could just call me Ches, which is short for my first name – McChesney.

We ended up identifying a decent number of birds during our outings, but what we basically had, every other weekend, was a group therapy session. Along the way, I told them that one of my college roommates had been raped, and that she was still struggling with what happened. By the time they had all talked about what they'd been through, I still hadn't decided if I should tell them what happened to me.

On a clear and reasonably warm Saturday in early March, I drove six girls to a park in a bend of a river. We walked to an isolated spot at the edge of a meadow, and after a few minutes, four of the girls were lying in the grass and trying to get some sun on their legs. The other two were looking through their binoculars and scanning the edge of the woods for birds. I was a few feet away, sitting against a beech tree. I looked over at the only black girl in the group, who, of course, called herself Blondie.

She was smiling and there was a playful look in her eyes. "Okay, *Ches*, I have a question. When we have discussions in class, you always tell us to join in. Well, we've been spilling our guts, and so far all you've done is listen. Did anything ever happen to you... I mean *way back* when you were in high school?"

The girls who had been looking for birds lowered their binoculars. They were all staring at me.

"Yeah... I have a story. But if anybody doesn't want to hear about it, you need to say something."

They were all listening. And waiting.

"Okay. Here goes. When I was almost fifteen, I was on spring break at the beach with one of my friends and her parents. One morning there I was – *innocent little me* – walking beside the ocean. Looking for shells. All by myself. I heard somebody right behind me, and then there was a hand up between my legs. And I felt fingers touch my *sacred crevice*. I turned around and saw the guy who did it. He looked like he was in college. A couple of other guys were standing a few yards behind him, and they were both laughing.

"I was trying not to freak out, but when I saw his beady little reptilian eyes and the horny little smirk on his face, I started laughing. That definitely ruined the moment for him. I think he already knew he sucked, and he got mad. He called me a bitch when he was walking away, but I couldn't make out what else he said."

I couldn't resist going for a laugh. "Maybe it wouldn't have been so bad if he'd had a halfway decent body. Or *at least* a chin."

I wanted to tell them what they needed to hear. It was a lot more than I'd just told them.

"I got back home a few days later, and when I told my mother what happened, she wasn't surprised. She'd already warned me about stuff like that. Then she told me what I'm about to tell you. The way she explained things… Well, it helped me understand what was going on. But before we get into all that, I want you to take turns and give a brief description of the guy who abused you."

Blondie blurted out, "Asshole." That got some laughs, but before I said anything she added, "Selfish."

Everybody made a contribution or two. Before long we had a fairly good description of an imaginary abuser. The girls decided to call him Biff.

"Okay, so now we have selfish but reasonably charming, vaguely handsome but rude, marginally popular but somewhat arrogant, moron, asshole, party boy Biff. *What* a guy. And there could also be a gay version of Biff, or some other variation. But we'll stick with the version that you guys had to deal with – presumably straight Biff."

My mother had come up with the approach I was about to use with the girls. After I named my abuser Chinless Ted, she had devised a scenario to explain why Chinless Ted had done what he did. I added a few details when I took Biff through the same scenario.

"Let's step back and take a deeper look at Biff. Maybe we can learn something. Imagine one brief period of his life. He's coming off a pretty bad cold. Phlegm has been plaguing him for a week. If he doesn't blow his nose every two minutes, he sneezes. The mucous is coming out one way or another. He doesn't feel all that great, but since he's a moron, he decides to go to a lake house with some of his friends and spend the weekend.

"There is – *surprise, surprise* – a large supply of alcohol on hand, and being a party boy, Biff does more than his share of drinking. At some point, he passes out, or maybe he just takes a nap. Either way, when he wakes up his bladder is *really* full. No problem. He just goes outside. Two or three minutes later, the water around the dock is *a lot* warmer than it was before.

"And, of course, the boys at the lake house also do a whole lot of eating. Biff, who can be a bit of a glutton, has six or eight giant bowls of chili, and at least two large pizzas with extra onions and pepperoni. He also consumes *massive* amounts of chips and cookies. On Sunday, around the time he's halfway home, he is under *extreme* intestinal duress, but he makes it back before anything *catastrophic* happens. And there you have it. For several days, Biff has been engaged in various acts of *compulsory* excretion."

I wondered if any of the girls could see what was coming next.

3

My mother's name was Carla. There were times when I called her *Mother*, but it was usually just Carla. If it hadn't been for Carla, the incident on the beach would've been a lot more traumatic than it was. Ever since I was in fifth or sixth grade, she'd been warning me about what could happen when I got older. By the time I was twelve, I was ready for all sorts of things. Things that were much worse than what eventually happened.

I was an only child, and because I didn't grow up with a father, Carla thought I had to be twice as prepared for what might be coming. She married young, and then she found out that she couldn't have children. End of story. But twenty years after her divorce, and after countless relationships, she discovered that I was on the way. She was in her mid-40s when I was born.

When she talked about it, she'd shake her head and smile. "An unmarried woman bringing a child into the world. How *scandalous*. I was almost as surprised as the Virgin Mary must've been."

I've never been able to sound as distinctive as Carla sounded. I still try to imitate the rhythm of her speech and the way she emphasized certain words, but I never get it just right. She was one of a kind. And it wasn't just the way she talked. It was everything. The girls were poised to hear what Carla had told me about males and sex, but it would've been a lot better if they could've heard it straight from her.

"During the week when he was suffering through his cold, and later on when he was at the lake house, Biff didn't give much thought to that *other* fluid building up in his body. He didn't have to think about it. It happened automatically. Like breathing or digesting his food. Producing reproductive fluid is just one more thing his body does – *all on its own.*"

I didn't detect any embarrassment among the bird watchers. I'd always wondered how Carla knew what I was about to tell them.

"The more Biff's fluid builds up, the more impact it has on his brain. Or at least on one part of his brain. The primitive part of every human brain is located at the back of the skull, near the base. The part that came along later is higher up, near the forehead. The lower brain regulates all kinds of basic functions. Breathing. Sleep. Heartbeats. And sex.

"Back when pre-humans only had lower brains, sex would've been *a lot* less complicated. Their bodies were programmed to reproduce. When their breeding instinct kicked in, there wasn't much holding them back. But fast forward to their less-than-impressive teenage descendant, Biff."

Blondie and the other birdwatchers were locked in.

"It doesn't take much to set off a teenage boy, so imagine what happens when Biff is full of rocket fuel and he sees a girl who rocks his world. And what if it's summer and she's in a bikini? His sexual response gets triggered. Big time. If his brain was being monitored, an MRI would show a lot of change when he sees a girl like that. Or when he looks at porn.

"As soon as the switch on Biff's lower brain gets flipped, his hormones are off and running. Hormones are natural drugs. If Biff acts like he's on drugs sometimes, it's because he *is* on drugs. And the more attracted and stimulated he is, the more his brain chemistry changes. But does that *in any way* entitle the Biffs of the world to do what was done to you girls? *Of course not. No.* And *Hell no.*"

"Biff didn't have to do what he did. Because he *also* has a higher brain. The one behind his forehead. His higher brain is asexual. It doesn't care about sex. Along with having the ability to foresee consequences, the higher brain is there to help him decide what's right and what's wrong. To balance everything out.

"So even though Biff isn't on track to be a rocket scientist, his higher brain usually overrides his lower brain. It keeps him in line. It helps him consider what could happen if he groped the girl in the bikini. Or if he makes a move on his friend's girlfriend. Or on his friend's mother. Or on his mother's friend, or on whoever else flips the switch in his lower brain. His upper brain is there to remind him what's moral or dangerous, and it usually talks Biff out of doing anything especially idiotic.

"But if Biff is drunk, all bets are off. Alcohol doesn't slow down the primitive brain too much, but it basically shuts down the higher brain. That doesn't excuse anything, it's just important to know that there's a lot less holding him back. That's why drinking and sex are such a dangerous combination."

I didn't want to talk too long, but none of the girls were zoning out.

"Back when I started to experience what my mother called *inclinations of the flesh,* she said that when it comes to sex, not to do *anything* I didn't want to do. And she said it was easy to confuse love and sex."

Blondie got me back on topic. "So when we look good to a boy, we're like a drug? Well, that sure explains a lot."

I needed to clarify. "When it comes to their lower brains, I think we *are* like drugs. If we're nice and smart, their upper brains might appreciate us for how kind and brilliant we are, but their lower brains see us as sex objects. Or as *non-sex* objects.

"That's right – guys *objectify* us. And guess what? Even though most of us aren't nearly as awkward about it as guys are, we do the same thing. I *strongly* suspect that some of you have done some objectifying of your own. And guess what else? Turning somebody else on – having the right person want you… That can feel like a drug, too.

"It's more obvious in the summer. Maybe you're at a swimming pool. Or maybe you're just walking down the street. You start looking around. You only glance at most people for a nanosecond. Children? No. Meh-looking kids your own age? No. Dads and moms with their dad and mom bods and their dad and mom faces? *Nope*. Grandpa and Mee Maw with all their sagging, wrinkled flesh? *Oh God no*. But *then*… Then you see a particular face or a physique. Or something else that triggers your *inner life force*. Your brain releases hormones, and *tah dah*, you're on drugs."

A flock of geese flew almost directly above us. They were low enough that we could hear their wings flapping. I took it as a sign, and after a few minutes, we got up and started walking. Seven deer ran out from the edge of the woods when we were close to the river. And right after that, we heard something that was between a call and a shriek. Then it turned into what sounded like a laugh. It was from less than two hundred feet away. I took a couple of steps back and got ready to run.

Blondie looked over at me and smirked. "Well, I guess *somebody* never heard a barred owl before. Don't worry, Ches. They don't *usually* feed on humans."

After that there was another call. 'Caw caw, ca-caw. Caw caw, ca-cawwww.' Blondie said it was supposed to sound like, 'Who cooks for you, who cooks for youuuu.' I thought it was closer to, 'Who *looks* for you, who looks for youuuu.'

We had three more outings. The girls opened up with each other more and more, and some of them got pretty interested in the birds they were seeing. But that day at the park when I talked about sex, one girl recorded what I said on her phone. She eventually sent the recording to one of her friends, and when her friend's mother found it on her daughter's phone, she alerted a couple of mothers who had girls in the club. When they didn't express any concern, she went to see the head of the school.

I was summoned to the office of the headmistress. She had a transcript of what I said. She told me that I hadn't followed school protocol. That I'd made it look like she didn't have control of her faculty. She said that the Ornithology Club was being disbanded, and that I needed to apologize to the girls and their parents.

I told her I appreciated being given another chance, but that I'd done what I did because it needed to be done. I said I wouldn't be much of a teacher if I didn't try to help girls who needed help. I also told her that I wasn't big on making insincere apologies. She seemed relieved when I told her that it would be best if I finished out the school year and then moved on. That's how I ended up in Iowa.

4

When I was on my way to the athletic center to interview Sam and John Armstrong, I thought I knew what to expect. I got there a little after dawn to film their morning workout. Except for two members of the cleaning crew, we were the only ones there. Sam and John were all business. They didn't say a word while they were lifting weights, or while they were executing takedown moves on the mat. They finally sat down in folding chairs, and I turned on the camera.

Sam was breathing hard, and he wiped off his face with a towel. He looked at his brother. "Hey John, how many Democrats does it take to change a light bulb?"

"I have no idea."

"It takes eleven. Ten to sign a petition saying that darkness is unfair, and one to call a handicapped trans electrician."

"Okay Sammy, how many Republicans does it take to change a light bulb?"

"I don't know, John, how many?"

"Four. One to call a Mexican electrician, and three to deport him as soon as he screws in the bulb."

Sam was quiet for a few seconds. "Well, how many Democrats does it take to screw in a light bulb in *the kitchen*?"

"I don't know, how many?"

"It's hard to say. As soon as the light comes on, they all run under the refrigerator."

John nodded and smiled. "Do you know why the Republican crossed the road?"

Sam shrugged. "Nope."

"Because a hungry child was crying on the sidewalk."

The first time I met the Armstrong brothers, I assumed that John was a fervent Republican, and Sam was a stolid Democrat. After they stopped telling jokes, Sam put his towel on the floor and looked at me.

I was zooming in on his face when he asked me a question. "Well, what do you think?"

"You mean about how you and John changed political parties?"

He smiled. "No. I mean the jokes."

"The jokes were good, but... let's back up. Let's start at the beginning. I want to know about your background."

Sam nodded. "Okay. We live out in the country. Between Storm Lake and Emmetsburg. Before our father died, he did some farming and he managed a little restaurant. Our mother is the school librarian and she does some bookkeeping on the side. John and I are the only kids. Money has always been tight. Our father hated debt. So does our mother. That meant student loans were *not* an option. If we hadn't gotten scholarships, we wouldn't have gone to college."

He was quiet for a few seconds, and I zoomed in on his face. "I'm glad this is where we're going to school. We're both good students, and we've turned out to be pretty good wrestlers. Anyway, I'm a senior. After I graduate, unless something changes, I'll be the assistant wrestling coach here. It's just part-time, but I've already been offered the job. I'm pretty sure I'll end up taking some business courses, too. John is a year behind me, and when he graduates..."

Sam broke into a diabolical laugh. "When he graduates, we'll put our *brilliant* plan into action."

It didn't take him long to explain what they had in mind. He and John wanted to see if they could become professional wrestlers. They would bulk up and find a manager, and then they'd find a circuit where they could wrestle as a tag team. Sam already had a name in mind – *The Magnificent Armstrongs*. I didn't know anything about pro wrestling, but if looks mattered, they'd do okay. They'd do better than okay.

I zoomed back out. "Now I understand why you joke around so much about politics. It's your angle. If you can bring some comedy into the ring, it'll be easier to get bookings. You're working on your act."

John was nodding. "Yeah, promoters want the crowd to be part of the show. Sometimes we go to matches just to see what fires up the audience. The more jokes and insults we can learn, the better.

"We don't get to as many matches as we'd like. Especially during wrestling season. We've driven as far as Omaha and Des Moines, but most of the time we just go over to Sioux City. We watch what goes on in the ring – the techniques and all. And like I said, we watch the crowds.

Sam started to say something. "We've only known you for a few days, but is it okay if we call you Ches?"

"Well, let's see. It *is* my name, so..."

He smiled and shook his head. "Okay, *Ches,* I have an idea. Tomorrow night we're heading up to Mason City to check out some matches. It'll be pretty low-rent, but it might help you understand what we're up to. So if you're interested..."

Sam was right. It was low rent. Six or seven hundred people had come to a high school gymnasium to see what was called a smackdown. I wondered if I was seeing something that happened in small towns all across America. After we sat down in the bleachers, I asked him about the fans.

"They're pretty much the same everywhere we've been. I guess they're the same everywhere."

One of the preliminary matches was off the charts. A black wrestler named *Lord Blackstone* was up against a big white guy named the *Amarillo Cyclone.* When *Blackstone* threw the *Cyclone* through the ropes and out onto the arena floor, a woman a couple of rows in front of us started screaming. She was a big, a *really big*, fan of the *Cyclone*. She was yelling at *Lord Blackstone* and calling him all sorts of names.

She was yelling n this and n that, and calling him anything else she could come up with. *Lord Blackstone* was trying not to laugh. Then he started to strut. He was staring right at her. He'd strut a few steps in one direction, and then he'd turn around and strut back. Just to make her mad. And after that, he puffed out his cheeks like he was as fat as she was. He waddled around like he weighed 500 pounds.

The more he mocked her, the madder she got. She was sitting back down by then. She was all spread out on the bleachers, but she kept yelling as loud as she could. The people on her side of the ring forgot about the smackdown. They were just watching her go after *Lord Blackstone*.

She kept screaming at him, and he finally cupped his hand behind his ear. "What's that Big Momma?" She just kept screaming. Then he said, "I can't hear you Big Momma. How about closing your legs?"

She wasn't sure what he meant. "What did you say, *boy*?"

"I said you need to put your legs together. I'm picking up an echo."

The people around her started laughing. She picked up a big cup that was half full of whatever she was drinking, and threw it at *Lord Blackstone*. Most of it hit a man and a woman on the front row. The man didn't do anything, but the woman turned around and started yelling profanities at Big Momma. Big Momma tried to get up and go after the woman, but she lost her balance. She fell down sideways, and she wedged between the seats. The other woman climbed over the people behind her, and started pounding on Big Momma. Then it seemed like the whole section was fighting.

The wrestlers took a break while a couple of sheriff's deputies tried to get things under control. Big Momma's blouse was torn and her hair was messed up, and her face was red and scratched. While they were taking her out of the stands, she was yelling and she gave *Lord Blackstone* the finger. But she was smiling.

I tried to look serious. "So, how long have you guys wanted to be professional wrestlers?"

Sam was laughing. "For a long time. Our Dad was a wrestling fan. He grew up in the South in the 50s and 60s. He'd talk about going to see wrestlers like Jackie Fargo and Tojo Yamamoto, and watching Gorgeous George on television. He took us to a few matches when we were little kids. As soon as we got home, we'd put our mattresses on the floor and turn our bedroom into a ring. It drove our mother crazy, but she usually let us get away with it. And just so you'll know, we've never seen fans get in a fight before."

The longer I listened to Sam and John, the easier it was to imagine them becoming pro wrestlers.

I shot fifteen or twenty hours of video over the next month. The conference tournament was held in the athletic center, and I filmed all their matches. John made it to the finals for the second year in a row. The guy he wrestled hadn't lost all year, but John took the match down to the wire and only lost by two points. Sam was favored to win his division again, but he hurt his right wrist at the end of the second period. He had to finish the match with one hand. He was in a lot of pain, but the other guy never could pin him.

I got some good shots of them holding each other after Sam's match, and then I filmed them sitting together at the medical center when the doctor came out and showed Sam the x-ray of his fractured wrist. The documentary couldn't be longer than an hour, and I had to cut what they said about going into professional wrestling. The faculty committee really liked what I'd done, and before the end of the spring semester, there were three separate showings in the campus theater.

I didn't stick around for graduation. I didn't need to hear a stranger tell me about the meaning of life, and then listen to somebody else spend a half hour reading the names of people I didn't know. I just sublet my apartment for the summer and flew home.

5

Carla pulled up to the terminal at the Santa Fe Airport in a late model jeep. She wasn't that far from eighty – an age she had been contemplating for as long as I could remember. I'd heard one of her pronouncements more times than I could count. "Even if I'm eighty, if I ever start driving an old lady car, you must *swear* that you will kill me."

She'd given her murder a lot of thought. "I only have two requirements. I don't want to feel any pain *whatsoever*, and my corpse must *not* be disfigured. Just slip some sort of potion into my wine glass. It should probably be a drug to make me feel drowsy. And then I can drift off into a deeper and deeper sleep. As for the car that made you kill me, just donate it to some charity."

I put my suitcase in the back, and got in the passenger seat. Then I gave Carla a kiss and a long hug. I hadn't seen her in almost a year. We would've spent the previous summer together, but she had been traveling through New Zealand. It was one of the few places she'd never been. She moved a little more slowly than since the last time I saw her, but her color was good. Her skin always seemed to glow.

She looked at me and smiled. "What do you think of my vehicle?"

"Well, I guess I don't have to kill you yet."

Carla glanced at me. "I tried to make that *abundantly* clear."

After we drove to her condominium on the outskirts of town, she announced that after she had a nap, we were going to a new downtown restaurant. "I want to be at my best tonight. We have *so much* catching up to do."

It was a sunny afternoon and I took the jeep and drove around for a while. In a few hours we would be sitting in a restaurant. She'd tell me all about New Zealand. Then I'd talk about Sam and John and the documentary. Immediately after that, I'd have to tell her that *no*, I hadn't slept with either one of them. And *no*, I wasn't in a serious relationship with anybody else.

Carla was a piece of work. There couldn't have been anybody else like her. That was pretty evident from her unique style of parenting.

Just after I got out of seventh grade, I went to a swimming party. I was standing beside the pool in my white two-piece, and some of the boys were laughing at me. Then they put their arms out like they were airplanes, and started running by me yelling, "Tora, Tora, Tora!" And they made sounds like machine guns and exploding bombs. One of my friends finally saw what was going on, and she came up and handed me a towel. On our way to where we changed, she pointed at the lower part of my bathing suit. My period had started. It looked like I was wearing the middle of a Japanese flag.

When I got home from the party, I got a typical Carla reaction. "Just look on the bright side, Ches. At least nobody thinks you're pregnant."

And then there was Christmas. Carla saw it as a perfect time to embarrass me. Or at least try. It was part of our holiday ritual. The Christmas I turned fourteen, there was a gift from Santa Claus under our tree. I opened it and pulled out several extremely oversized bras.

She picked them up one at a time, and then she glanced at my chest and tried to look confused. I would've laughed, but I didn't want to encourage her. The next year my present was an assortment of enormous panties. She insisted on holding up each pair and making inappropriate comments, but I just shrugged.

She never stopped trying to make me blush. When I was older, there was everything from risque undergarments to adult *paraphernalia*. All I did was look at her and smile. And on Christmas morning, I usually received a couple of framed photographs she'd taken of me during the year. The more unflattering they were, the more delighted Carla was. Me asleep with my mouth open. And drooling. Or with a trophy zit and zero makeup. And awful hair. Picking wax out of my ear. The list went on and on. Needless to say, I *always* made it a point to lock the bathroom door.

That night, dinner went pretty much the way I expected – at least at first. It was warmer than usual for early May, and we sat across from each other at a candle-lit corner table on the heated patio of the restaurant. The air was still. While Carla was going through the last several months of her life, her gaze kept shifting from my eyes to the slowly moving flame of the candle. The sky had turned cloudy, but from time to time she looked up like she was searching for stars.

After I told her about the Armstrong brothers, I waited for the interrogation to start. She perked up when I mentioned how good-looking they were, but instead of asking for detailed physical descriptions, she went back to staring at the candle.

I finally broke the silence. "You're less inquisitive than usual. Are you still tired?"

Carla closed her eyes. "Ches, I have some things to tell you, and I'm not sure where I should start."

She shook her head and it was a few seconds before she said anything else. "I don't like the way I sounded just then. It was too ominous. There should be *music* in my voice, so I'll start over." She took a deep breath and smiled. "My dearest *darling* daughter, I… well I might as well just cut to the chase.

"It appears that you will never be called upon to poison my wine. And according to the physicians who have examined me, I will be spared the *ordeal* of ending up in some assisted living facility. I don't feel especially bad. Just more fatigued than I was."

I understood what Carla was telling me. Emptiness was swallowing me whole, but I tried to focus on what she was saying.

"I've been diagnosed with ovarian cancer, Ches. My doctors insist that it cannot be cured."

I was too numb to gasp. Or cry. I wouldn't let myself think about what she was facing. Or what the world would be like without her. I just tried to keep everything from becoming a blur.

She was determined, as she always was, to display her sense of humor. And her independent spirit. "When the time is right, I plan to revisit my earlier affinity for drugs. *Thank God* I'll have time to indulge in some hedonism before I drift off into the great beyond. I want to make my farewell tour a *celebration.* Knowing that I won't end up having my diaper changed in some *depressing* facility for the elderly is a good reason to celebrate. Don't you agree?"

Carla had spent almost as much time preparing me for her eventual death, as she'd spent warning me about hormone-crazed males. I'd always hated the thought of her living out her final years surrounded by people with worn-out minds and worn-out bodies. I was glad she found a silver lining, but that didn't change the way I felt.

She went on to say that although her particular type of cancer could be aggressive, it was difficult to predict. Some people were more impaired than others. And while there were patients who lived for less than a year with ovarian cancer, a few survived for as much as a decade.

"Ches, I'm more than happy to stay alive as long as I'm having fun. But I intend to make my grand exit *well* before things become grim. We can go into all that later on. I'm not that far from eighty, and the last thing I want to be is feeble and *ninety*. I don't care about longevity, but I'm still quite interested in *levity*."

She released a long breath. "Now are you ready for the *rest* of my news?"

"You mean there's *even more*?"

"Yes, dear. I have two more headlines. Here's the first one. I'm moving back to Nashville. But no, I am *not* going home to die."

I was surprised she was going back. Just about all she ever had to say about Nashville was that it was where she grew up. Carla hadn't been close to her parents. Even though they both lived into my teens, I never met either one of them. I didn't know much about that part of her life. Every once in a while, she talked about how unhappy she'd been, but most of the information I got came in bits and pieces.

Her family had been wealthy. "Sitting on a throne is toxic for the soul. There was *so* much arrogance. And I find arrogance *extremely* off-putting – particularly when it emanates from people of means. I tried to remind myself that I was *not* the one who built the kingdom – *or* the throne."

She had mostly navigated childhood on her own. "My mother and father were *considerably* more interested in playing bridge and attending social events, than in being parents. They rarely took me and my sister along when they went on vacation. They had each *mastered* the art of the perfunctory relationship. Especially when it came to their children."

She kept staring at the flame of the candle, and she ended up telling me a story I remembered hearing when I was a teenager. "When I was a sophomore in high school, I was the only girl in my class without breasts. My nickname was IB, which stood for *ironing board*. There was no point in mentioning it to my mother. She was *incapable* of sitting down with me and saying anything helpful. It would've made her too uncomfortable. She would've just passed the problem along to my father. After he told his secretary to write a letter of complaint to the school, he would've just signed it, and had it mailed to the headmistress."

I'd heard Carla describe her emergence into womanhood in a number of different ways. My favorite was, "At long last, my estrogen awoke from its long, deep slumber."

She had much more to say about the life she lived after she went away to college.

"When I left home I had a clean slate, *so to speak*, but my slate did not stay *pristine* for long. Judging from the attention I began to receive, I was forced to conclude that I had become at least *moderately* attractive. And by the end of my first year, a law student developed an interest in me – an interest that soon escalated to matters of a *carnal* nature. He was older and quite handsome, and he swept me off my feet. I was naive, and the next year, right after he graduated from law school, we married. I was still a teenager. What could have *possibly* gone wrong?"

Carla's husband had made it clear that he wanted children, and that he wanted them right away. "We expended a *great deal* of effort in pursuit of that particular goal. But it was, alas, to no avail. I was examined – quite *thoroughly* – by our physician, and then by a specialist. The specialist tried to be kind. He merely said it was *highly* unlikely that I would ever bear children. But by then I was able to be somewhat *philosophical.*"

She already suspected that her husband was seeing another woman, and then she found out that an affair had been going on since before her marriage. Carla usually laughed about that part of her life. "He was such a *damnable cad.* Getting me pregnant was just a strategy to establish himself financially and socially, and to give his child – or children – a place at *the trough* when my father's estate was eventually doled out. I was naïve, but in the end I learned my lesson."

Carla was facing the restaurant. She couldn't see the traces of lightning in the sky behind her. A thunderhead was slowly sliding into view.

"I was much less disappointed by the divorce than by what I learned from the doctors. I'd always wanted children. I'd always liked them *considerably* more than I liked adults. But all I could do was move on. So I moved on."

Once I got to be around sixteen, Carla was more open about the life she'd lived after her divorce. "I had *a lot* to make up for, or at least I thought I did. The years of being ignored in high school. Being married to *the cad* and missing out on most of college. Being told that I couldn't have children. Being haunted by the thought of growing old alone. But I must say that exploring *debauchery…* That was a rather *delicious* way to take revenge on my all-too-virtuous past."

Carla lived for a time in a commune in New Mexico, but in the early 1970s – not long before she turned thirty – she came home.

"Word of my *loose* lifestyle had somehow reached Nashville. And my mother, no doubt *deafened* by the whispers of society, *persuaded* me to come home. She delegated our family attorney to inform me that my trust fund had some *strings* attached. But he tried to be polite. He said that if I did as I was told – if I began behaving with a degree of *discretion* – I would continue to enjoy the fruits of my economic good fortune."

The thunderhead was closer, but we couldn't hear any thunder.

"My father offered to buy me a house, but I didn't want a house. I didn't want all the *headaches* that came with having a place of my own. I ended up living in my sister's guest cottage. In exchange for her *generosity*, I helped with her children. She and my brother-in-law were *sadly* lacking as parents, but I really liked their kids.

"For the first few years, I was everything from their chauffeur to their cook to their tutor. I managed to have several *reasonably discrete* flings along the way, and then my life took something of *a turn*."

Most of the time, when Carla talked about her life, she sounded like an actress delivering lines in an old movie. She would speak a little more slowly than usual, and she took delight in bestowing theatrical emphasis on certain words. But her cadence had changed.

"If I ever write my autobiography… Well, one of the most compelling sections would begin in the mid-1970s, when I met a rather unusual young man."

Carla finished her wine, and she looked at me. "I said that I had *two* headlines. There's a little park just down the road. It would be a good place to tell you the rest of what I have to say."

I hoped it was far enough from the lights of town to give us a good look at the thunderhead that was moving in.

6

The thunderhead was massive and brimming with light, but there still wasn't any thunder. It towered above the landscape. Every time it erupted, the park was briefly illuminated. I was telling myself the same thing over and over. If my mother was ever going to tell me what I'd been waiting so long to hear, it would be then. Right after she told me she was dying.

I wasn't in suspense for long. "Ches, it's time you knew about your father. Maybe I should've done this five or ten years ago, but I wanted you to know about him – and meet him – at the right time."

I'd always assumed he was alive. Carla would've told me about him if he was dead. There were times when I wondered if he was a drug addict or an abusive drunk. She could've been waiting to see if he would get past whatever his problems were.

I'd never stopped asking Carla about my father. When I was younger, she just deflected my questions. Or ignored them altogether. But the older I got, the more I ached to know who he was. And the more persistent I was. I tried everything I could think of. I'd be rational and convincing. When that didn't work, I was emotional. But no matter how much I begged or cried, or threatened to run away from home, she wouldn't budge. I ended up telling myself that she must have a good reason for holding back. That's what I told myself, but I wasn't sure it was true.

Carla touched my arm. "I haven't told you his name, but I've mentioned him before. We became friends back in 1976."

I knew who she was talking about. "You mean the guy who made you laugh all the time?"

Bursts of lightning surged inside the thunderhead and illuminated her face.

"Yes, dear. His name is Mac Allen – McChesney Allen. I gave you his first name."

Back when I was an insecure girl trying to disappear, I hated having a name that made me stand out. Having a name like McChesney was bad enough. But being called Ches was worse. I knew that Carla's nickname had been Ironing Board. If I ended up being as flat as she was, at least as flat as she'd been at first – or if some recessive gene with a sense of humor cursed me with a big rack – I knew what would happen. It wouldn't be long before Ches became *Chest*. Thank God that what I ended up with didn't subject me to any ridicule. By the time I was sixteen, I really liked my name.

I was overflowing with questions, but I kept quiet. Carla said that she and my father had known each other for over ten years by the time I was conceived. "We met when I was thirty-three. Even though Mac was in his late twenties, there were times when he seemed like a teenager. But there were other times… There were times when he could be *pretty* wise. But however young or old he acted didn't matter. From the first time we met, I felt like I'd known him my whole life. And I've never understood why."

She said that my father had spent something like forty years coaching grade school boys in sports. "Mac always said that the reason he was good with kids was because he was still a kid himself." And she told me that one of his passions was researching the history of his neighborhood. "At some point, I asked him why he did it. He said it was to keep good things from being forgotten."

The thunderhead erupted again. "Before you start asking questions, I'll tell you a little about Mac. He and his wife have four grown children. The last time I saw him was right after I found out I was pregnant with you."

"By then we'd been friends – well we were clearly a good deal *more* than friends – for eleven years. We'd see each other off and on, but we also saw other people. At one point I spent a year in Spain. But no matter how long I was away, when we got back together… it was like we'd never been apart. He'd have periodic *dalliances*, but he was usually preoccupied with some girl who was too young for him. I'll let him tell you about all that.

"When he was in his late thirties, he fell for a young woman named Elinor. She was in her mid-twenties. He'd known her back when she was in high school. He talked about her a lot, but she was engaged to somebody else. Mac and I just kept doing what we'd always done. Seeing other people, and from time to time seeing each other."

The thunderhead was still silent. "Mac had been talking about history for as long as I'd known him. Maybe that's why I finally got curious about the history of my family. Right around the time I turned forty-four, I got motivated. My parents were spending the winter in Hawaii, and I was staying in their house. At some point, my mother had paid a genealogist to research our ancestry. I remembered seeing a large envelope with the information that had been compiled. I had to look around for a while, but I finally found it in a box in the attic."

The tone of Carla's voice changed. She sounded like she had

walked out onto a stage. The thunderhead lit up, and I glanced at her. Her chin was raised, and her eyes were properly expressive. "And *what* a surprise. I didn't just find the envelope – I also found a small brown *packet.* And the packet contained my adoption papers. I had always been told that I was born in Miami, where my parents were staying at their vacation home during the war. But the papers I found showed that I had been adopted in Tennessee. The woman who I *assumed* was my mother… She had *somehow* neglected to tell me that I was *not* her biological child.

"I read through everything in the packet several times. Then I walked around the house for a while. My mind wouldn't slow down, and I finally called Mac. When he walked in the door, he was singing *Someday My Prince Will Come*, from the movie, Cinderella. And he started right in on me. 'Some aristocrat *you* turned out to be. Shouldn't you be back in the kitchen, scrubbing the floor? Are you missing a glass slipper?' He ended up keeping me company for two or three days."

The thunderhead was finally close enough for us to hear a low rumble. "And that is *precisely* when my reproductive system – defying the *dire* predictions of medical science – allowed me to become pregnant with you. And an abortion was out of the question. I fell in love with you as soon as I knew you were part of me.

"I would've told Mac I was pregnant the minute I found out, but from the way he talked about Elinor… I had to find out if they could end up together. If he knew I was carrying his child, he would've *done the noble thing*. If Elinor really was his soul mate… I couldn't take that away from him."

Distant thunder rolled across the park again. "Mac had always wanted me to meet Elinor, and it wasn't long before the three of us went out to dinner. I'd been wondering about the same thing for eleven years. Whether Mac and *I* might be soul mates. There were times when I thought we might be, but he'd never looked at me the way he looked at Elinor that night. We can talk about tears and loss some other time. I think they already knew that they belonged together.

"I left town not long before I started to show. I still called Mac every couple of weeks, just in case I was wrong about his relationship with Elinor. But I wasn't wrong. She broke off her engagement to the other guy, and that was that. You were around two when she and Mac got married, and that was *really* that."

There was a light rush of wind along with the thunder.

"And here's the rest of it. Mac doesn't know about you. He has no idea that he has a daughter. Elinor started having children right off the bat, and I never told him. By the time you turned twelve, you had three half-brothers and a half-sister. What kind of relationship could you and Mac have had? Maybe I was wrong, but I didn't think it would be good for you to know about him, or for him to know about you.

"He and I wrote back and forth for a few years, but the letters got farther and farther apart. We eventually just stopped writing. Maybe I felt guilty for not telling him about you. But I have a friend who kept me up to date about Mac and his family. He and Elinor live in the country, a few miles out of Nashville. Even though I haven't seen him for over thirty years, I know how he'll react when he hears about you. He'll be stunned at first, but trust me – he'll be fine. I'll let him know about you as soon as I move back.

"If I had the energy, I could spend the next three months telling you about him, but I wouldn't know where to start. There's so much you should know."

I could hear some fatigue in her voice. I said that she should pace herself. That we'd have plenty of time to talk about it later. But she got a second wind and told stories for another hour. I finally said that we both needed to get some sleep. Mac Allen sounded like he was at least as far off the bell curve as I was – which was saying a lot.

He and Elinor lived in a log house out in the woods, and they mostly kept to themselves. Mac had written a few books that not many people had read. Some were about local history, and some were about people he knew. People who were dying. He thought they'd lived consequential lives, and he hadn't wanted their stories to be lost. One of Carla's friends had sent her copies of the books he'd written, and she'd read them all.

She told me that not long after they became friends, he'd written a novel. She didn't read it until the mid-1980s, when he was thinking about getting it published. She said I'd learn a whole lot about Mac if I read it. She sounded like she was smiling.

We got back to the condominium, and after she went to her room, I took the jeep and rode around for a while. I jumped back and forth between Carla dying, and finding out about my father. Knowing his name – just hearing Carla say, *McChesney Allen* – made me feel like I was in a dream. I almost lost it a couple of times. I pulled off the road, but there was too much to cry about, and I didn't end up crying at all.

When I got back to Carla's, I didn't get on the Internet and look for my father's photograph. When I saw him for the first time, I wanted him to be right in front of me. And I didn't want to read about him online, or hear any more about him from Carla. I wanted to hear everything straight from him. It was a little before dawn when my brain finally started slowing down. I didn't wake up until the next afternoon.

7

Carla didn't have as much energy as she'd had the year before, but she made all the arrangements to move back to Nashville. Just about all I did was help her pack boxes. A few days after I got to Santa Fe, we were clearing out a bureau in her bedroom.

She opened a drawer and looked over at me. "Are you ready to hear more of my *compelling* life story?"

I wasn't sure if she was about to tell me about her adoption, or talk about her parents. Or about Mac. "I've been ready."

Carla raised her eyebrows and took on a British accent. "My sensitive, *precious* child, all you had to do is ask."

I pretended to be a child in Victorian England. "Oh, Mother dear, *do* tell me another story!"

Carla dropped her accent. "Well, *dear*, this chapter explains why we live so well. It starts with when I discovered that I was adopted. I thought about not telling Mother what I'd found out. Leave things the way they were. Just shut up and keep on *pretending*."

I hoped that she was about to turn herself loose.

"But I was too *angry* to pretend. And I wasn't just mad at my *supposed* mother, I was mad at myself. My intuition had been *screaming* at me for years. Like an air raid siren. I'd always been different from the rest of the family, but it wasn't just that.

"My mother had always kept me at a distance. I watched my friends and their mothers. How their mothers kissed them. Gave them hugs and stroked their hair. The only times I got that from Mother was when she thought somebody was watching. And she was almost that distant with my sister."

Carla closed the drawer of her dresser, and a small frown crossed her face.

"When she came back from Hawaii, just after she got home, she brushed my cheek with her lips. The same way she always did. It was her version of a kiss. A couple of days later, I ambushed her in the breakfast room. I didn't show any emotion. Or any disappointment. I just told her about finding my adoption papers.

"She stared at me for a few seconds and then she looked away. She was irritated. 'Well now what? I suppose you have all sorts of *questions*.'

"I only had a few. When I asked her why she hadn't told me I was adopted, she said that if I'd known, I wouldn't have felt like a member of the family. Then I asked her – as casually as I could – who else knew about it. 'Except for our doctor and your father and our attorney, no one knows who matters.'

"I didn't need to ask her why I'd been adopted. Or why my adoption was such a deep, dark secret. It was obvious. While her friends were having babies, she had remained childless. She absolutely *hated* being seen as inadequate – biologically, or in any other way.

"As soon as they knew they were going to adopt me, she and my father had to come up with a cover story. People would've known that I wasn't their biological daughter if they had stayed in Nashville. But if my parents left town, she didn't have to look pregnant. She wouldn't have to eventually explain why her child looked older than she should've been.

"They decided to spend several months at their vacation home. They spread the word to everybody they knew. And just before they left, Mother confided to her *closest* friends that although she wasn't certain, there was *just a chance* that she was expecting.

"The adoption paperwork had already been completed, and within a day or two, they picked me up from wherever I was and they took me to Florida. At some point they must have written home and conveyed the *joyous* news. That she was, indeed, with child. And because she was in such a *fragile* state, the doctors thought that the long trip home was ill-advised. Sometime later, when I no longer looked suspiciously *old*, I was brought home and finally introduced to the people *who really mattered*.

"And after expending all that effort convincing her friends and acquaintances that she had become a mother, guess what? A few weeks later, she *did* get pregnant. If it had happened any earlier, she would've had an abortion. The timing would've been too close for comfort. I'm sure she was proud of how *fertile* she appeared to be. She had *two* daughters to show off. I was always aware that Mother felt closer to my sister than she felt to me. By the time I found out I was adopted, I'd spent over forty years of my life trying to understand why."

She walked to a window and looked outside.

"You've already heard about how I grew up in the *lap of luxury*. But you need to know what happened when I told Mother I was pregnant with you. She was well aware of what my out-of-wedlock pregnancy would do to her image. Of course, she assumed that I would have an abortion.

"When I informed her that I was determined to have you, *and* raise you… Well, she was more than a bit *miffed*. Her ladylike demeanor *entirely* disappeared. She raved and ranted, and then, *of course*, she said that if I did not do as I was told, I would be disinherited. It didn't work. In 1973, when I came home from the commune, I had been dependent on my usual income. But after that, I paid *considerably* more attention to financial matters.

"I received quarterly disbursements from the family trust, and over the next decade and a half, I managed to make a number of *exceedingly fortunate* investments. After I told her I had all the money I needed, she was fuming. I stayed calm, and that infuriated her even more. Then I let her know that I had my eye on a *very* nice home. Just off Belle Meade Boulevard. I said it was in a *delightful* neighborhood. That it was an *ideal* place to raise a child. She kept imagining her *illegitimate* grandchild growing up in full view of the leading members of local society, and the social humiliation she would experience. I enjoyed watching her fall apart.

"That gave me *a lot* of leverage. I could've been magnanimous, but I thought a lesson might be in order. My mother and my father were both *obsessed* with money. One of their mantras was, 'Never leave a dollar on the table.' I wanted to show them that their advice had not fallen on deaf ears.

"Mother was still glaring at me, but her expression changed – at least slightly – when I said I had a solution. I said I understood how *awkward* it might be if I raised my daughter in Nashville. I told her that I would consider moving away, but that I had two conditions. The first condition was that my portion of the family trust would be converted into a new trust – one benefiting me and any children I might have. The second condition was that the first condition was not negotiable. She was *beyond* resentful and *beyond* furious, but she didn't have a choice and she knew it. And what made her even more resentful – and even more furious – was that she understood that I knew it, too."

Carla never saw either one of her parents again. When they died, she didn't go back for either funeral.

She sealed up another box. "One of my Nashville friends told me that Mother cooked up an elaborate explanation for why I left town and never came back. She told her friends that I had become engaged to an older European divorcee. She let it be known that she hadn't approved of the marriage, but that I had married anyway. She said she still loved me very much, *so* very much, but in the wake of my *defiance*, we had become estranged. She claimed that the subject was so painful, so *very* painful, that she just couldn't bring herself to discuss it."

Carla tilted her head and smiled. "Well, she was *nothing* if not creative. And she pulled it off. She and my father and our doctor and our lawyer are all dead – and so is my sister – so none of the people who *mattered* ever knew I was adopted. Or had any idea about what became of me. I only had three friends who knew about you, or why I left, and every one of them could keep a secret."

8

The house Carla bought in Tennessee wouldn't be ready for several weeks, and she had to postpone moving in. We flew to Portland and rented a car, and we spent nearly a month driving down the Pacific Coast Highway. After we got back to Santa Fe, we packed up the rest of what Carla was taking to Nashville. By then I'd decided to move there, too.

When Carla made what she described as her *triumphant* return to Nashville, the first thing she did was take a detour and cruise through her old Belle Meade neighborhood in her jeep. Then she drove several miles to her new house, which was in an area where nobody would know who she was. I planned to live with her until I found a place of my own, but I needed to go back to the college and clear out my apartment.

After I bought a nondescript used car in Nashville, I left for Iowa. It took me a couple of days to get to my apartment, and I went straight from there to the athletic center. Even though it was the summer semester, I expected to find Sam and John practicing moves on the wrestling mat, or working out in the weight room. But they weren't around. I went back three more times without seeing them. After a few days, I was ready to leave for Nashville, and I decided to give it one more try. I talked to a woman on the cleaning crew. She had heard that Sam was sick, but she didn't know any details.

I finally found another guy on the wrestling team. He said that Sam had been in the hospital, and he gave me Mrs. Armstrong's phone number and address. I didn't get an answer when I called, and I ended up driving an hour and a half to their house.

When I pulled into the driveway, John was leaning back in a chair in the shade of a big tree. He got up and came over as soon as he saw me. He looked worn out. His mother had taken Sam to dialysis. We went inside and he got me a glass of tea. It was the first time I'd seen him when his eyes didn't sparkle. We sat down and he told me what had happened.

"There was a cage match in Sioux City, and Sammy and I went over to check it out. It was pretty good. We'd gotten to know a couple of the guys who work security. They said there was this bar where the wrestlers went whenever they were in town. We were curious about what went on after a match, and we got there a few minutes before they showed up.

"They were drinking a lot of beer, but they were pretty laid back. Then some girls walked in and sat down in a booth on the opposite side of the bar. One girl was wearing a T-shirt with a big American flag on the front, and this huge wrestler – he calls himself *Brando* – he started talking to the girl. It wasn't long before he got obnoxious. The girl tried to ignore him, but he kept standing over her. When she and the other girls tried to leave, he wouldn't let them.

"One of the other wrestlers went over and tried to get *Brando* away from her. *Brando* pushed the guy into a table and some beer bottles fell off and broke on the floor. Her friends got away, but the girl in the flag T-shirt couldn't get past *Brando.* When she started crying, Sammy and I got up. All he said was, 'Watch my back.'

"*Brando* saw us coming. 'Well what do we have here? Looks like somebody's lookin' to get their asses kicked.'

"Sammy had a big smile on his face. 'No sir. We're just fans. We saw you wrestle tonight at the Arena, and we hope you'll let us buy you a beer.'

"Sammy wrestled at 197 pounds, but it was off-season and he weighed about 220. *Brando* was around six-foot-six, and he weighed at least 320. Sammy was only twenty feet away from *Brando.* He'd stopped walking, and I was a few steps behind him. I looked over at the other wrestlers. They were just watching. *Brando* had turned away from the girl in the booth, and he seemed to relax a little. But when she saw an opening and tried to get up, *Brando* reached out and shoved her back into the booth.

"She started crying harder, and as soon as Sammy took a step toward her, *Brando* charged. I backed up and Sammy made a quick move behind a table, but he slipped in the beer and hit the floor. *Brando* almost fell, too, but he caught himself on a chair. He kicked the chair over, and while Sammy scrambled up, *Brando* threw the table out of the way. I got the girl, and after we made it to the kitchen, she ran out the back door.

"When I got back to Sammy, *Brando* was trying to corner him. But Sammy was too quick. He faked to the left, then he cut behind a couple of tables, and we both took off. We got away, and I thought we'd be laughing and talking about how Sammy's first match against a professional wrestler was a draw. But when we got in the car, blood was dripping from his right wrist.

"He'd cut it on a piece of broken glass when he was getting off the floor. I thought we should find a hospital and have it stitched up, but he said it could wait until morning. He held a T-shirt against it the whole way home. It stopped bleeding by the time we went to bed, and after breakfast, I drove him to see our doctor. Sammy got eight stitches. He was mad about the workouts he'd have to miss, but we started smiling about what the other wrestlers would say about *Brando* trying to beat up a couple of college kids."

Four days later Sam woke up during the night with a fever. By morning his heart was racing and he was confused. "Our doctor saw him, and admitted him to the hospital. He was diagnosed with a sepsis infection that probably came from the cut on his wrist. Within a few hours, he was transferred to intensive care and put on a ventilator. Six days later he woke up from a medically-induced coma. His kidneys weren't functioning, but his condition had stabilized."

I couldn't think of anything to say. John looked over at me. All he said was, "Ches… I know." I was pretty sure he didn't want to be alone. I fixed sandwiches, and we were eating outside when Sam got back with his mother. He struggled a little getting out of the car. He walked like an old man. He'd lost some muscle, but his eyes were still full of life. I talked to Mrs. Armstrong for a few minutes, and after she excused herself, John went for a run.

Sam was sitting across from me at the kitchen table. I must have looked as sad as I felt, and he reached over and squeezed my shoulder. "Okay Ches, here's the way I see it. If I can't be Johnny's partner, there's no reason I can't be his manager."

He brightened up. "I've already come up with a name. *The Iowa Farm Boy*. When he climbs into the ring, maybe he'll be wearing red white and blue overalls. With some stars and stripes. He can still use our jokes, and there's plenty of time to come up with more material. He doesn't want to hear it, but there's an advantage to what happened. Instead of wrestling at 184 pounds next year, he gets to move up to 197. When he has to bulk up later on, he won't have as far to go."

Not long after I got there, we were sitting under the tree in front of his house. After he told me a few jokes he'd come up with, I finally asked him what he and John really thought when it came to politics. He said they saw things pretty much the same way.

"We have friends, and some relatives, who argue about politics all the time. But we're mostly middle-of-the-road. Like if immigration comes up, one side wants to turn away every migrant who shows up at the border, and the other side wants to let almost everybody in. But immigration is complicated. We can't take everybody, but so many of those people are heroic. They were living through hell back where they were, and they need help.

"One side says women shouldn't be able to get abortions, and the other side says women should make their own decisions. Destroying a fetus seems unnatural, but it doesn't seem right for the government to decide what happens when a woman gets pregnant.

"One side wants to see most murderers get executed. The other side thinks society should look at why criminals do what they do. Sometimes we'll hear about a killing. We'll talk about how much we'd like to tear the guy apart. But later on, if we read that the killer got beaten up by his drunk father all the time when he was little, we end up feeling sorry for the guy.

"And when it comes to gun rights, one side says everybody should be able to carry a gun, and the other side says almost nobody should. Some people hunt, and people need to protect themselves, but a whole lot more people – innocent people and kids – get killed by guns in America than anywhere else in the world.

"But when it comes to the environment… Well, we're both pretty clear on that one. People we care about keep saying that human beings don't have anything to do with the climate. But way before we were born, scientists were predicting exactly what's happening to the environment right now. They've been saying the same thing for over a century. If there's too much carbon in the atmosphere, the planet will keep getting hotter and droughts will get worse, and all the rest of it. Some people still want to argue about it, but that's exactly what's happening. All people have to do is open their eyes and look around."

9

Sam shook his head. "Has the world always been this messed up, Ches?"

I pretended to be insulted. "How old do you think I am? *Ninety-five*? Well, hold on a minute. Let me put on my spectacles and look for my walker. Then I might be able to find my teeth and answer your question."

Sam was smiling. "This seems like a good time to change the subject. There's something I've been wondering about. We've gotten to be friends, and I... I want to know more about your life."

"Like what?"

"Well, like boyfriends you've had. Or if you've ever come close to getting married. But if that's too personal..."

"I don't mind personal. So, boyfriends... Let's see. I had one in high school, but it wasn't all that serious. My first heartbreak was in college. His name was Les. He was movie star good-looking. And authentic. He wasn't curious about the world and we didn't have much to talk about, but I really don't have anything bad to say about him. We just didn't fit together. But *God* was he good to look at.

"The next one was Andy. He was *a lot* brighter than Les. His parents were both social workers, and even though that's what he said he wanted to be, I couldn't see it. He was a nice guy, but he was pretty materialistic. And he spent way too much time looking in the mirror. His ex-girlfriend – the one he had right before I came along – you know what she told me? She said he was so vain, that he yelled out his own name during sex. I thought she was kidding, but later on, I wasn't so sure.

"Then there was Jan. He was off-the-charts smart. He said he felt closer to me than he'd ever felt to anybody in his life. I felt the same way about him. It was a long time before I figured something out. Pretending to be intimate was a game for him. The whole time we were seeing each other, he was giving a couple of his friends a running account of what he and I talked about. And what we were doing. Jan would've been a great spy. I guess he got a rush from being deceptive."

I didn't go into it with Sam, but all those relationships had one thing in common. I wanted to know as much as I could about each one of those guys. Who they were. How they looked at the world. We talked a lot at first, but the longer we were together, the less they had to say. I wanted to know more about them than they wanted to know about me. I didn't understand it, and it bothered me.

I couldn't tell if Sam wanted me to keep talking.

After a few seconds, he glanced over at me. "I don't know the best way to ask this, but how… how does it feel to look back on all that? I mean do any of those relationships still mean anything? The reason I'm asking… Well, I've been in love – I mean I guess it's love – since my last year of high school."

I knew what to say. "What's her name?"

"Liza. And she's great. She just got tired of having to compete with wrestling. We stayed together until my second year in college. I was working out and studying all the time, and she finally pulled the plug. We talked about getting back together, but now… She's called a couple of times, and she wants to come by. I don't want her to see me like this. I mean, what's the point?"

I tried to be careful. "You asked me about my old relationships. I guess I'm not too good at moving on. I think about Les and Andy and Jan every day. Most of what we had was real – even with Jan the spy. I still care about those guys. I hate the idea that those relationships… That they could end up not meaning anything.

"I'm sure you don't want Liza to feel… empty every time she thinks about you. Every time she looks back on the way you felt about each other. You've been part of her life, and she's been part of your life. The way I see it, she needs to see you. You need to see each other."

That was as hard as I needed to push. She came to see Sam the next day.

A couple of hours after we talked, Sam was resting. I was outside with John, and I asked him how he saw the future.

"Well, Sammy will keep getting his treatments until he has a kidney transplant. I wish I could be a donor, but I'm not a match. I guess that would've been too easy. If I stay in school, he'll do some coaching and take a few classes. If I go ahead and turn pro, I'll need a manager. If he finds something else he wants to do, that's okay, but I'm pretty sure he wants to manage me."

Then he stared into my eyes. "I'm not sure when it'll happen, Ches, but I'll catch up with *Brando*. I'm gonna make him pay for what he… did to Sammy."

The day before I left for Nashville, Sam and I were in the house alone. I had a feeling there was something he wanted to tell me.

"My doctor says I should have a hope button and a reality button.

The hope button is thinking that I can get a kidney transplant. Or that there could be some kind of medical breakthrough. The reality button is understanding that I might not make it through this. You've already told part of our story. If something happens to me, I want you to do another documentary. Maybe the story of John becoming a professional wrestler. Or maybe just the story of him trying.

"I'm worried, Ches. About what'll happen if I check out. Wrestling can keep him connected with me. If you did another documentary, I would be part of something that's still going on. I know it's a lot to ask, but..."

I didn't let him finish. "You know what they say about great minds. I'm already thinking about part two. You can cross that off your list. I'll do it. I promise. And you'll be part of it."

After he told me how much it meant to see Liza again, he talked about missing his father. Then he said how much he loved John. And the love he had for his mother, and the way he felt about wrestling, and about where he lived, and how blessed he was to have the life he'd had. By then he was getting tired. When he went to his room to lie down, I went outside and took a walk. I stayed on the road until I saw an abandoned farm. I walked across a field and went behind a shed, and I cried until I couldn't cry anymore.

10

It was a long drive back to Nashville. The further away I got from Sam and John, the more I thought about McChesney Allen. I would've tried to prepare myself, but I didn't know what to prepare myself for. I kept trying to imagine the moment when I'd meet him. What he'd be like. What I'd be like. I'd go through one door, and then I'd go through another one. I finally just turned everything loose. Whatever happened, would happen.

I got to Carla's house early the next afternoon. The home she bought was in a neighborhood about ten miles south of downtown Nashville. It had originally been a farmhouse, and in the 1940s it was enlarged into a good-sized residence. In the front was a sea of big houses and big yards, but behind it there was a hill that was too steep to build on.

I helped her make dinner. That's when I told her about Sam Armstrong. After we ate, we went out onto the back porch. Carla sat down on an outdoor couch and looked over at me.

"Ches, I'm getting in touch with Mac in the morning."

I was afraid she might've already called him. And that he hadn't wanted to see her. Or me.

"Unless he's changed – and I'm *highly* confident that he hasn't – he'll be… Well, he'll be *more* than glad to hear from me.

"I've told you some of this before, but when I left here in 1987… In some ways, Mac and I were as close as we'd ever been. A few years after that, I wrote him a letter. I told him it might be a while before he heard from me. I said I'd always love him, and that the next time I saw him we'd have *a lot* to talk about. After thirty years most people would assume a relationship is over, but Mac is not most people."

I slept late the next morning. Carla was gone by the time I got up. I tried to imagine the conversation she was having with my father. My heart was beating too fast, and I had to take some deep breaths. I ended up climbing over the back fence and hiking up to the top of the hill behind the house. I walked around for a while, and when I came back down, there were burrs all over my socks and my jeans. Then I took a shower. It seemed like time had stopped.

It was late afternoon when Carla finally came home. She smiled and gave me a long hug. "Like I said last night, Mac Allen is *not* most people."

Carla had called him at 9AM and by 11:30 they were eating lunch. She didn't go into much detail. She knew that I wanted to have as few preconceptions about him as possible, but she told me a little about what happened. She let Mac know that she'd read all of his books, and that she knew a little about each one of his children.

"While we were waiting for our food, Mac said, 'This *might* be a pretty good time to tell me why we haven't seen each other in thirty-two years.'

"Ches, I'd memorized how I was going to tell him about you, but I changed my mind. All I said was, 'Remember what the doctors said? About how I'd never have children?'

"He didn't move. He just stared at me for what seemed like a full minute. Then he said, 'So I take it that you had a child?'

"When I told him about you, all he said was, 'Are you sure it's yours?' It was classic Mac. He hasn't changed. When he doesn't know what to say, he comes up with one-liners.

"Then I said, 'Yes, Mac. I'm *fairly* sure the child you fathered – the child I named after you – is mine. She goes by Ches. She is brilliant and wonderful, and I think you'll love her as soon as you meet her.'

"Mac had a big smile on his face, but he started signaling for a timeout. He said before I told him anything else, he had to call Elinor. He wanted her to know what was happening. We all got together a couple of hours later. And Elinor... Well, she has just as much grace as she had before. If she was gritting her teeth, I couldn't tell. She said it might take her a while to get used to being a stepmother, but she's looking forward to meeting you."

I felt like laughing and crying at the same time. Questions were swirling around, and I swooped in and devoured one at the edge of the swirl. "So he really said, 'Are you sure it's yours?'" There was something comical about the look on Carla's face. It set me off, and as soon as I started laughing, so did she. It took us a long time to stop.

After I got in bed and turned off the light, the questions started swirling again. Would he like me? Would I like *him*? Would he see me as an obligation? Could he end up loving me? Thoughts hovered and darted away. Like hummingbirds. Carla had waited thirty years to tell him about me. What would he say? What would he *keep* himself from saying? How much would he want to know about me? How much should I tell him? I didn't fall asleep until it was starting to get light outside.

11

Carla talked to Mac again the next morning. She suggested that we meet at a little neighborhood playground in Nashville. It was called Woodmont Park, and it was close to where he grew up. I got there right after lunch. I was a half-hour early. The sun was out and it was the middle of June, but a cold front had moved through during the night, and it wasn't especially hot.

Two mothers were watching their kids playing in the sandbox. A guy with a backpack was pushing a stroller on a walkway that ran along the perimeter of a grassy field. And an older man was standing at the far end of the park. He was wearing jeans and standing near a baseball backstop. He was looking at me, but I wasn't sure it was Mac Allen. Then he put his right forearm across his waist and bowed. After I gave my best version of a curtsy, we started walking toward each other. A breeze was flowing into the park, and I felt it touching my face.

I kept walking, but I felt like I was floating. When we were four or five feet away from each other, we both stopped. I was close enough to look into his eyes, and I saw the same emotion I was feeling. I stared at him until I couldn't see through my tears. I was trying to hold on, and when I felt his arms go around me, I almost broke.

He held me until I took a deep breath, and then he let go and wiped his eyes. He didn't say anything until we started walking to a picnic table under a tree.

He tried to lighten things up. "I sure hope your name is Ches."

I didn't want to start crying, and I tried to look surprised. "Ches? You mean you're not my Uncle George?"

He pretended to be confused. "Somewhere along the way I got old. I'm not always sure who I am, but I'm pretty sure that Ches is my biological daughter. I wish I could tell you about her, but I didn't know she existed until yesterday."

I stayed in character. "I'm a little curious. If Ches… if she happens to show up. I mean what are you planning to say, you know… to the daughter you just found out you have?"

Mac closed his eyes. "I've been trying to figure that out since yesterday. I guess I'll have to play it by ear. I just don't want what I say to be… hollow."

"What if she shows up and you don't recognize her?"

He looked at me and smiled. "That won't be a problem. I'll know her as soon as I see her."

We held each other again, and then we sat down at the picnic table. Before long I was telling him a lot more than I thought I would. He heard all about my childhood, and how I felt about growing up without a father. Then I told him how Carla had gotten me through the worst of my angst-ridden junior high and high school years.

I was talking about college – telling Mac about majoring in English – when we both noticed a green inchworm swinging back and forth between us. It was suspended by a barely visible thread.

When the angle of the light changed, the filament disappeared from view, and the inchworm seemed to be floating above the picnic table. The breeze came and went, and the worm kept moving from side to side.

After I finished talking about college and a couple of the boyfriends I had, I talked about teaching, and why I gave it up. He didn't say anything until after I told him about Sam and John, and about the documentary I'd made.

He looked over at the inchworm. "I've been thinking about what I would've done, what I *could've* done, to help you. I mean if I'd known… If Carla had told me. I like to think that things would've been better for you. And for me. But it might not have gone that way. I'm looking at how you've turned out. What I'm about to say… It isn't because I'm in shock. You are… *spectacular*. There were probably times when it would've been good to have me around, but maybe you didn't need me."

I thought about saying, "Aw Shucks," or telling him he might end up changing his mind, but I let it go. All I said was thanks. The inchworm lowered itself onto the table and started crawling, and I told Mac it was his turn to talk.

He smiled and took a comically deep breath. "I'm not surprised that Carla wanted us to meet here. Woodmont Park would be just another subdivision if it hadn't been for her."

He shook his head. "But I need to back up a little. A lot of what I want to tell you, about this park and everything else, is in a book I wrote back when I was about to turn thirty.

"Not long after your mother and I got to be friends, my life turned upside down. Instead of going crazy, I wrote the book. Most of it is autobiographical, but not everything. So that makes it a novel. It's too long and too complicated, but ten years after I wrote it, I decided to take a crack at getting it published.

"A lot of it was about Carla, and I had to make sure she was okay with what I'd written. I let her read it, but she took off before we could talk about it. Yesterday she said she still has it. I told her it's fine with me if you read it, but... Well, some of it..."

I was trying not to smile at how uncomfortable he looked.

"Even though I tried to be tasteful, there are a couple of parts you might want to skip over."

He didn't need to worry. "I'm well aware that my mother was, and is... a free spirit. She's been making me cringe since I was little. I'm pretty sure I'll survive no matter what you wrote."

Mac grinned at me and shrugged. "Well, if you end up finding out more than you want to know, it isn't my fault."

We went back to watching the inchworm. He didn't say anything else until the worm got to the edge of the table. "I just thought of something. You're almost the same age I was when I wrote the book. One minute I was thirty, and the next minute I was wondering what in the hell happened to all those years. And the minute after that, I'm looking at you and trying to figure out if I'm hallucinating."

12

Mac said that Woodmont School, where he went in the 1950s, had stood right where we were sitting. He told me a little about growing up, and before long he was talking about how much he'd loved his neighborhood and how hard it was to watch it change. "When you're a kid, you think the world you're growing up in... You think it'll last forever."

Mac was a teenager when he started coaching grade school boys – along with an occasional girl – in basketball, baseball, and football. He didn't stop until four decades later, after he'd coached his own children. "I held onto my childhood for about as long as I could." Then he pointed to where the baseball field had been. "There were times when working with kids was closer to group therapy than it was to sports. There was so much more to coaching than taking infield and batting practice. Or blocking and tackling. Or working on rebounding and fast breaks."

He glanced down at the inchworm. It was exploring the edge of the picnic table.

"Just about every year during baseball season, one of my players would come across an inchworm. I'd stop what we were doing and get them to watch how it moved. Just like we're doing now. See how its midsection arches up when it brings its back legs close to its front legs? And how its back gets flat when it stretches out its front legs? I'd ask the kids why inchworms move that way. Scrunching and unscrunching, instead of just crawling.

"It took a while, but somebody would eventually figure out that they move that way because they don't have legs in the middle of their bodies. Then I'd let them guess what they eventually turn into – if they don't get eaten by birds first. They were usually surprised that they turned into moths. They thought they'd be butterflies."

Mac tilted his head a little. "And there's something else about an inchworm. Know what it is?"

Something had already occurred to me, and I wanted to impress him. "Well inchworms are a pretty good metaphor for American politics. If they had support from the middle, they'd move a lot better."

He smiled and shook his head. "And the blue ribbon goes to Ches Thompson."

I wanted him to keep talking. "But what were you going to say? You know, about the inchworm."

He ran his fingers along the edge of the table. "Well, I don't know if there's room for another metaphor about political moderation, but here goes. When an inchworm arches its back, it looks a whole lot like the last Greek letter. Omega. *The grand finale.* What happens to a society when it loses its middle class. And its political moderates."

I didn't want to start talking about the sorry state of American politics. Not yet. It would change what was happening between us. Before we said anything else, the inchworm raised up on its rear legs. It seemed to be looking around.

Mac looked at me and smiled. "I guess we all need to get our bearings from time to time."

We kept watching the inchworm, and Mac went back to talking about his life.

He told me why he didn't marry until he was forty-two. "I'd done an *excellent* job of staying immature." How he thought he'd done as a father. "It's better to be lucky than good. And to have a great wife." Why he immersed himself in the history of his neighborhood. "The way neighborhoods change over time says a lot about the arc of the country."

When I asked how he felt when Carla told him about me, he didn't say anything for a few seconds. "Well at first I thought she might be kidding. Then I felt numb. I shouldn't have worried about how Elinor would take it. She wasn't happy about it at first, but then she smiled and said, 'Well isn't life interesting?' After that, we took turns imitating the way our kids will react when we tell them about you. Elinor is a lot funnier than I am, but my impression of our daughter made her crack up."

We talked until the shadow of the tree we were under had stretched all the way across the field. By the time the shadow faded away, the inchworm had disappeared under the picnic table. Mac tried to find it before we left to meet Elinor for dinner, but it was gone.

After we left the park, we met Elinor at a restaurant. She couldn't have been too thrilled that I turned up, but she was friendly and gracious. I didn't know how I would've responded. She was smart and funny, and she had no idea how beautiful she was. Two days later, Carla and I were invited to Mac and Elinor's log house out in the country. To meet their children.

I wondered how they'd feel about having a half-sibling suddenly show up. Or how I felt about having three half-brothers and a half-sister. It was a strange situation. There was a little awkwardness at first, but it probably came from me. They were mostly curious. I didn't know how close we'd end up being, but before long, the little bit of tension there had been was pretty much gone.

I was only a little older than Mac and Elinor's oldest son. He had been married for a couple of years. He and his wife were kind and quiet and authentic, and his younger brothers were both open and friendly. My new half-sister was eight years younger than I was. She and Mac never stopped exchanging insults, and they kept everybody laughing.

We were halfway home before Carla said anything. "If I'd known Mac's kids would be that welcoming… I should've told you everything a long time ago. All those times you asked about him… And not telling you until you're thirty. If you're still angry…"

"It's been a long time since that made me angry. You just thought it was better to wait. It was a judgment call. You handled it the way you thought you should. And you didn't know how they'd feel about me. Having a stray child show up at the door… If I'd met them when I was ten, or when I was twenty, it might not have been the way it is now."

After sitting under the tree and talking to Mac at Woodmont Park, and then seeing the way he was with his children, I was getting an idea of who he was. When I got back to Carla's, she pulled out her copy of Mac's typed manuscript. I could tell that she'd read it more than once. It was called *Parables of Light.*

I thought I'd read a couple of chapters after dinner, but I had a hard time putting it down. It wasn't what I expected. I stayed up late that night, and the more I read, the more questions I had.

13

By the time Mac and Elinor left town for a family wedding a few days later, I'd finished reading his book. None of the parts he was worried about had made me uncomfortable, but I never would've guessed what he was involved in. Or what he'd gone through. I asked a lot of questions over the next few months, and I got plenty of answers.

Not long after I read the book, I was eating breakfast with Carla on her back porch. My cell phone rang, and it was John Armstrong. His voice was hollow. He told me that Sam had pneumonia, and that he was getting sicker. And weaker. After I packed a couple of bags and got my camera, I was on my way to Iowa.

I tried to forget the fear I'd heard in John's voice. Sam would be better by the time I got there. I went over everything I'd say, and I thought about all the questions I'd ask him when we did our next interview.

I drove as far as I could before I stopped at a little motel not far from Des Moines. I got an early start the next morning. I called John when I was about a half hour away. He didn't answer. When I got to the Armstrong's house, it looked like nobody was home. I knocked anyway, and an older lady – a neighbor – finally came to the door. She was crying. Sam had died about an hour earlier.

She didn't know when John and Mrs. Armstrong would be back. The phone in the parlor rang, and after the lady excused herself, I started walking around outside. I wanted to feel as much as I could. I wanted to hurt.

I imagined John and his mother standing beside the hospital bed. Sam's last wisp of life fading away. The two of them lingering in the room after he was gone. A hospital tech finally pulling up the sheet and covering Sam's face. His body lying in the stillness until it was taken away.

I was in a daze, but I'd made Sam a promise. After a few minutes, I got my camera out of the trunk, and filmed the desolation of the Armstrong place through my grief. It wasn't desolate for long.

Relatives and friends and neighbors started driving up, but I kept filming. They parked their cars in the field next to the side yard, and they brought in food and arrangements of flowers. I tried to be as unobtrusive as I could. I got some glances and nods, but no one asked me who I was. By the time John and his mother came home, the front porch was decorated with flowers. A table had been put up under the big tree in the front yard, and it was heaped with food. I stopped filming when John walked up.

The pain had settled deep in his face. He gave me a long hug. "I don't know how you got here so fast." I nodded at the camera and started to explain, but he shook his head. "I'll let people know what you're doing. Film anything you want."

A young married couple was walking toward John, but he looked up and stared into my eyes. "Give me a few days and we'll…"

I squeezed his arm. "I'm not going anywhere."

Mrs. Armstrong had a spare bedroom. She invited me to stay there, but I ended up going to a motel about ten miles away. I wanted to be alone when I cried. When I screamed into my pillow. During the next couple of days, I interviewed people who were close to Sam. I got plenty of stories about how inseparable he and John had always been, and how beloved they were in their community.

A nice-looking guy showed up at the house the night before the funeral. He wasn't much older than I was. He must've been the only person of color within thirty or forty miles. He came back the next morning before the service, and he spent a long time talking to John and his mother. I wondered if he was somebody I should interview, but he left before I asked John who he was.

The visitation and the funeral came and went. Sam was buried beside his father in the family graveyard – a few hundred feet from the house. It was a relief when all the activity settled down. When nobody was around, I went out to the cemetery and talked about how I thought the documentary should unfold. At some point, I had to interview John about Sam's death. I was dreading it.

If John ever broke down, I wasn't there to see it. He went for long runs in the morning, and I'd see him doing pullups on the bar that he and Sam had put up at the top of their bedroom door, back when they were in high school.

Two days after the funeral, John said he was going on a road trip the next day. He wanted me to go with him. Driving all the way to Sioux City to watch a professional wrestling extravaganza sounded about as appealing as a six-hour pelvic exam, but there's no way I would've turned John down.

It was an hour and a half to Sioux City. I kept waiting for John to start talking about Sam, but we just listened to CDs. I got the feeling I was hearing the same music that he and Sam had listened to on their way to the last match they would ever see together.

John got a couple of calls, and I watched him while he was on the phone. The road he thought he'd be traveling with Sam had turned solitary. I didn't want the rest of his life to be diminished – or defined – by what happened with the career he wanted to pursue.

The Event Center in Sioux City was the region's main venue for professional wrestling. John said that ticket sales had fallen off over the last few years, but on that night, the arena was mostly full. Our seats were only about fifty feet from the ring. It was several minutes before the first match, and I was studying the fans sitting nearby.

Two guys at the far end of the row in front of us had beards and tattoos, and they were both wearing camouflage pants, tank tops, and baseball caps. There was a clean-cut young couple in our row, just a few seats down from us. They were in their late twenties or early thirties, and they'd brought along a couple of toddlers. On the other side, there were three drunk teenage boys. And sitting right in front of us – between two counselors – were five men and three women from what must have been an adult group home. One man seemed almost catatonic, and there was a young woman with Down syndrome. She looked like she might start bouncing off the walls. She was jumping around, and every time one of the spotlights swept across her, she let out a squeal.

A few people in the crowd were carrying signs. Some had the name of their favorite wrestler. Others said insulting things about wrestlers they hated. When it came to wrestling, there was something I was curious about. I would've asked John what percentage of the audience thought that what they were seeing was real, but it was hard to hear anything above the mix of heavy metal and country music that echoed through the arena.

After a few minutes, the center got dark, and when red, white, and blue lights started sweeping across the crowd, there was a huge roar.

Born in the USA was blaring from the overhead amplifiers, and before long, just about everybody around us was singing. The singing continued during the national anthem, and a couple of minutes later, the first group of wrestlers came out of the tunnel and made their way up into the ring.

The crowd heated up even more, and I kept studying the people around me. I remembered Carla smirking on the rare occasions when the subject of professional wrestling came up. Before I met Sam and John, I'd never watched wrestling on TV. I just didn't think about it. I saw it as fake wrestling. It took me by surprise.

I was surprised that the wrestlers – both the men and the women – were so athletic. And a lot of what they did was dangerous. I hadn't expected to see a 300-pound bodybuilder get on top of the ropes – and then jump on a guy who was just as big as he was, and drive him to the canvas. It was choreographed, but the falls and collisions were real.

When a wrestler was introduced, spotlights swept across the audience. Lasers flashed from the ceiling to the floor. Music reverberated, and most of the people in the arena cheered. Sometimes a popular wrestler picked up a microphone and talked to the fans, or a villain taunted the crowd. The jeers and boos got louder as the night wore on.

Some people in the crowd were getting revved up on beer, but the animated young woman from the group home didn't need any alcohol. Nobody was more absorbed in what she was seeing than she was. She cheered when her wrestlers were winning, and when they were losing, she booed and grimaced and put her face in her hands.

The seats behind us were empty at first, but then a family – a mother and father, and a girl and a boy who looked like they were in junior high school – showed up. The kids didn't cheer for anybody, but when the villains made their entrance, the mother and father started screaming and cursing, and then they stood up and screamed and cursed some more. The parents were vitriolic, but their kids weren't paying attention.

I could feel spit hitting my neck during the most passionate parental eruptions. John was getting hit, too. He was irritated, and he finally leaned over and said there was somebody he wanted me to meet. I looked back as we were leaving. The man and his wife who had been yelling were resting up for the next match. They were staring straight ahead and holding cups of beer. Their kids were looking at their phones.

We went around to the entrance of the main tunnel. John talked to a security guard who waved us through. The tunnel led to a corridor, and we walked a few hundred feet before we came to an open office door and went inside.

The young black guy I'd seen at the Armstrong's house was sitting at a desk. He was on his phone. He looked across the room and nodded at John, and then he smiled at me. There were four large TV monitors on the wall. Two showed the wrestling ring, and the other two showed various sections of the crowd. I assumed I was there to meet the guy behind the desk. After a couple of minutes, I was still trying to figure out who he was and why John wanted me to meet him.

When he finally put down the phone, he stood up and walked over to me. His name was Cassius Caruthers, but he went by Cash.

14

"It's really good to meet you, Ches. I've been hearing about you ever since... Well, since right after John and Sam met you. I've watched your documentary four times. We have a lot to talk about. I mean as soon as you're up for a conversation."

Whenever Cash was in town, an official at the Event Center let him use the office. John sat at the desk and started watching the match on the TV monitor. I followed Cash to a sofa near the door.

I had some questions, but Cash spoke up before I said anything. "I'm sure you're wondering how I met the Armstrongs. Three years ago, Sam wrote me a letter. I was working for the WWE."

I must've looked lost.

He smiled. "I apologize for the acronym. WWE stands for World Wrestling Entertainment. It's a multinational corporation, and I'd just started working there. Since I was the new guy, I had to deal with random letters like the one Sam wrote. He was in his first year of college. In his letter, he said he was writing an English paper.

He was researching a professional wrestler named Owen Hart, who died back in 1999. Hart had fallen about eighty feet while he was being lowered into the ring in Kansas City. I could tell from the letter that Sam was pretty bright. I couldn't understand why a college freshman would want to write about a dead wrestler. I was intrigued."

And I was intrigued by Cassius Caruthers. Not many people would respond that way to a letter from a random college kid.

"Anyway, I sent him a good bit of information about Owen Hart. Later on, he mailed me a copy of his paper. It knocked me out. Here's a kid out in Iowa, and he writes something that's at least as good as what underclassmen in Ivy League schools turn out. I went to graduate school at Princeton, and I still don't write as well as Sam did back then."

I was wondering how a guy who went to Princeton ended up in the wrestling business.

"We stayed in touch after that. The next year there was a cage match in Des Moines, and I sent him a couple of tickets. Sam brought John along, of course, and we got to hang out afterward. I couldn't get over how driven and intelligent – and how funny – they both were.

When I came back through a couple of months later, I stopped by their college and saw them wrestle. By then Sam was already asking how they could turn pro after college. They were both tall and they had big frames, and they were both good athletes. I didn't see any reason why they couldn't gain enough weight, and get strong enough, to eventually compete."

I wanted to know more about Cash's background. "I have some questions. If I don't ask them now, I might forget what I want to know."

It didn't take him long to fill in the blanks. He was named for an uncle who'd been named for Cassius Clay. He was an only child, and he'd lived in Illinois and Indiana before his family moved to

Minnesota. His father was the pastor of a fundamentalist church. His mother was a social worker, and she was a fixture in her husband's congregation.

Cash had played football and wrestled when he was in high school. "I wasn't all-world, but I held my own." He was a good student. "I worked pretty hard and I read all the time." And he went to the same Bible college his father had attended. "I should've gone to a big school and had a little fun."

He majored in theology and minored in history. "Back then I thought they were the same thing. I had professors who said I asked too many questions, but I kept seeing contradictions in the Bible and I was looking for answers." After college, he worked for a year and got a student loan, and then he enrolled in Divinity School at Princeton. "I was still a believer, but my fundamentalism didn't survive my first semester."

Following his graduation, he became an assistant minister in a small-town church. "I enjoyed getting to know the people in the congregation, and I wasn't half bad at giving sermons." He fell for the daughter of a local black business leader, but she broke off their engagement. "Her parents kept telling her how hard it would be to raise a family on a preacher's salary." He resigned after two years. "I'd been getting less and less sure about what I believed. My parents still haven't gotten over the last time we talked about religion."

Then he joined the Marine Corps. "I started out as a chaplain, but I ended up as an intelligence analyst in Okinawa. That's where I was when I figured out what I wanted to do."

Cash leaned back on the sofa. "I remembered a sermon I'd given, back when I was pastoring my church. It was about how television evangelists were undermining Christianity. I talked about all the smoke and mirrors and showmanship, and went into how televangelism was a lot like professional wrestling. But what came to me when I was in Okinawa didn't have anything to do with religion. It was about how to make money, a *lot* of money, in the wrestling business.

"I'd always had a morbid curiosity about showbiz wrestling, but I wasn't a big fan or anything. The athletic part is important, but people want to see a lot more than that. They want to see stories. They want to see plays. I figured out that professional wrestling is missing a huge opportunity.

"What goes on in the ring has gotten way too predictable. It's stale. *News flash!* America is politically divided. The wrestling audience – the people who go to events and buy merchandise and pay to watch matches on television – I'm convinced that those people are ready to see a lot more politics in wrestling rings."

Cash leaned forward. He was talking a little louder and a little faster than before. "Why not have characters represent political issues? Have a generic Republican against a generic Democrat. Have a doctor who supposedly performs abortions wrestle against somebody pretending to be a pro-life activist. A black protester against a Klansman. A gun-rights fanatic against a school shooting survivor. The possibilities go on and on. They could scream at each other and rile up the crowd before every match. And after it's over, whoever won could insult everybody who was booing."

It was a couple of seconds before I said anything. "You'd have to spend a whole lot of money on security."

Cash didn't miss a beat. "You're right. But most wrestling revenue doesn't come from fans who go to arenas. Most of the money comes from network deals and home subscriptions and selling merchandise."

After the match he was watching was over, John stood up and yawned. Then he went out to stretch his legs.

Cash didn't say anything until John closed the door behind him. "You've probably figured out why he wanted us to meet."

I decided to flirt a little. "Well let's see. John wants to be a professional wrestler. Isn't that the business *you're* in? Could it have *anything* to do with the documentary I'm about to make about John? Could *that* be why I'm here? And when I first met the Armstrong brothers, they were already working on their act. Is it possible that they've had a mentor in the wrestling business this *entire* time?"

Cash was smiling. "How do you feel about the input I've been providing?"

"I'm not sure. I have a few hundred more questions, but for now… I guess I should just be glad that John has this… this *dream* to go after."

He looked over at me. "I feel the same way, Ches."

I liked it when he said my name.

He was quiet for a few seconds. "I… he needs both of us right now. I promised Sam that I'd help John any way I could. It won't be easy, but I'm pretty sure he can make it as a wrestler. I meant to come up and introduce myself… you know, when I saw you back before Sam's funeral. But at that point, I was barely keeping myself together. It wasn't the right time.

"A documentary could really help his career. Some parts of entertainment wrestling can be pretty opaque, so if there's anything you don't understand – or want to know – I hope you'll ask me. And I need to tell you something, in case John hasn't already told you. He's skipping his last year of college. I'll be his agent, and I'm trying to line up a trainer. Right now he probably weighs around 210, but he needs to put on *at least* fifty pounds before he gets in the ring with anybody."

He glanced over at the door. "And there's one other thing. I assume you know how Sam got sepsis."

I just nodded.

"When it comes to *Brando*, John is playing a long game. Last week we were just driving around. He hadn't said anything for at least an hour. I thought he was asleep. I looked over and he was staring straight ahead. He had this, I don't know, this... grim expression on his face. He just said, "It'll take me a while, but I'll get him."

I needed to interview John and Cash as soon as I could. I wanted to film them talking about what was ahead. Capturing John that early in his journey could take the documentary to another level.

John came back a few minutes later. We told Cash goodbye and went back out to our seats. The man and woman behind us were on their feet, screaming at a tall, muscular wrestler with long red hair. Their son and their daughter were still looking at their phones. The young woman from the group home had lost some of her energy, but from time to time she stood up and let out a high-pitched boo.

I still wondered how many people in the crowd understood that they were watching a mixture of scripted moves and impromptu theater. I was sure that the woman from the group home believed she was seeing a fight between two enemies. The khaki-wearing guys at the end of the row in front of me were really into the violence. When they stood up and started yelling, their fists were clenched and there was anger in their faces. It was pretty clear they believed, or wanted to believe, that the wrestlers had a deep hatred for each other.

The teenage boys sitting next to the aisle seemed to know what was going on. Instead of watching the matches, they were laughing at the other people in the crowd. From what I could tell, the couple behind us thought the wrestlers were really fighting. I wondered if they hated their lives, and if screaming was how they got rid of their anger.

And I wondered how many people in the crowd were at least a little turned on by how the wrestlers looked. It was pretty obvious that muscular, bare-chested young men in tights, and athletic young women showing plenty of skin, helped bring in the crowd.

After a while, I came up with a different way of looking at the matches. I told myself that when a wrestler was standing on top of the turnbuckle, just before he dove down into the ring, he wasn't taking on the other wrestler. He was taking on *the Phantom*.

The Phantom was the ligament damage and the dislocated shoulder that was only one miscalculation away. When wrestlers were thrown through the ropes – when they landed on a concrete arena floor – *the Phantom* was the cuts and sprains and broken bones that were bound to come along sooner or later. And when wrestlers were being held upside down, just before being driven headfirst into the canvas, *the Phantom* was the broken neck that could send them to the hospital and end their careers.

After another hour of flashing lights and booming music and body slams and contrived hostility, the last match finally came to a close. I was worn out, but I still had a long ride ahead of me. On our way out of the Event Center, John and I were a few feet behind a well-built young guy with a military haircut. He was walking beside a high school kid who was limping. They were probably brothers.

The younger kid looked like he had cerebral palsy, and he was moving as fast as he could. In front of us, and right behind the two brothers, were a couple of big drunk guys. They were in their thirties and they were wearing sleeveless shirts. One of them yelled, "*God Dammit! Get movin'*!"

The kid's older brother was average-sized. He kept walking, but he half-turned his head to see what he was dealing with. Then the guy behind him yelled again. "I said get out of the way, you little *gimp*!"

In one motion, the older brother spun around and grabbed the drunk by the throat. The drunk fell over backward, and the young guy didn't let go of his throat until the back of the drunk's head hit the floor. The other drunk looked stunned and he just stood there. The two brothers started walking again. There wasn't time to be scared. John didn't say a word, but he was smiling. It was the first time I'd seen him smile since Sam died.

15

I stayed in Iowa long enough to interview both Cash and John. I asked a question every now and then, but mostly I just listened. I learned a little more about what lay ahead for John. He had lost five pounds since his brother died. He only weighed 205, but he thought he could get up to 260 in the next few months. Some heavyweights, including *Brando*, were a whole lot bigger than that. When I asked John if he was worried about being able to pick up and body slam larger opponents, he just said he was stronger than he looked.

I didn't ask either one of them if John planned on using steroids – or human growth hormones or testosterone injections or something else – to get bigger. I didn't ask if they were worried about what gaining fifty or sixty pounds could eventually do to his health. And I didn't question the wisdom of helping a grieving twenty-one-year-old move into a world that seemed so psychologically toxic.

John was determined to take vengeance on *Brando*. He was putting himself under a lot of pressure, and I couldn't help him. I was leaving town when he needed somebody to talk to. The college had an excellent counseling service, but he didn't respond either time I brought it up.

My interview with Cash was more like a conversation. After three hours I felt like I was getting to know him, but whenever he started straying off into politics, he caught himself and changed the subject.

I finally brought it up. "It's okay to talk about politics. I've been curious about how you see the world since… Ever since the other day, when you talked about portraying wrestlers as abortion providers and Klansmen and whoever else. But every time politics comes up, you…"

He leaned back in his chair, and he was smiling. "I know. I must sound like *such* a tease. I don't want to talk about politics until we know each other better. One of my most egregious flaws is that when I'm passionate about something, I talk about it too much. Politics is one of those things. If I subjected you to one of my discourses, you'd probably run away and hide. I'm trying to tone it down, but I'm not there yet."

It was a long way back to Tennessee. The counties came and went. When the Iowa countryside turned into the Missouri countryside, I was still trying to process what had happened over the past week. I was worried about John's journey turning into a tragedy. And along with Sam and John and professional wrestling, I kept thinking about Cash Caruthers. I couldn't help it. It wasn't just because of the way he looked, or because of any particular thing he said. I wasn't sure what it was.

It took a while before I finally started to shift gears. Clutch in and downshift. I was going back to help Carla. Downshift again. I was on my way back to be with my father.

I'd been thinking about Mac's love for history, and how it eventually led Carla to find her adoption records. She didn't mention family history when I was growing up, but maybe she was more curious about where she came from than I thought. There was a chance that Carla wouldn't have another birthday. If she wanted to learn something about her parents and about her ancestry, I was going to find as many answers as I could get before she died.

As soon as I was back in Nashville, I told Mac what I wanted to do. His first suggestion was to order DNA collection kits from two different family tree sites. He said if the results lined up, it would confirm that the information was accurate. The kits were both delivered within a few days. After Carla ran the swabs from each kit along the inside of her cheek, I sealed them in plastic vials and mailed them back. After two or three weeks, we were supposed to receive the reports.

I didn't tell Carla that I had more in mind than DNA. Mac said that even if her report didn't lead her to anybody with matching genetic markers, it still might be possible to identify one or both of her parents through genealogical research.

Back when Carla found her records, Mac had gone through the file and made notes. Along with official forms, there were a few letters between Carla's mother and an adoption attorney. Mac had put away his notes, but he was pretty sure he could find them. He said he never threw anything away.

I got together with Mac as much as I could. Sometimes Elinor came with us, but it was usually just Mac and me. We got along great and we had a number of similarities, but we didn't see everything the same way. He had a *challenging* sense of humor. The more inappropriate something was, the more he liked saying it.

At some point, he'd created a character he called Ricky Wayne Redneck. "I'll tell you one thing, by God. My wife's pretty much up for grabs, but the guv'ment best not come after my guns. Or my truck. Or my beer. Or my skanky girlfriend. If they do, I'll have to open me up a great big can of whup-ass. Then there's gonna be *hell* to pay, by God." When he was portraying Ricky Wayne, his most colorful rants were about gays and blacks. But he didn't call them gays and blacks.

And he liked going after left-wingers just about as much as right-wingers. If political correctness came up, he'd turn into Larry the Leftist, who was offended by just about everything he saw or heard. He'd fan himself like he was having a hot flash. "I tried to read *Huckleberry Finn,* and then I tried to read *To Kill a Mockingbird.* But they were both just *too upsetting* to finish. I was so triggered by all the racist language, that I've had to go into therapy. Again."

After having Carla for a mother, Mac's impersonations and his jokes – even his worst ones – weren't a problem. He said if I'd grown up when he grew up – and where he grew up – that my sense of humor would probably be about like his was.

And we were different in a couple of other ways. He was more of a dreamer than I was. And more philosophical. That would've probably been the case whenever I was born, and wherever I grew up.

The first analysis of Carla's DNA came in the mail on a Saturday, and the other report arrived the following Tuesday. They were essentially the same. As she would've expected, she was almost entirely of European extraction. But parts of her heritage were a surprise. Her markers varied a little, but they indicated that she was around 3% Southern European, 2% Native American, 2% Ashkenazi Jew, and 1% Sub-Saharan African.

Carla was delighted. "What I wouldn't *give* to have Mother here to share this moment! Her shame would've been… *overwhelming*."

She began to portray her mother, and put the back of her hand against her forehead. "Oh, the *humiliation*. Being Italian and Indian is bad enough, but part *Jewish*? And *Negro*?"

Mac picked it up from there as Ricky Wayne Redneck. "A sub-Saharan *African*? Oh *hell* no. I've fathered a child with… with a… I can't even *say* it." Then he turned around and bent over, and he started to gag. I didn't try to keep from laughing.

The first report included the names of two people whose markers indicated close kinship to Carla, and the second report contained an additional name. She continued to revel in what she referred to as her *exotic* genetic profile. I didn't let her know that I was planning to contact all three of her three DNA matches.

16

I sent emails to each of Carla's genetic matches. The only one who replied was a woman in Kentucky named Sherry Smith. She wrote that ever since she submitted her DNA, she'd been waiting to get the email I sent. Because of all the markers she shared with Carla, and because her mother had a younger sister who was taken from the family as an infant, Sherry was convinced that Carla was her aunt and that I was her first cousin.

I went ahead and called her. Three days later, Sherry and I met at a restaurant outside of Bowling Green, Kentucky. It was about halfway between Nashville and the little town where she lived. I wanted Carla to hear the conversation later on, and Sherry didn't mind when I asked if I could record what she was about to say. I didn't expect anything close to what I heard.

"Momma was born in 1938. She died just last year. She was about to turn eighty. Momma's name was Ruth Lynn – Ruth Lynn Pearcy. She grew up down the river from Louisville, but before that, back before the war, she lived in Tennessee. They were country people. They lived on a farm in Cannon County. Momma said it was sixty-something miles from Nashville. Momma's father was named Jimmy

Pearcy. He was a sharecropper. Back durin' the Depression he usually worked two jobs, and there were times when he worked three. I prob'ly don't have to tell you how hard times was back then. Momma's daddy got killed in 1943. Momma was five. He fell asleep while he was drivin' a tractor. It ran off a bank, and it ended up on top of him in a creek.

"Momma's mother was Susie Cunningham back before she married. Everybody called her Sugar. Momma didn't know much about Sugar's father. She was pretty sure his first name was Roy. They was barely gettin' by, and when Granddaddy Jimmy got killed, Sugar was pregnant. Well Sugar, she was a good-lookin' woman. She wasn't but twenty years old when her husband died. Jimmy had been workin' for Mister J.A. Buford. The Buford farm was ten or twelve miles out from town. He was a widower, and he had some half-growed children.

"Sugar was still carryin' Jimmy Pearcy's baby when she and J.A. got married. When the baby was born, Sugar named her Lucy May. She was a beautiful child, but she was prone to havin' colic. Momma said that J.A. was alright as long as he was sober, but he was ill-tempered when he drank. It wasn't long before he got tired of hearin' Lucy cry. And before long he told Sugar she had to give up her baby. But she wouldn't do it. One day when Sugar was out in the barn, J.A. just… He'd been drinkin', and he just snatched the baby right up out of her crib. Then he put her in his truck and drove away.

"Momma ran to the barn and told Sugar. Well, Sugar… she just broke down. She didn't know what J.A. would do – him bein' drunk and all. They didn't have no telephones that far out in the county. The nearest neighbors was a half-mile away. She ran down there and asked for a ride to Woodbury, but they owed J.A. some money and they wouldn't help her.

"J.A. stopped off to do some more drinkin', and he didn't get back till way after dark. When he sat down at the kitchen table, Sugar pulled a knife out of her apron and put it to his throat. Momma saw her do it. He swore he hadn't hurt Lucy, but he wouldn't say where she was at.

"A few weeks later, J.A. got drunk and beat Sugar up. Said he was done hearin' about the baby. As soon as she could, she took his truck and she drove Momma up to Kentucky. Sugar got a job at a diner. J.A. finally tracked her down, but when he showed up, it wasn't Sugar he talked to. He had to deal with Buck Welch. Buck ran the diner. He and Sugar had gotten to know each other, and he'd heard all about J.A. by then. He'd lost half his foot at Guadalcanal, but J.A. could tell that Buck was the wrong man to tangle with.

"Buck told J.A. how things was goin' to be. He told J.A. that he had one chance to tell him what he'd done with Lucy, and J.A. told him. He said he'd gone to Murfreesboro and left the baby just outside the front door of the courthouse. He waited across the street till somebody came up and carried her inside. That was the last he saw of her. Then Buck took Sugar and J.A. to a lawyer. After they signed some papers, Buck gave J.A. his truck back. All he said to J.A. was that if he ever saw him again, he'd kill him right there and then.

"When the divorce papers was final, Sugar and Buck went ahead and got married. Buck treated Momma like she was his own daughter. Sugar and Buck tried to find Lucy, but they never got nowhere. Sugar… she was sure the baby had been adopted – bein' that she was so pretty and all. But she never got over losin' Lucy. She and Buck died just two months apart. It was back in 1999. They was together more than fifty years.

"Like I said, Momma passed away a year ago. I couldn't have children, and every now and then she'd say that unless Lucy had children, I was the end of the line. She had dreams about Lucy right up till the month she died. It would've meant the world to Momma to know she had a sister – and a niece. And it means the world to me that I have an aunt. And a cousin."

After I finished talking to Sherry, I called Mac. I wanted to see his face when he heard the recording, but I couldn't wait. I went ahead and played it over the phone.

All he said was, "We have a lot of work to do."

He picked me up the next morning and we drove into Nashville. We spent the day at the State Library and Archives. At some point, Carla had told me that Mac was a history addict. She wasn't exaggerating. Most of the records from Cannon County were on microfilm, and I watched him go through reel after reel of deeds and wills and census records. I finally started looking through the local history section. I spent the rest of the day reading about the place where Carla almost grew up. Where she would've lived if her father hadn't fallen asleep on a tractor back in 1943.

We stayed until closing time. Mac found more than he thought he would about the Cunningham and Pearcy families, and about the neighborhood where they lived. And I came across a few accounts from people who lived in Cannon County back in the 1800s. Mac wanted to read what I found, and while I drove back to Carla's, he sat beside me and devoured all the copies I'd made.

17

Three days later, Mac and I were on our way to Woodbury, the county seat of Cannon County. We went through Murfreesboro, where J.A. Buford had abandoned the baby who grew up to be my mother. Murfreesboro was a typical fast-growing town, but the old courthouse where he dropped her off was still there. I saw the place where J.A. left her. It got to me more than I thought it would.

Cannon County was the next county to the east. There was a four-lane highway from Murfreesboro to Woodbury, but Mac took the old road. The same road Carla had ridden down beside her drunken stepfather in 1943.

Mac was quiet at first, but before long he was talking about the remote section of Cannon County where Carla's ancestors had lived before the Civil War. "The Pearcy and Cunningham families settled up near Short Mountain. There were a few small farms up there. Mostly rocky land. Hardly any slaves. A lot of guerilla activity during the war. Probably as many Union sympathizers as Confederates, but they were mostly folks who wanted to be left alone. There wasn't much law. Old scores got settled. New feuds got started.

"After the war it was poverty. And ignorance. Lots of moonshine being made. That was one way people survived. Things hadn't changed much by the time Carla was born. Up around Short Mountain, World War Two didn't put an end to the Depression. Children still didn't have shoes. No electricity once you got outside of Woodbury. Nobody had much money. Or much of anything else, unless you count little country churches and old-time religion. Rough times. Rough people, but mostly good God-fearing people. That's the world Carla came into."

We came over a hill, and a tractor pulling a hay wagon was turning onto the highway. Mac had to brake pretty hard, but we didn't skid. We stayed behind the tractor for two or three miles.

Mac started talking about Carla's family. "Jimmy Pearcy married Susie Cunningham on the fifth of July, 1938. He was eighteen and Sugar was fifteen. Sherry Smith said her mother was born in the same year, so it's pretty clear why they got married. Anyway, the Pearcys and the Cunninghams came to that part of the county back in the late 1830s. Carla's great-grandfather, Huell Pearcy, fought for the South, and her Cunningham great-grandfather fought for the Union. But if there were any hard feelings, they must not have lasted very long.

"I should be able to put together a pretty good family tree for Carla. But I want to give her more than names and dates and a few anecdotes. The reason we're going to Cannon County is to see if we can find the right person."

I had no idea what he was talking about. "The right person?"

"Yeah. Just about every community has somebody who knows more about the history of that place than anybody else. But I'm not talking about a whole county or a city. I'm talking about a locale. A neighborhood. A place where certain families lived."

"It sounds like you've done this before."

He glanced over at me and winked. "Just a time or two. There's a small library in Woodbury. With a little luck, the librarian will know who we need to talk to."

The old road ended, and we took the highway until we were near the courthouse. The library was on a side street, and I followed Mac inside. He reminded me of a hunter stalking his prey. It didn't look too promising at first. There was just a young guy sitting behind a desk. He looked like he was a volunteer. But then Mac looked over and saw a small room that had been set aside for genealogy. A middle-aged man was bending over a table and looking at a map.

The man was an amateur genealogist from Woodbury, and he knew exactly who we needed to see. "Oh, you should talk to Millie Warwick. If it happened in this county, she probably knows about it. And if she doesn't know about it, it probably didn't happen."

He said she was over in the courthouse, which was only two or three minutes away. We found Miss Warwick in a room on the second floor. She was sitting at a long table, and she was going through a large box of old court documents. She was framed by the sunlight coming through the window. It would've made a good photograph. She didn't look up until Mac knocked on the open door.

Miss Warwick looked like she was in her late seventies, but later on she mentioned that she was ninety-one. She closed her eyes while Mac told her why we were there. She nodded when he mentioned the Pearcy family, and she nodded again when he mentioned the Cunninghams. She was happy for me to record what she had to say.

"Well, the Cunninghams… they were from up in Mason Hollow. The Pearcys came from the other side of the ridge. That's Young Hollow. There were still little communities up there before the war. I remember the old folks saying that some Melungeons used to live on that side of the mountain. They were supposed to be a mix. You know – descendants of Indians and slaves and everybody else.

"Eula Cunningham sure looked that way. When I was a girl, she was around the age I am now, so she must've been born around… around 1850. Her complexion was pretty dark, but she had a blonde granddaughter. I don't know how many Melungeons were up there, but there ended up being plenty of moonshiners."

Mac must've had as many questions as I did.

"When I was little, my family lived out on Gassaway Road. For a couple of years, I went to a little school up on Sugar Tree Knob. That's where the children from Mason Hollow and Young Hollow would go. I heard about the Cunninghams and Pearcys, but I don't recall any of them being in school when I was there."

Mac spoke up. "Do you know anything about a girl named Ruth Lynn Pearcy?"

Miss Warwick closed her eyes and thought for a few seconds. "I don't believe so. Did she grow up in Young Hollow?"

Mac nodded. "Yes Mam. Her mother was Susan Pearcy."

The old woman sat back in her chair. "Susan Pearcy? *Oh*, you're talking about *Sugar*. She was a Cunningham back before she married. She's the one I was just talking about. The blonde girl – old Eula Cunningham's grandchild. I remember Sugar. She wasn't just pretty, people said she was probably the smartest girl in the county."

She was smiling and then she looked back and forth between Mac and me. "I'm guessing that you're her kin."

Mac reached over and touched my shoulder. "Well, I'm afraid I'm just an in-law. But my daughter… From what we understand, Ches is Sugar's granddaughter.

18

Miss Warwick put her hands on the edge of the table, and pushed herself to her feet. She didn't say anything at first. She was studying my face. "I was around fifteen the last time I saw Sugar. I'm picturing her right now. I can see her in you – especially in your eyes."

I had to say something. "I don't know what to... Thank you. I'd never even heard of Sugar until a few days ago. I've talked to her other granddaughter and... well it's a pretty long story. I recorded what she told us. Would you like to hear what she said?"

Miss Warwick kept nodding while she listened to Sherry Smith describe what happened to Carla. When the recording was over, she sat down and said there was more that I needed to know.

"Before Jimmy died, he went to Nashville to enlist in the Army. They turned him down, but pretty soon after that, he was drafted. He was about to leave for basic training when he got killed. After the accident, my father rode out to the Buford place with the sheriff and the coroner. Part of the tractor came down on Jimmy's neck. Daddy was pretty sure that Jimmy never knew what happened.

"Everybody liked Jimmy. He was a hard worker. Good to people. And he was right nice looking. Sugar's daddy was dead, but her family could've caused Jimmy some grief when they found out that Sugar was carrying his child. I was young at the time. I didn't know what was going on, but I heard all about it a few years later. I guess her people figured that she and Jimmy would wind up together anyway, and they didn't bother him about it. They got married downstairs – right here in this courthouse.

"I'd forgotten Ruth Lynn's name, and I never knew what Sugar named the other child. But everybody around here, including me, we… Well, we all heard about it when J.A. took away that baby. Sugar had to talk her uncles and cousins out of killing J.A. right then. It wasn't long after that when she took off with the older girl.

"Nobody knew where she went. And nobody understood why she never came back. You know, especially after J.A. was dead. A year or two later he got tied to a tree out in front of his house. When his body was found, there were five bullet holes in his stomach. The holes were in the shape of a cross. The sheriff asked a few questions, but folks didn't have much use for J.A., and there wasn't an investigation."

I had to keep reminding myself that I was hearing the history of my own family. After I told Miss Warwick about Carla, I gave her a quick account of her life in Nashville.

A few minutes later, Miss Warwick leaned back in her chair. "It's been nearly eighty years since Sugar left. The Cunninghams are all dead, and I might be the only one left who knew her. I wish I remembered more than I do, but I do know one story. And it's something people around don't know anything about. If it hadn't been for my brother, Vernal, I wouldn't have known about it either. Jimmy and Sugar… Well, they found a cave up on Short Mountain.

"A little after the war, Vernal was hunting up above Young Hollow Branch, on the west slope of the mountain. He shot a buck, but he didn't kill it. He had to track it for a while. By the time he found the buck and got through dressing it, a storm was coming up.

"There were some big rocks up above where he was. Vernal thought he might be able to find a place to stay dry, and he climbed up to take a look. There was an overhang where some rock had broken away from the mountain, and when he climbed up and got under the ledge, he saw an opening to a cave. After the storm let up, when he was leaving, he saw a broken slab of rock. He told me there were two names and a date on the rock. *Jimmy* and *Sugar 1937*.

"There are a few other caves up around there. They have names written all over them. But there were only those two names outside the cave Vernal found. That's why he thought Sugar and Jimmy were the ones who discovered it. He never went back to see how far back it went. He'd gone into a cave when he was little, and he said one cave was enough. I'm pretty sure I'm the only one that Vernal ever told.

"With Jimmy dead and Sugar gone, Vernal didn't want people going up there and tromping around. Writing their names and making a mess. And he didn't want people making up stories about how the cave was where Jimmy got Sugar pregnant. He said whatever happened between them wasn't anybody else's business."

Miss Warwick looked at Mac and then she looked at me. "But there was probably another reason why he didn't talk about the cave. The hunting was pretty good up through there, and if people started poking around, they would've run off all the game. I expect that Vernal was right. There would've been all sorts of stories. I just wish I'd asked him more about exactly where the cave was."

I wondered if I could find the rock. I imagined showing Carla a photograph of the rock when I told her about her parents.

Miss Warwick had been talking to both Mac and me, but then she was just looking at me.

"I don't know if you'd ever want to go up there and take a look. If you do, you might want to hold off till winter. It's a lot easier to get around once the leaves are down. If you wait till the first hard frost, you won't have to worry about snakes or ticks, or any of the critters in between. If that's something you want to do, you should probably let me know. Like I said before, a good bit of moonshine used to be made up around Short Mountain. And later on they grew marijuana. A lot of that has played out, but there could still be some pretty rough folks up in there.

"If you let me know you're coming, I might be able to find somebody to go with you. My first cousin has a grandson named Wilton. Sometimes he hunts on Short Mountain. He probably wouldn't mind showing you around. Wilton keeps to himself. If you found that cave, I doubt that he'd say anything."

I got Miss Warwick's phone number and her address, and after we thanked her, we went out to Mac's car.

He looked at me and smiled. "She's right about waiting for cold weather. But how do you feel about driving up and taking a look around? As long as we stay on paved roads, we should be able to avoid whoever, or whatever, might be *lurking* in the hollows of Short Mountain."

I wanted to see what it looked like, but I wasn't sure how much more I could take in.

19

Before we left Woodbury, I pulled up a topographical map of the area around Short Mountain on my phone. There wouldn't be any cell service once we got outside of town. We looked at the map, and the best view of the mountain seemed to be from Sugar Tree Knob, where Miss Warwick had gone to school when she was a child.

Sugar Tree Knob looked like it was only five or six miles from Woodbury, but it turned out to be a lot further away than that. To get there, we had to wind through the countryside on a couple of long, narrow country roads. We passed three or four cars, and then we were by ourselves.

What I knew about my ancestry had always been next to nothing. I'd never given it much thought. But I was riding on roads that my grandparents, and *their* grandparents, must have traveled all the time. I was passing the same creeks and fields and woods, and some of the same trees, they had passed back when they were alive.

I had gone from having Carla as the only ancestor I knew about, to having all sorts of people rustling around in the branches of my family tree. I'd read about Mac's parents and grandparents in his book, and along with Sugar and Jimmy and my dark-skinned great-

great-grandmother, Eula Cunningham, I was about to learn about people whose names I'd never heard before.

We finally turned onto a smaller road that led up into a hollow. Except for the road, what we were seeing probably hadn't changed for thousands of years. The land kept getting steeper, and the further we went into the shadows of Short Mountain, the cooler the July day became.

When we got up to the knob, it was like coming back to civilization. There were patches of cleared land and an occasional house, and then we came to a small church. It was made of concrete blocks that were painted white, and there was a cemetery beside it. Mac pulled off the road and parked in the shade of a couple of big trees. Nobody else was around, and we got out of the car and walked out into the cemetery. We could see Short Mountain through the trees. It was across a valley, overlooking Sugar Tree Knob.

Mac walked around until he found a fairly unobstructed view of the mountain. "I've done a little reading about the geology of this area. If we went twenty miles further to the east, we'd get to the Cumberland Plateau. It's a stretch of high ground that goes from West Virginia all the way down into northern Alabama. The plateau is about a thousand feet higher than the land on either side. And guess what? The top of the Cumberland Plateau has the same elevation as the top of Short Mountain."

He was about to tell me something, but I had no idea what it was.

"There was a time when Short Mountain was part of the plateau. It took a few hundred million years of erosion to separate it from the plateau."

I was a lot more interested in the cemetery than I was in geology. I assumed that Sugar's grave was somewhere up in Kentucky, but we hadn't asked Miss Warwick where Jimmy was buried. I had to keep reminding myself that he was my grandfather. I knew it was a long shot, but I started going from grave to grave in case he was there. The oldest tombstone I saw was for somebody whose name had long since weathered away. Only the lower portion of the stone was legible. Whoever was buried there had been born in 1822, and lived to be ninety. I kept wondering if that person, or anybody else in the cemetery, was kin to me.

I was looking at the crumbling gravestone when Mac walked over. "Are you doing okay?"

"Well as some of the folks in this cemetery must have said from time to time, 'I spect I'm doin' right tolable.'"

Mac raised his eyebrows. "Where did you pick up that little colloquialism?"

"I have no idea. I could be channeling the spirit of one of these dead people, but it's probably something I heard in a movie."

He bent down and read the bottom part of the tombstone. "What's all this been like for you? I mean things are coming at you pretty fast. First, you find out about me and my family, and now there's everything you're learning about Carla's people."

"I guess it's a little like… an avalanche. I've gone from not having any family history to having more than I can process."

He looked at me and smiled. "There was something I used to do with the kids on my team. You know, back when I was coaching. Can you handle a little insight into family history?"

It sounded like we were about to have a father-daughter moment. "If all I have to do is listen, I'll probably be okay."

"When I tried to tell my players anything about history, they'd usually just look at each other and roll their eyes. I finally tried a different approach. Bribery. I said we were going to have a contest, and the winner would get a football or a basketball or a baseball –

something like that. I told them to go home and ask their parents how they met each other. If a kid's parents were divorced, he could ask his grandparents the same question. And if somebody was adopted, he could ask his adoptive parents."

I wanted to take in everything Mac was saying, but my mind was starting to drift.

"At the next practice, after the kids had explained how their parents met, I'd go story by story. We'd talk about all the things that could've kept their mothers and fathers from meeting each other. If a kid said his parents met in college, I'd get him to find out how close they came to going to different schools.

"By then I'd already asked if anybody thought he would've been born if his parents hadn't ever met. Every now and then somebody would say he would've been born anyway. The other kids would start laughing and tell him why that was impossible, and it wouldn't be long before he changed his mind. I wanted the kids to know that they wouldn't exist if things hadn't happened exactly the way they happened. Once they understood that, they got a little more interested in the past."

I was struggling to stay focused. "Should I pretend to be one of your players?"

Mac had a playful look on his face. "You sure?"

"Yeah. Let's give it a shot. You and Carla met each other because you were coaching her nephew in basketball. If you hadn't decided to coach that particular team, you probably wouldn't have met each other. And you never would've met if her nephew had gone to a different school, or if he hadn't wanted to play basketball. And you and Carla not only had to like each other, you had to stay friends for… the next *eleven* years. After all that, Carla had to get curious about her ancestry. Which is why she found her adoption records.

And that set the stage for me to be conceived. How am I doing so far? Am I in the running for a prize?"

"It's too early to tell. The next step is to go back another generation. You already understand this, but most of the kids hadn't thought about it. If their grandparents never met, their parents wouldn't have been born."

I was pretty sure I knew where he was going. "Well, thanks to your book and to what Miss Warwick told us, I know a little about my grandparents. And I get it. Everything had to happen just like it did for you and Carla – and for me – to be born. What comes next?"

"The number of ancestors you have… it doubles with every generation you go back."

It wasn't hard to do the math. "All right, my four grandparents came from my eight great-grandparents, and the generation before that I had sixteen great-greats, and so on and so on. I get that, too. No matter how far back I go – no matter how many ancestors I have – everything had to happen exactly like it did for me to be born."

Mac was nodding. And smiling. "It's been almost two and a half centuries since America was established. If three generations are born every century, eight generations of your ancestors have probably been born since 1776. And *that* means you had something like… 128 great-great-great-great-great-grandparents when the Declaration of Independence was signed."

He looked off toward Short Mountain. "Almost all of them lived in the same place as the person they married. And there were *reasons* why people lived where they lived. They usually ended up where they were because, before that, they were dealing with things like famine and war and religious persecution. One way or another, they lived where they lived because of historical events."

"Did the kids on your teams get it? I mean did they start listening to what you had to say about history?"

"One or two usually did. But I ended up thinking that most kids, and most *people*, just aren't wired to understand complexity."

He was quiet for a few seconds. "I keep going back to something you said. That you didn't think you had a family history. But you *always* had one. And so did the adopted kids I coached. So does everybody. The further back in time you go, the more that family history becomes world history. Can you see where this is going?"

I tried to do the calculation in my head. "I think so. If I had 128 ancestors in 1776, a hundred years earlier, in 1676, that number would…"

I pulled out my phone and used the calculator. "One century before that – three generations earlier – I'd have 1024 ancestors. In another century, in the year 1576 – I'd have… more than eight thousand. Like you said, the number doubles with each generation."

Mac was still nodding. "Some people brag about tracing their ancestry back to Charlemagne. I guess they think that having an emperor in their family tree makes them look better. Charlemagne has been dead for a little over twelve hundred years. Twelve centuries ago is something like thirty-six generations back. If I remember right, at thirty-six generations there would be almost seventy *billion* slots for ancestors on a family tree. But that's about ten times as many people as there are today. How could that be? It's because of how closely related people are. Cousins married cousins back through countless generations. That means the same individuals can fill thousands, or millions, of different slots on the same family tree."

He raised his hand like he was taking an oath. "I'm almost through. I promise."

I hoped I hadn't looked bored.

"One time a kid asked me about the Romans. He wanted to know if any of his ancestors could've been Roman soldiers. I tried to explain what the gene pool is, and then I answered his question. I said he wasn't just descended from *thousands* of Roman soldiers, he was probably descended from hundreds of thousands – or millions – of people who lived in the Roman Empire. From female slaves and barbarians, to queens and emperors.

"The further back you go, the more that history and family history become the same thing. It varies from continent to continent, but at some point, everybody goes back to the same individuals. None of us would've been born if history had unfolded in any other way than the way it did."

Mac looked at me and smiled. "Ches, you've always had a family history. So has everybody else. It's called *history*."

I was pretty sure he had more to tell me, but I didn't ask any questions.

20

I stayed busy for the rest of the summer. Mac and I spent two or three days a week at the State Library, learning as much as we could about the Cunninghams and the Pearcys and their Cannon County relations. Before long I was determined to find the rock where Carla's parents had written their names.

Even though Carla was getting sicker, it was happening too slowly to notice. I was pretty sure that Mac and I had time to get back to Short Mountain, but at times she woke up feeling lousy. That's when I was tempted to tell her about Sugar and Jimmy and her other ancestors.

One morning, pretty soon after Mac and I got back from Cannon County, I was having breakfast with Carla in the kitchen. She had finished eating, and she saw me glance at the food that was still on her plate.

She gave me a look that said, "Oh *really*?"

After a few seconds, she stood up. "And now a decree from the Queen. Henceforth, no notice *whatsoever* shall be taken of any decline, real or imagined, in Her Majesty's health. From the state of her complexion, to the amount of food she consumes, to the nature of the royal *stools*, there shall be no comments and no questions.

"Should assistance be required, a royal request will be issued. No sad countenances are to be displayed at any time. Subjects shall not *surreptitiously* monitor the health of the Queen, nor shall any unsolicited offers be made to accompany Her Majesty when she visits her royal physician. The Queen hereby proclaims that those throughout her kingdom shall give thanks for her long reign, and for the many blessings with which she has *thus far* been favored."

Then Carla began to nod and wave to a nonexistent audience.

I couldn't resist. "Yes, Your Majesty. Of course, Your Majesty. But how do you expect to keep any color in your cheeks if you don't eat? Just look at *all the fiber* you still have on your plate."

She was trying to keep from smiling. She casually picked up a piece of broccoli and tossed it at me.

I caught it and pretended she was a child. "Now you know what they say, 'Some broccoli each day keeps the roughage in play.'"

Then she threw a half-eaten roll across the table.

It hit me on the shoulder, but I caught it before it fell in my lap. I held it up. "And there's nothing like a little bread to keep on weight."

We restrained ourselves. We'd had a few food fights over the years, and we didn't want to clean up the mess later on. After that, things stayed pretty much the way they'd been. I'd pretend that she didn't have cancer, and she'd pretend not to know how much I worried about her.

One afternoon I was walking with Mac around a lake in a nature preserve. We stopped to look at a row of turtles on a log near the bank. I wanted to tell him more about Cash, but I ended up asking him a question about Carla. There was something I couldn't figure out. Considering what happened to her when she was a baby, and the way she was treated by her parents when she was growing up, I couldn't understand how she turned out to be such a great mother. But before I said anything about Carla, Mac asked me if I thought I'd ever be a mother.

I kept myself from giving him a half-answer. "I'd love to find my soulmate someday. I really want that. Settle down and see if it's *actually possible* to live happily ever after. I like children. I used to think I'd have kids, but America is falling apart. The world is crashing. The planet is getting hotter and hotter. More crowded. More polluted. Natural disasters. Mass extinctions. I just can't see bringing children into a nightmare."

Mac was staring up the trail. "Couldn't things turn around?"

I didn't want to sound hopeless, but I went ahead and told him what I thought. "I… I wish we had a better chance than we do. But look at the politicians we have. Look at the *electorate* we have. A few *billion* people might need to die off to save the planet. What does that say about how bad things are?"

He just kept staring across the lake.

One day that fall, we went back to Woodmont Park. We were sitting at the same picnic table where we sat the first time we met. The leaves had started to change color. They were falling three or four at a time. He was telling me about going to the school carnival at the end of his fifth-grade year. By then I wasn't surprised at how much he remembered.

He leaned back and closed his eyes, and then he took a deep breath. "*Ah, the dreams of our youth. How beautiful they are… and how perishable.* I wish that I'd come up with that, but Mark Twain beat me to it. This place… The school that we had… We knew we'd have to leave Woodmont, but we thought the school would always be here. We all knew we'd get older, but the future wasn't real for any of us."

"If you could go back to the Woodmont Carnival, is there any... What would you tell yourself?"

"You mean if I snapped my fingers and it was suddenly 1958?"

"Yeah. You'd be back at the Woodmont Carnival, and you'd see your boyhood self. Would you say anything?"

He leaned forward. "Well, if it would change the way my life has turned out, I wouldn't say a word. But if I could pass along some wisdom, and still keep all the good things I've experienced – Elinor, our children, you, Carla, the kids I coached, and all the rest of it – there's a lot I would've said."

He thought for a few seconds. "Here's one thing, but it might sound pretty innocuous. My mother and father always told me how great I was. They kept saying I could do anything if I wanted to do it badly enough. That I could be anything I wanted to be. What I wanted was to be the best athlete in my class. And to be popular and make straight A's. I thought it was my fault when none of those things happened. There were times when I hated myself for what I wasn't.

"So I'd say that I needed to forgive myself if I wasn't good at something. I'd tell myself to do the best I could. To keep trying new things until I found what I'm wired to do. I spent *way* too long feeling bad about myself."

Mac and Carla were on my mind a lot, and so were John Armstrong and Cassius Caruthers. When I wasn't with Mac or Carla, I spent a lot of time editing the documentary about John. Watching the interviews. I kept seeing Sam the way he was when I first met him, and then the last time I saw him. It was brutal. Going back through my interviews with John was a different kind of bad. The innocent kid joking around and laughing all the time, becoming a young man bent on revenge.

The same questions kept swirling around in my head. What was gaining so much weight doing to his body? What was vengeance doing to his spirit? And what would happen to his spirit if he failed?

And there was Cash. The way he looked at Sam's funeral. His smile on the night we met. The way he said my name. How bright he was. Wondering if I was just seeing him through my loneliness. And on. And on.

21

I flew to Des Moines just after Halloween. I hadn't seen John in over four months. He'd gotten bigger. He weighed just under 250 pounds, and he looked taller. I didn't ask him if he was taking anything, but I was sure he was. He was living with a trainer Cash had hired. He could walk from his apartment to the gym. He was friendly and warm, but there were no jokes. There was no playfulness.

I checked into a hotel, and the next day I got to the gym early. I spent the first three hours filming him working out with weights and jumping rope, and doing crunches and pullups. After lunch, we did a long interview. He spent every morning in the gym. In the afternoon he alternated between working out with a gymnastics coach, and learning Brazilian jujitsu. He didn't move the way he had before. He reminded me of a powerful jungle cat.

It was difficult for him, but he finally talked a little about Sam. I zoomed in to capture the pain in his eyes. What I saw was numb resignation. The resignation that came from living in the shadow of loss. And I saw determination. Grim determination. When I asked if he was ready to see the last interview I did with Sam, he just shook his head.

He waited until the camera was off before he said anything about *Brando*. "I've watched him wrestle three times so far, Ches. Studied his patterns. Looked for weaknesses. He's bigger than he was. He's a monster. The last match I saw was a couple of weeks ago. He made it seem like an accident, but he broke a guy's shoulder. He's getting a reputation. Cash says he's on his way to being a star."

Cash called John at least once a week, and he came through town whenever he got a chance. My timing was good. A couple of days later I was back at the gym. I'd just finished another interview with John. I hadn't expected to see Cash, but I looked up and there he was. With his muscular shoulders. With his shining eyes. With his perfect smile.

There was something I'd promised myself that I'd do the next time I saw him. On the rare occasions when I met a man I wanted to know better, I'd always played it safe. But the older I got, the more I disliked being passive. It made me feel weak. It took a while, but I finally decided to open up and say what I wanted to say. If that ran him off, at least I would've given it a shot.

But telling myself I'd be open wasn't the same as *being* open. We made small talk while we watched John go back and do an extra set of bench presses. After he went into the locker room and rinsed off, he took off for his gymnastics workout. I was ready to lay it on the line with Cash.

"I have two things I want to talk about. The first one is John. He's changed a lot in three months. He's a lot bigger and stronger now. And his career plans… They've probably changed, too. I want to catch up on, you know, the latest strategy."

I made myself look into his eyes. "There's something else. I want you to know that… you've been on my mind. You've been on my mind *a lot*."

Cash smiled. I waited, but he didn't say anything.

After a few seconds, I lowered my voice. "Really Ches?"

He was still smiling, and I tried to make my voice a little deeper. "You… you've *really* been thinking about me? *A lot?*"

He took a deep breath and started to say something, but I cut him off. "Gosh Ches, I don't know what to say."

I kept talking. About what drew me to him. How intelligent he was. The way he was helping John. How much I liked the way he looked. I'd never been that open with a guy I barely knew. It felt good. The truth. What a concept.

He started to say something, but I held up my hand. I tried to imitate an announcer in a TV commercial.

"But wait! There's *more*! A lot of how I feel – it's based on intuition. And my intuition keeps telling me to be completely honest with you. If I'm wrong… Then I'm making a *complete* fool of myself right now."

Cash didn't say a word. He just looked at his watch and stood up. "*Good Lord*! I didn't realize how late it was. I'd love to stay here and talk, but… I was supposed to be on a conference call five minutes ago. I have *got* to get going."

He walked to the front of the gym. When he got to the door, he looked at his watch again. Then he turned around. "But hold on. I think I've gotten my days mixed up. That call isn't until tomorrow."

I pretended to be looking at my phone.

He walked back to where I was sitting. "Here's to your intuition. And I have a confession to make. I didn't just *happen* to show up. I told John to let me know the next time you were in town. I've been wanting to tell you… well, pretty much what you just said to me. But I need to say a little bit more than *ditto*.

"After Sam and John told me about you – how kind and talented and intelligent you are – I really wanted to meet you. They also used the term 'hot.' And even though it's a characterization that I find *demeaning* and *horrific*, it did magnify my interest."

I started taking my pulse with my fingertips. "Well, my heart is still beating, so I guess I've *somehow* survived the shock of being objectified in such a *blatantly* sexist way."

Cash got back to business. "I think I've already mentioned the first time I saw you. Sam had just died. I didn't want to meet you in the middle of a tragedy. Then I saw you in Sioux City. You were everything John and Sam said you were. Smart. Kind. *Hot*. All of it."

He was smiling. I hadn't told him how much I liked his smile.

He took his turn at imitating an announcer. "But *hold on*! There's *even* more!"

He dropped his TV voice. "It's about relationships I've had. A couple of times I thought I'd found what I was looking for, but it turned out to be biology. I have plenty of hormones rolling around right now, but this... feels different."

Cash started speaking more slowly. "Just about all we have right now is what we sense in each other. But it seems like I've known you for a long time. We have a million things to talk about, and a million questions to ask each other. I hope we like the answers we get. I want to believe that if something is supposed to happen, telling the truth can't mess it up. I don't know if that's true, but I hope it is."

I wanted everything to slow down. I was trying to memorize the moment, but it was moving too fast. I was going a hundred miles an hour down a one-lane road with the sun in my eyes. Cash looked like he felt the same way. It was fairly nice outside, and we ended up taking a walk.

I finally asked him a question. "If we're right about each other – if we're both such *spectacular* specimens of humanity – how come we're both so *spectacularly* alone?"

He looked like he had an answer. "Well, here's a *possible* explanation. At least when it comes to me. I've already told you about getting dumped – back when I was a preacher. After that, I fell for a woman named Laurie. Right before she split, she told me that I thought too much. That I just needed to let things be. Then there was Beth. She said I analyzed things to death, and then she was gone, too. And after that, I was really into Christine. She told me the same thing. She said she'd liked the way I tried to figure everything out, at least she had at first. But then it got annoying. I'm not positive, but there *seems* to be something of a pattern."

Cash glanced over at me. "What's your story?"

"It's something you've probably heard a thousand times. Girl meets boy. Girl wants to understand boy. Boy tells girl that she asks too many questions, and he says to lighten up. Girl and boy have less and less to talk about. Boy and girl break up. Times three."

He wanted details, and he got them. I told him all about Les, who'd been in front of the line when it came to looks, but at the very back when it came to intellectual curiosity. He heard about Andy the narcissist, and about Jan, the manipulator. When I told Cash how I felt about not having them in my life, he reached down and squeezed my hand.

22

We stopped at a little restaurant not far from the gym. It was nearly empty. It seemed like a good place to have an intimate conversation, if that's what we were about to have. But first, we had to talk about John.

I got right to it. "Okay, Cash. I want to know how John is getting so big. What's he taking? And there's all the grief and anger he's carrying around. Is it time to send him to a psychologist?

He looked at me across the table. "About his size. He's been working out like crazy. And after we got the go-ahead from a physician, and input from Billy, his trainer, he started taking creatine. The studies I saw said that as long as he didn't take it for more than five years, there wouldn't be any negative effects. He should be done with wrestling way before that.

"And there's his personality. You're right, Ches. He's changing. Billy keeps me plugged in, and every couple of weeks I give John a nudge about getting some counseling. He always says he'll think about it, but that's as far as it's gone."

Cash took a drink of water. "It's good that he's staying busy. Between his workouts and gymnastics and jujitsu, and going to watch *Brando* wrestle, he usually has something going on. And he keeps saying he needs to work on his kicks. I wouldn't be surprised if he gets into Tae Kwan Do."

The server came out and took our orders.

Cash answered my next question before I asked it. "I've never seen anybody as dedicated as John is. At first, I wondered if he'd stay focused. Not anymore. So, here's how this should play out. He'll keep training, and when he's almost big enough and strong enough to have a chance with *Brando*, he'll start practicing against a heavyweight.

"I found a guy who just retired. He's already lined up. When they're just getting started, most guys don't know what they're doing. That's when they get hurt. There are several techniques – especially how to fall – that he'll have to master before I put him on a circuit."

"How will you decide which circuit?"

"It'll be whichever one *Brando* is on. By the time John is ready, *Brando* might've moved up to the next level. He's been making a name for himself, but not in a good way. He's an outlaw. If he wasn't pulling in so many fans, nobody would get near him.

"John is worried about *Brando* getting banned – or put in prison – before he gets a crack at him. Last week he told me that waiting too long would be a lot worse than not waiting long enough. He wants to get at *Brando* as soon as he can. John is really gifted, and when the time comes…"

I interrupted. "Is he gifted enough?"

Cash gave a half-shrug. "I think he'd have a chance."

"Okay. What happens, you know, leading up to the big showdown?"

"After he turns pro, he'll have a few matches. And when he's as ready as he'll get, I'll line up the match with *Brando*. That part should be easy. *Brando's* manager is already having a hard time finding opponents. Most wrestlers won't take him on. He's too crazy. He keeps hurting people, but that's bringing in fans."

Cash must have seen the look on my face. "I know this sounds scary, Ches. It *is* scary. But *Brando* won't have any idea who John is. He'll think it's just another match. And John has a pretty solid strategy. At some point, probably right before the match, he'll say something to make *Brando* mad. To provoke him. *Brando* has to attack John while they're in the ring. John has to come off like he's defending himself against a guy with a violent reputation. He can't look like the aggressor when league officials – and maybe the police – review what happens."

He was talking a little slower. "The cameras will be recording a real fight. John will have some control when it comes to provoking *Brando*, but what happens after that is… unpredictable. *Brando* won't have any idea what to expect from John. Whatever John is able to do, he might not have long to do it. If *Brando* starts losing – if it's a real fight – people could run in and break it up.

"When it comes to hurting *Brando*, John hasn't said how far he'll take things. He understands that the less I know, the better. But I'm sure that John wants to end *Brando's* career.

"And if he pulls it off… To say that his career would take off is an understatement. When the time comes, I'm planning to shoot video from multiple angles. It'll be all over the internet and on television news. It could get hundreds of millions of views on YouTube. A whole lot of people will want to know all about the kid who took on a thug in a real fight. And there would be a bidding war for rights to your documentary."

Even though we hadn't been served yet, Cash was holding his fork.

"The match with *Brando* will launch John's career. But he won't be wrestling as John Armstrong. He wants to use that name Sam came up with – *The Iowa Farm Boy*."

He smiled at me across the table. He tried to sound like a cheesy promoter. "Brave. Clean-cut. Handsome. The kind of guy that boys worship, and grown men admire. The kind of young man that single women want, and older women want their daughters to marry."

He went back to his normal voice. "The fans should love his authenticity, but they'll expect some showbiz. So will the sponsors. He might be wearing overalls and a baseball cap when he comes into the ring, but that's about as far as we've gotten."

I couldn't resist. "And he could carry around a sack of... of corn cobs, or something. He could throw them out to the crowd. What do you think?"

Cash was smiling and shaking his head. "I think you understand pro wrestling better than I thought."

After we left the restaurant, we took a walk. Before long we came to a bridge that led across the Des Moines River. When we were halfway over the bridge, I stopped and looked down at the water.

I spoke up before Cash said anything. "I want to say a couple of things about John. Letting him go straight into the same circuit that *Brando* is in... That's good. The less time he has to carry his anger around, the better. Provoking *Brando* makes sense, too. And turning John into *The Iowa Farm Boy* is great marketing."

He glanced over at me, but he didn't say anything.

"You're probably right about *The Iowa Farm Boy* becoming a sensation. About being on YouTube and all the rest of it. But I'm worried about the world he'll be in. John is a great kid. He doesn't need to spend the next fifteen years of his life flopping around in arenas with his shirt off. He doesn't need to spend all that time traveling. Just so he can entertain audiences full of… gullible fans. What would that do to his soul?"

Cash had more of an answer than I expected. "I've always been straight with John. The first time he asked me to help him, I said I didn't want to be involved. I didn't want to help him destroy himself. But we kept talking. Nothing was going to keep him from trying to hurt *Brando*. That was going to happen whether I helped him or not.

"And if he can pull it off, guess what he'll do with the money he makes? After he gets his mother taken care of, he wants to set up a scholarship fund in Sam's name at the college. I've told him what professional wrestling is. He gets it. But there's a lot I still haven't told you. There's a bigger plan. If he takes down *Brando*…"

I interrupted him. "But what if wrestling turns out to be his drug? What if he's *really* successful? What if he gets hooked on… I don't know. Money. Being famous. Women. Or whatever else there is."

He looked over at me. "Here's why that won't happen. And this is where our conversation goes down a rabbit hole."

I kept myself from saying anything about carrots, or being all ears. A canoe paddle floated out from under the bridge, and we watched it drift away.

It was another minute before he started telling me what was down the rabbit hole. "Sam and John and I talked a lot about what's happening in the world. From politics to the state of the planet. They were a whole lot more aware of what's going on than most guys their age. I didn't have to convince them that things are moving past the tipping point. They could see that America and the Earth are falling apart at the same time. They knew it wasn't a coincidence.

"Things might get bad, Ches. It could all hit the fan tomorrow, or we might limp along for a few more years. The people who make it through whatever might be coming… They'll be the ones who are prepared. And part of being prepared takes money."

Cash was getting ahead of where I wanted him to be. I held up my hand. "Before you get into your survival strategy, I want to hear why you're so confident that the world is crashing."

He started walking a little slower. "Remember when you interviewed me? Right after Sam died? When you wanted me to talk about politics?"

"Yeah. You were afraid I'd freak out or something. You said you didn't want to sound too… analytical. How contradictory. A former military analyst who doesn't want to sound analytical."

He gave me a quick smile. "What can I say? I wanted to impress you. I didn't want to sound like one of those clowns who just keeps repeating the latest piece of propaganda he's heard. They always act like it's something they came up with themselves. But I feel you. I've put this off longer than I should have. I can't explain why the world is collapsing unless I get into politics. You're about to experience what I warned you about. Just remember – I tried to protect you."

23

After we went across the bridge, we took some stairs down to a walkway. It led along the Des Moines River, and we headed upstream. We could hear an ambulance in the distance.

Cash started talking. "You know what makes a good intelligence report? Providing as much relevant context as possible. The colonel who ran our unit in Okinawa always wanted a lot of detail. I'm pretty obsessive, so you might want to buckle up. And if you need to tap out, I'll understand."

I made sure he saw me roll my eyes. "Do I need a safe word?"

He almost laughed. "That's not a bad idea. Or you could be dramatic and just throw yourself in the river."

I got the feeling that he'd like to see me in the water. "Enough stalling. It's showtime. I'm ready to find out how you've managed to run off *so* many women."

He put his shoulders back and cleared his throat. "Okay. Here's some context. I'll start with prehistoric people – when they came up with stories to help them understand how the world came to be. Some of their stories evolved into beliefs. It took a while, but a few beliefs developed into religions. Storytellers became holy men, and after writing and reading came along, narratives gradually became holy scriptures."

"Then things got more complicated. Look how it went with Judaism and Christianity and Islam. All those rabbis and preachers and mullahs claimed that their scriptures came straight from God. That they were interpreting scripture the way God intended. But in each religion, there were arguments about what the scriptures meant. That didn't bother the holy men. They just said that any cleric within their religion, if he was teaching a different interpretation of scripture from the version they taught, was a heretic."

I didn't tell Cash that he was preaching to the choir. I liked hearing him preach.

"Temples and cathedrals and mosques were built, and traditions and rituals were put in place. Rewards in the afterlife were promised to the faithful. Believers who didn't follow the teachings of the one true God were threatened with damnation. And the holy men said that the clerics and worshipers of rival faiths were infidels. War after war was fought, and as the centuries passed, millions of innocent people were killed in the name of the *one true God*."

I glanced over at an outdoor ice skating rink we were passing.

"Here we are in the twenty-first century, and some things haven't changed all that much. Picture two remote villages, hundreds of miles apart in Afghanistan. One village is Shiite and one is Sunni. Each village has a mullah, and the mullahs are the only ones in either village who can read. There isn't any radio or TV or Internet. The only information the villagers get comes from their mullah.

"The Shiite mullah teaches that the Sunnis are heretics, and the Sunni mullah says the same thing about Shiites. The villagers, at least most of them, are *absolutely sure* that they are worshipping the one true God. And how many Jewish and Christian fundamentalists – or

Buddhist and Hindu fundamentalists – are the same way? How many are absolutely certain that they know the absolute truth? How many people on Earth are *absolutely certain* that the God they worship is the one true God?"

Cash sounded more like a professor than an ex-preacher. A heron was flying slowly upstream. It was moving along the bank, just ten or fifteen feet above the water.

"People know that religions and denominations and sects have conflicting beliefs, but they don't think about what that means. Welcome to one of humanity's fatal flaws. An *astounding* lack of discernment. Most people don't reach the obvious conclusion. When it comes to God and holy scriptures, either every group of believers in the world is wrong *except one*, or they're *all* wrong.

"It's the same with politics. People will believe just about anything they're told. And once they're *absolutely certain* that what they've been told is true, they stop questioning what they believe. Somebody said this a long time ago. 'It ain't what you don't know that gets you into trouble. It's what you know for sure that just ain't so.' And being gullible and undiscerning keeps getting us in trouble."

I didn't know whether to say, 'Beware of the arrogance of certainty,' or just 'Amen.'

"We're vulnerable to all kinds of narratives. If advertising didn't work, corporations wouldn't spend billions of dollars a year getting us to buy their products. 'Our soap is the best soap!' 'Our car is the best car!' 'Our burgers taste better!' We're *really* vulnerable to propaganda. Human beings are suckers."

He looked out across the river. "Is it time for me to shut up yet? This is when the women I told you about would usually shut down. This is when I'd see the light drain out of their eyes."

I shook my head. "Well, I'm not over here praying for a merciful death, if that's what you mean. At least not yet. Don't pump the brakes. Keep talking."

"Okay. Here's the next part. Political narratives are taking the place of religious narratives. Look at what oozes out of political narratives. It used to be 'Joe Smith will raise your taxes!' Then it was, 'Joe Smith is a communist!' Now it's, 'Joe Smith is a Satan-worshiping pedophile who eats the flesh of babies!' The crazier it is, the more entertaining it is. And John and Mary Doe sure love to be entertained. They'll believe almost anything if they hear it enough.

"And it's about to get a whole lot worse. It won't be long before technology will be able to create video images of any politician on the planet, present or past. The images will say whatever they've been programmed to say. Franklin Delano Roosevelt surrendering to Japan and begging for mercy after Pearl Harbor. President Kennedy giving a press conference after surviving the assassination attempt in Dallas. Ronald Reagan announcing his membership in the Communist Party. Trump receiving the Congressional Medal of Honor for heroism in Vietnam. The facts barely matter as it is. What happens when computer-generated images like that start showing up?

"Propaganda works. And state propaganda *really* works. Look at Third Reich. How many German citizens believed every lie the Nazis dreamed up to justify the persecution of the Jewish people? And a majority of Russians are *absolutely sure* that their country annexed Crimea in 2014 to stop people from being persecuted by Nazis."

We came to a pedestrian bridge that was suspended from an arch. It was just a few feet upstream from where the river was cascading over a shelf of rock. Two young men were holding hands on the bridge, and looking down at the rushing water.

"Political propaganda is mostly made up of lies. Whether they come from the right wing or the left wing, political lies are… They create political partisans. They might as well be creating cancer."

"I'm not sure I'm following you."

"Partisans are always sure they're right. If you disagree with them, you're the enemy. They refuse to consider different points of view. There's no compromise. They're like cancer cells. The mass movements they can create – like Nazism – are like tumors. Malignant tumors that can destroy democracy. And society.

"Extremists on the left have always been a threat to democracy. But for now at least, right-wing extremists are much more dangerous. They're spreading a lot faster. Most people on the radical right say they love America. But if they destroy democracy, the America they claim to love so much will become a dictatorship. If that happens, how long will it be before a Hitler or a Stalin – or a Putin – takes power in Washington?"

"Okay, why do you think the radical right is metastasizing?"

"It's the power of technology. And it's how well they use propaganda – the way they use narratives. The left does it, too, but the right wing is… masterful. They've been using fear as a political strategy for decades. Fear of black people. Fear of communism. Fear of labor unions. It used to be, 'Blacks want to rape your wives and your daughters!' Then it was, 'The communists are taking over the world!' Now it's, 'The government is your enemy!'"

Professor Caruthers was teaching a political science class.

"And when the old targets start losing their flavor? No problem. The right-wing think tanks just come up with new targets. Welcome to the culture wars. They kept blacks on their list, of course. And they added Muslims, gays, trans people, immigrants, liberals – any group that was easy to vilify. 'Immigrants are taking over the country! Gays and transsexuals want to turn your children into perverts! All Muslims want to subject America to Sharia law!'"

Cash left out Jews. He probably thought it was too obvious to mention.

"It's fear and simple narratives. Smoke and mirrors. Look at climate change. Scientists try to explain why the planet is heating up. How fossil fuels release carbon atoms into the atmosphere and into the oceans. They try to keep it simple, but it's a lot more complicated than what the right wing tells its base. 'Climate change is a lie being used by the left to justify government control. Complex explanations are all fake news. Anything you don't understand is a lie.'"

There was a gate, and the walkway led into an oriental garden. After a few steps, we came to twelve massive stone blocks arranged in a circle.

Cash stopped walking. "Just what we need. A serene place where we can contemplate the demise of America. But if you're ready to jump in the river, the water is right over there."

I couldn't keep myself from flirting. "What? I'm sorry. What were you saying again?"

Cash looked over at me. "I asked if you're giving any thought to jumping in the river."

I shook my head. "No. I mean before that. You know, back when we were next to that skating rink. I must've zoned out for a while. Weren't you saying something about prehistoric people and stories?"

He tried to grab me, but I sidestepped him and got him in a bear hug. I started to lift him off the ground, but I got distracted by how good his body felt. I let him go and pushed him back. When he came at me again, I didn't try to get away. Then I was in his arms. Then we had our first kiss.

24

We weren't alone for long. We heard somebody behind us, and a short, bowlegged man was coming up the walkway. Cash and I let each other go, and we watched the man until he was out of sight. I wasn't sure what would happen next. I was up for round two, but Cash went back to what he wanted to tell me.

"It isn't just the simple narratives and the fear-mongering that gives the right wing an advantage. Part of what makes the left wing so secondary is how incoherent it is. It should have a focused strategy, but it doesn't. It goes off in every direction at once. It's tough to explain the positions it already has, and it keeps taking up more issues. It keeps picking up more balls to juggle.

"And some of the causes that the left wing takes up... They just give the right wing more power. Like when it embraces the Word Police. *God forbid* that somebody might get offended by something that's written or said. The left keeps diverting time and energy to causes that are easy for the right to use against them – like racial reparations. The left always chooses idealism over pragmatism. It insists on fighting losing battles. And then there's the arrogance. The intellectual brittleness."

Cash was on a roll. I'd already thought about most of what he was saying, but I hadn't heard anybody put it together all at once.

He shrugged. "How do you change people's minds after they've been radicalized? Fifty years ago, it was still possible to have a conversation about whether cells in the process of forming into an embryo are the same thing as a child. But that was before right-wing propaganda made abortion a political issue. That was before millions of people became *absolutely sure* that every abortion was murder.

"And there was a time when there could be conversations about what the Second Amendment actually says. But then the propagandists saw how much gun rights issues could help get their candidates elected. It wasn't long before tens of millions of people were *absolutely sure* that it was unconstitutional to prevent an eighteen-year-old with mental health problems from having an assault rifle."

We started walking again, and we came to a little bridge. It led over a pond to an open-air pagoda. We went across, and we started kissing again in a shaded corner of the pagoda. I was on my way to a place I hadn't been – or at least where I hadn't been for a while. But then, *of course*, an elderly woman showed up walking her fat little dog. And she decided to stick around for a while. She sat down a few feet away, and she kept smiling at us.

After a couple of minutes, we went out and stood on a bridge on the far side of the pagoda. A kayaker was paddling down the river. Cash hadn't lost his focus. Of course.

"The radical right wing has become a confederation of the angry and the fearful. And the hateful. The worst faction is a modern version of the Brownshirts who served Hitler in the years leading up to World War II. It's ninety years later, and gangs of American thugs are following in their footsteps. Lurking in the shadows with their AR-15s and their hand grenades."

There was some anger in his voice. "Misfits pretending to be patriots. The worst of the worst. They can't *wait* to start killing some of the people they've been taught to despise. They can't *wait* to be destructive. They're like the street criminals who use left-wing protests as an opportunity to loot stores and burn buildings. If they didn't have the support of the rest of their… *coalition,* they'd just slink back into the shadows. But they sure are useful to their masters."

"Their masters?"

"Yeah. The politicians who use them to intimidate the opposition. Or create chaos. Or to make headlines. Like what happened with the white nationalists a couple of years ago in Charlottesville.

"But most of the people who've been sucked into the right-wing narrative aren't Neo-Nazis or white supremacists or Klansmen. They just vote like they are. Ninety-nine percent of the people swirling around inside the right-wing vortex see themselves as good Americans. They'd deny that they're collaborating with groups that want to uproot democracy. But they don't condemn the Brownshirts. They protect them."

We started walking again. It wasn't long before we came to a display of six boulders inscribed with Chinese characters. After he pretended to read the inscriptions, Cash ceremonially cleared his throat. And just like that, he was back to explaining the decline of the nation.

"A lot of right wingers… they remind me of the characters in *Invasion of the Body Snatchers.* That movie from back in the 1950s. Aliens made exact copies of people, and then they replaced people with their duplicates. But the duplicates didn't have human emotions. Or any individuality. I know a lot of really good people who have turned into right-wing partisans. It's like they were taken over by aliens."

I'd seen *Invasion of the Body Snatchers* when I was in high school. The same thought had occurred to me, but I just kept walking.

"Back when I was in college, I was around plenty of people who called themselves Christian Conservatives. And I was around even more when I was a preacher. They'd been hearing simple stories their whole lives. Adam and Eve. Noah's Ark. David and Goliath. Their religious beliefs led them straight into right-wing politics, and before long, right-wing politics was their religion."

He left out Jonah and the Whale. We were getting close to a large overpass. There was the continual woosh of cars and trucks moving above us, and the sound of tires bumping over uneven sections of pavement.

"And plenty of people who *aren't* religious buy into the right-wing narrative. I'll run into a moron every now and then, but most right-wing partisans aren't stupid. A lot of them are just frustrated. They might hate their jobs. They might be in debt. Or maybe they hate the way the world is changing. They're angry. They're afraid. And some just go along with the crowd. But one way or another, they get drawn into the anger and frustration the right keeps serving up."

I was thinking about what happens when a pair of acoustic guitars are put next to each other. Pluck a string on one guitar, and a string on the other guitar starts vibrating. The resonance of resentment. And he left something out. A lot of people just need something to believe in.

"Whether they're on the right or on the left, people can get pulled into a partisan vortex for all sorts of reasons. It takes a lot of effort to understand political issues. Some people don't have the time. Or maybe they just aren't very analytical. When they go looking for answers, guess what they find? They find the multi-billion-dollar propaganda industry. TV networks. Syndicated radio programs. They go online and find websites, and pretty soon they're part of a community. They're part of a movement."

When we emerged from the shadow of the overpass, the dome of a building in a botanical garden was right in front of us.

"Here's the playbook for radical right-wing and left-wing propaganda. Cater to your audience. Tell people what they already believe. Only report what reinforces your narrative. Keep it simple. Create fear. Dehumanize the other side. *Demonize* the other side. Provoke anger and indignation. Feed it to your audience until they're addicted. And always project *absolute certainty*.

"Like I said, the radical right is a lot more effective than the radical left. Here's what they've gotten *millions* of their followers to believe. 'The victims in mass shootings are all actors!' 'Gay and trans people want to seduce your children!' 'Human-related global warming is a hoax!' 'The government wants to take away all your guns!' 'The press is the enemy of the people!' And it goes on from there. The right-wing narrative thrives by producing outrage."

It didn't take much to turn people into grievance junkies. Into anger addicts.

"A lot of my friends have disappeared into the right-wing whirlpool. A few years ago, I took a trip with a bunch of guys I'd known since high school. We were on our way to the beach, and we'd been drinking a little. Telling stories and laughing. We were listening to Aretha Franklin, and right in the middle of *Respect*, somebody said, 'Hey – it's eight o'clock!' Then it wasn't Aretha anymore. Some radio multi-millionaire had a show coming on. Everybody got quiet, and for the next hour, they listened while the guy spewed out all sorts of lies and nonsense.

"And they lapped it all up. They were like little kids being read to at bedtime. They were good guys, but every one of them had been sucked into the radical narrative."

Cash took in a deep breath. "And I don't think any of the guys in that car will go back to who they used to be. They'll never admit they're wrong. They'd lose too many relationships if they ever left the fold. They only let themselves hear what they already believe. And it'll be that way for the rest of their lives.

"Millions of people are the same way. And they keep calling themselves conservatives. They are *not* conservatives. They're radicals. A conservative would protect American democracy – not undermine it. A conservative would work to sustain the environment of the planet – not deny the science that explains climate change. But they keep thrashing around in their partisan fog. And they're all sure – they're all *absolutely sure* – that every single thing they believe is true."

We walked onto the grounds of the botanical garden. The bumping from the overpass sounded like a distant artillery barrage.

"If enough people get poisoned by propaganda, America will fall apart. But the partisans who want to disrupt the government – or cripple it, or kill it – they won't end up with what they're expecting. They'll end up living in a nightmare."

25

It was a lot to take in, but I wasn't on the verge of throwing myself in the river. I wanted to understand the way Cash thought.

"How do you see things going… you know, if America falls apart?

He glanced at the dome that overlooked the botanical garden. "The chaos would vary from place to place. Most people who live in rural areas vote with the right wing. Most people in the cities vote with the left wing. They've lived in harmony for a long time. But when things get hot enough, people will take to the streets. There might be a few areas where opposing factions would negotiate with each other, but think about the politicians we have. Particularly the ones who cater to right-wing radicals. Can you see them compromising? On anything?"

The path we were on led us through a rolling landscape of flower beds and ponds.

"Demonstrations and counter-demonstrations would turn into attacks and counter-attacks. Violence would escalate. The Brownshirts would make sure of that. So would the left-wing radicals and the looters. There would be fighting in nearly every city in America. In some places, it would be over pretty fast. It wouldn't take long for the right wing or the left wing to take control of regions where they're already in power. But left-wing cities located inside right-wing territory could become killing grounds."

My brain was in overdrive. From the way he saw the world. From the emotion in his voice. From the look in his eyes. From how beautiful he was when he was passionate.

"And I'll go ahead and throw this in. I can't see most people of color staying on the sidelines and hoping that things will work out. If we're living in a place where democracy looks like it's getting replaced by an authoritarian right-wing state, black people, brown people, African-Americans, whatever we call ourselves... We'll know we're in trouble. Big trouble."

We were moving past a pond with a lot of water plants, and I stopped to see which ones I recognized. Cash was looking at the pond, too, but his mind was someplace else.

"Whether they're on the right or the left, the radicals who want to turn America upside-down... They're irresponsible. They're *idiots.* They have no idea how much fire they're playing with. If Neo-Nazi militias start fighting against the government, or against the left, what would black gangs do? What would Latino gangs do? Would the police break into opposing factions, and fight against each other? What about the National Guard? And who would command the United States military? Would some of those units end up fighting against each other, too?"

The sidewalk led between two long rows of trees, but Cash was moving down a path of his own.

"It wouldn't be long before there were mass migrations in both directions. People moving from right-wing territory into left-wing territory. And from left-wing territory into right-wing territory. But even after the fighting died down and new boundaries were drawn, millions of people would've stayed where they were. Guerilla attacks could go on for decades.

"How would our infrastructure survive all that? We have a highly integrated system. It would be vulnerable even in a small-scale conflict. What happens if the fighting goes on for years? How long would the power grid function? What about the availability of water? Who would operate the sewer system? What about financial services? What about everything else? Cell towers. Sanitation. Prisons and courts. Hospitals and schools. Highways. Railroads and airports. The infrastructure – the system everybody depends on – is only as strong as the society it serves.

"And how would the supply chain function in a war zone? How would food and fuel and medicine be transported? If things come crashing down, how much death and how many years of hardship will people have to endure? It would be a disaster. America would probably end up as two or three different countries."

I touched him on the arm. "Okay, I get it. A lot of right wingers – and some anarchists on the left – want to destroy the federal government. Are you saying that's inevitable?"

He didn't say anything at first. "No, it isn't inevitable. But that's the road we're on right now. I keep looking for something that can keep it from happening."

I'd been watching his eyes and the expression on his face. Along with his passion, I saw sadness. The sidewalk led to an oval pool with a fountain in the middle. Neither one of us said anything for a few minutes. Then we started walking back between the trees.

"Are you still friends with any of those guys you knew in high school? The ones you went with to the beach?"

He didn't say anything until I stopped to watch a Blue Jay perched a few feet away in a tree. "After they changed… well, we avoided politics after that. Then we just quit talking. I couldn't tell them what I thought. That they were way too smart to buy into a movement led by one of the most contemptible… one of the most *despicable* public figures this country has ever produced.

"How do you tell people that a lot of what they believe – what they believe with absolute *certainty* – is absolute *bullshit*? That it's a show. That it's just propaganda. How do you tell people, people you care about, that they've been manipulated? What's the point in saying that they're complicit in a movement that's destroying America? That what they're caught up in is… I don't even know what to call it."

I jumped in. "You mean in addition to a malignant tumor?"

"Yeah."

I remembered something Mac had written. "How about a cult of ignorance?"

Cash was thinking. "Or a *malignant* cult of ignorance?"

It just needed a little more tweaking. "What about a cult of snarling ignorance?"

Cash nodded. "That sounds about right."

We started walking again, and I went ahead and asked a question. "Okay, what'll things be like? I mean if the snarling cult ends up breaking America into pieces."

We were leaving the garden. There was a little smile on his face. "Oh good. This means there's still a chance."

"For what?"

"For my apocalyptic vision to drive you into the river."

"Bring it on, big boy. Give it your best shot."

Cash took a deep breath for dramatic effect. "Okay, if the country does break up… my guess is that whatever part ends up being controlled by the right wing – that part would become a Christian nation.

"It's hard to say which version of Christianity would come out on top, but it probably wouldn't matter for long. In the end, it wouldn't be about Jesus. It would be like it always is with dictatorships. It would be about keeping a few people in power. Destroy anybody and anything that threatens your regime. It would end up just like the theocracy that took over in Iran. The people who go along with the destruction of democracy… By the time they figure out what they've done, it'll be too late."

There was some fatigue in his voice. "It would be an updated version of *Nineteen Eighty-four*. Thought police. Electronic surveillance. Informants. Technology used as a tool for state control. More and more people losing themselves in the cyber world. An increasingly homogenized population. Easier for the state to control. Entertainment events staged to appease citizens. And to distract them. Who knows? Maybe they'll even bring back gladiators.

"And if America starts breaking up, the global power structure would turn inside-out. Our foreign military bases would shut down. Our intelligence capability? Gone. Our alliances? A total reset. Maybe the Chinese would be strong enough to just step in and take over the world. And it isn't just what China would do. What about Russia? What about Iran and North Korea? One way or another, our adversaries would get stronger and our allies would get weaker.

"All I know for sure is that things won't stay like they are. That's why I need to make enough money to get through whatever is coming. That's why I'm not worried about John spending his life as a professional wrestler. He won't do it for long, because he won't have long to do it."

When we got back to the riverwalk, Cash changed gears. "Here's the rest of what you should know. I'm putting together my own wrestling league. I've already lined up some good wrestlers, and like I already said, they'll have political identities. And I'm pretty far down the road with a major cable network.

"We started talking back before Sam got sick. The executives I'm working with love the concept. As soon as everything is lined up, they're ready to pull the trigger. The circuit will take off as soon as there's a network deal, and the rest of the pieces will fall into place right after that. Sponsors, advertisers, event bookings – everything. John will be a silent partner, and it shouldn't be long before the organization is worth a *lot* of money. Then we'll sell it."

There was another bridge ahead of us, and we stopped to look at the river. Nobody else was around. I wanted to hold him again. After we walked through a fringe of trees, we got to a street that led to the bridge. I had one more question before we started back across the river. "There's something I'm not clear about."

"Okay."

"You started out as a fundamentalist. But by the time you graduated from Divinity School, you weren't a fundamentalist anymore. And even though things had changed, you were still enough of a believer to lead a church. Then you were a chaplain. Now you sound… you sound pretty skeptical about religion."

"I guess I need to fill in some blanks."

We started walking again. "When it comes to religion, that could take *weeks* to unpack. Luckily I have a one-minute version."

That was a relief.

"Back when I was an evangelical Christian, I said, *I know,* way too much. After that, when I was a preacher, I said, *I believe*. Now I say, *I sense*. That isn't good enough for most religious people, but that's the way I'm wired. The presence of God is something I *sense*."

We stopped when we were halfway across the bridge, and I started looking down at the water.

I didn't say anything at first, but I finally turned toward Cash and touched his arm. "I think you're coming into focus. So is… you know, what's happening between us. I guess it's the same old story. Girl feels herself falling for boy. Girl asks boy why he thinks the world is falling apart. Boy is afraid of running her off, but he tells her anyway. Girl and boy make out beside a river and in a pagoda. Girl and boy keep talking. Girl doesn't jump in the river. Girl feels the most intense connection she has ever felt."

He was looking into my eyes, and he kept looking. "Boy meets girl. Boy…"

That was as far as he got. We started kissing, but it wasn't long before somebody drove by and yelled, "Get a room!"

Cash pretended to be thinking. "You know, that is *not* an altogether bad idea."

I tried to look offended. "Well if you think I'm *that* kind of girl, you can just… you can just come back with me to my hotel before I wake up from this dream I'm having.

26

The dream lasted until the next morning. Cash was lying on his back in bed. He was talking about where we would be in five years. John would've already gotten into the ring with *Brando*. Whatever was going to happen, would have happened. Cash said that even if America hadn't fallen by then, its limp would probably be a whole lot worse. He rolled over and looked at me. He said he didn't know where we'd be or what we'd be doing, but he wanted us to be together. Then he started talking about the children he hoped we'd have.

I wasn't surprised that he wanted kids, but until then I wasn't sure. I was afraid it would push us apart. I was determined to tell him the truth, but I didn't want to sound ominous. I tried to be playful.

I sat up and looked at him. "My what *interesting* timing."

He was still looking at me. "How so?"

"We spend a passionate night together, and the first thing you do the next morning is talk about having children."

Cash started smiling. "Well Ches, as I'm *pretty sure* you know, that wasn't the first thing I did this morning. Or the second thing. But what's so interesting about the timing?"

"Yesterday afternoon you spent a couple of hours talking about how the country is on the verge of collapse. Chaos. Destruction. Blood in the streets. And a day later, you're talking about children. What you described would be a terrible time to raise a child. Or to *be* one."

I was trying to read his face, and I kept talking. "It's not that I don't like kids. I *love* kids. I did more than my share of babysitting when I was growing up, and I've taught school. If it was thirty or forty years ago, I'd jump right in. I'd love to be a mother. But now… I don't know."

He wasn't smiling. "It sounds like you *do* know."

I kept looking at Cash. "I could say, 'Never say never,' but… I don't want to mislead you, so I'll say this. Unless something changes, I can't see bringing children into the world."

I tried to tell myself that it was my imagination, but it felt like the magic was being sucked out of the room. "God, I hope this isn't a deal-breaker for you. I want us to be together."

He didn't say anything at first. He just looked at me. Then he rolled onto his back again and started gazing at the ceiling. "I'd never want you to do something you didn't want to do. I shouldn't have even started this conversation. It was way too early to talk about… you know, us being parents. But it was on my mind and… I didn't want to keep anything from you."

I rolled onto my back, too. "I don't want you holding back. It would've come up anyway. Maybe… things can change."

Cash had already told me about having a meeting the next day in Miami. I should've said something about being open to adoption, but I wasn't thinking. I was worn out. We had our goodbye hug when he left for the airport. The hug felt empty. I felt empty. And sad. I wondered if Cash felt the same way I did.

Two days later I was back in Tennessee. I had braced myself when I was on my way to see Carla. I thought she might've gotten worse, but she looked the same. That night we were standing in the kitchen. She was on her second glass of wine when I mentioned that I shouldn't have been gone for so long.

She went into one of her routines. She stared out the window and tried to look forlorn. "Is this how you imagined me? Abandoned and confused? Pitiful? Or would you like to see me as I *actually was?*"

She walked away from the window and put her fists on her hips like she was a warrior queen. "While you were away, I managed to *entertain* a rather *vigorous* visitor. To spare you any discomfort, I'll just refer to him as an *old friend*."

She looked over at me. She half-closed her eyes and bit her lower lip. "This is how I appeared from time to time during your absence. Adventurous. Wanton. *Lascivious*."

Then she raised her glass. "To the blessings of modern pharmacology. To dark bedrooms. And to not outliving one's libido."

I put my hand over my mouth, and pretended I was about to vomit.

I thought about going to bed without saying anything, but I went ahead and got it over with. There was no point in concealing the way I felt. She always knew when I was depressed.

As soon as I started telling her about Cash, she lit up. "A young man of color! How *outrageous*! Yet another reason to wish that my purported mother had lived long enough to suffer a bit more. I would've had *so* much fun with this."

She finally settled down and listened. After I talked about falling for Cash, I told her how afraid I was that I was losing him.

She didn't say anything at first. "Hearing you talk about Cash… I was watching you while you were describing him. I kept having the same thought. There's a lot more pulling you together than pushing you apart. You've been looking for somebody like Cash for most of your life. And from what you said – from what he told you – he's been waiting just as long for you.

"Ches, I don't think you're losing each other. It might take a little while, but it wouldn't surprise me if everything works out. And as for the way you feel about having children, that's a conversation we can have when I'm not about to say good night."

Carla gave me a kiss, but before she started back to her bedroom, she gave me a sly smile. "I plan on sleeping late in the morning. I need to recover from the last few days, and *nights*. So much excess. So much *experimentation*."

She never missed an opportunity to gross me out. She didn't mind exaggerating for effect, but if she said she had a tryst – she definitely had a tryst.

I slept better than I had the night before, but the next morning I was just as sad about Cash. Clouds were low in the sky. Gloomy and gray. Grieving weather. After I didn't eat breakfast, I walked up the hill behind the house. There weren't many leaves left on the trees. I stayed outside for a couple of hours. I drank in the solitude until a light rain started falling, and then I went back down to the house. I thought about calling Mac, but I didn't want to spend all afternoon telling him about Cash. I ended up building a fire, and I started reading his book again.

Two days later I went to see him at his house. After a while he started showing me photographs of Mac's parents – my grandfather and grandmother – and a few of my earlier ancestors. Then I asked him if he had photographs of some of the other people I'd been reading about.

He looked at me and smiled. "I have *lots* of photos. As luck would have it, one of my many eccentricities is collecting old yearbooks."

I followed him up to the top of the stairs, to what he called his library. An entire wall was covered by a bookshelf. It was lined with rows of high school and college yearbooks.

"About fifty years ago, I went to a yard sale. A couple of high school annuals were on a table. They were from back in the 1940s. One had a withered corsage and a couple of love letters inside. They were a dollar each. After that, I went to other yard sales and to estate sales, and I started looking through old bookstores. I ended up with more yearbooks than I have room for. Who do you want to see?"

He showed me pictures of two girls, Callie and her friend Claire. He'd been especially drawn to both of them back when they were in high school. The last picture I saw was of a lady named Ann Woodmore. She was in a college yearbook from the early 1930s. She had been one of Mac's guiding lights when he was young. He'd written about how deeply kind she was, and I could see it in her eyes.

He put her yearbook back on the shelf. "And if you want to see any of the places you read about, I'd love to show you around."

27

By then we would've already gone back to Short Mountain. We would've already searched for the rock where Sugar and Jimmy had written their names. But it rained pretty hard for several days in a row, and we had to wait for the ground to dry out. After that, I had a cold. And then Mac came down with a sinus infection. When he finally got well, there was more rain, and he just started driving me around. I saw the house where he grew up, and he showed me what was left of the neighborhood he had tried to preserve. Almost every place he cared about was gone, but he wanted me to see where those places had been.

Then he drove me to what had been the campus of his old high school. The only remaining structures were the gymnasium and one renovated building, but he spent an hour showing me where things had happened almost sixty years earlier. Mac looked at me when we got back to his car. "I'm tired of showing you where things *used* to be. I think we should go somewhere that hasn't changed."

He started driving, and it was a couple of minutes before he said anything else. "Aren't you curious about where we're going?"

"I think I already know."

He glanced over. "Okay. Let's hear it."

"I think we're going to the cemetery where your parents are buried. And where your father's grandparents are."

He started smiling. "How did you figure it out?"

"Well, you said it was someplace that hasn't changed. And there was that scene in your book. When you went there with your father. I've been wanting to go. I would've asked, but… I didn't know how you'd feel about going."

Mac rolled through an intersection as the light turned yellow. "It isn't a problem. I don't go as much as I should, but I went right after you and I met. I told my mother and my father about you. I wish you could've known them."

"You mean they wouldn't have disowned you? I mean for fathering a kid with an unmarried woman?"

He laughed. "Are you kidding? They were *aching* for a grandchild. They had the misfortune of being the parents of an only child. And you've read my book. When it came to having serious relationships with women, I was a late bloomer. My mother would've thrown confetti, and my father would've given me a medal."

Mac reached up and adjusted the rearview mirror. "And what goes around has come around. Now I feel the same way they did. Elinor and I are still waiting for a grandchild. But there's something I want to ask you."

I wasn't sure what was coming. "Okay."

"It seems like you've been a little bit down ever since you got back from Iowa. At first I thought you might be having a problem with the documentary you're working on. But maybe something happened with that guy you told me about, back in the summer. The guy in the wrestling business."

I wasn't sure how much I wanted to say. "I would've told you more about Cash, but there wasn't much to tell. Now there is. Or at least there was."

I went ahead and told Mac why I loved Cash. I went back through what had happened to Sam, and I told him where things stood with John's vendetta against *Brando*. After I tried to explain the new wrestling league, I went into how Cash saw the world. But we got to the cemetery before I could tell him about Cash wanting children.

Mac didn't drive directly to where his parents were buried. He wanted me to get a sense of where we were. We didn't see any other cars in the sprawling, tree-filled cemetery. We drove past monuments that had been standing since the mid-1800s, and we finally turned onto a narrow side road. Mac pulled up and parked beside a massive oak. We got out of the car, and I followed him to where several members of his family were buried.

The graves of my grandmother and grandfather were under thick rectangular slabs of limestone. Along with their names, the inscriptions included when and where they were born, and when and where they died. I'd read about them in Mac's book. I knew intimate details of their lives. Secrets that their closest friends wouldn't have known.

When Mac introduced me to them, and them to me, I imagined they were there listening. Shadows and sunlight slid back and forth across their gravestones. He talked about me, and about both of them, and I could feel a connection beginning to form. By the time he put his arm around me, I was holding back a lot of emotion.

We eventually started walking around and looking at other graves. One of the earliest dates we saw was on a weathered limestone monument. There was an angel carved out of marble on top. The marker was for a woman who was born in 1775. She lived until 1871. Her ninety-six-year journey had been boiled down to a couple of dates and a hyphen. The front of the base had deteriorated, and the angel was leaning forward at a precarious angle.

Mac glanced over at me. "I was glad to hear about Cash and what he thinks about the world, but… Back when we were taking one of our walks, you told me a little about how you see the future. I'd love to know more about what *you* think."

I wanted to keep looking at gravestones. "Well, it took a while for Cash to lay out his dark vision of the future. I don't want to spend the next hour talking, but I can say a little about… you know, about America. I just wish I was more hopeful than I am."

I peered up at the angel. "Like I said before, I'm worried about the country. More and more Americans are giving up on democracy. If they can get what they want in the short run, too many people seem fine with having an authoritarian leader. It's like the voters who want America to keep being a democracy are driving a car. And the people who don't like the way the country is changing… they're trying to grab the steering wheel.

"They don't want America to be racially diverse. They don't like immigration. They don't like gay marriage. Or taxes. Or federal regulations. They don't like a lot of things. They think the only way to stop what's happening is to run the car into a ditch. Even if the ditch is a right-wing dictatorship."

I noticed how solemn the angel looked. "How long can democracy survive in America when millions of right-wing radicals, and left-wing extremists, are trying to tear it apart? And even if it does last for a while, what then? The climate is changing too fast for the environment to adapt. What's the difference between a democracy and an autocracy when the world is on fire?

"There's something I was about to tell you when we got here. Cash wants children, but I feel the same way I did when you and I took that walk back in the summer. I can't see bringing a child into a catastrophe. And I'm afraid that means I'll lose him."

"I don't want to push Cash away, but it would be wrong to build up his hopes. I love him, but I need time to think through everything. The other day I sent him a letter. I said it might be a while before he hears from me, but not to give up on us."

Mac was staring at the leaning angel on the monument. "I wish I could say you're wrong about what's happening to the world, but I can't. There's so much I want to tell you. There's too much. But I'll start with this. It's important to understand why things are happening the way they are.

"The world has gotten way too complicated for most people. How many people can explain how a cell phone works? Or even how a television works? Maybe one one-thousandth of one percent? It's the same when it comes to the problems the government has to deal with. How many people really understand even *one* complex political issue?

"Almost everybody has to rely on somebody else to explain what's going on. That was fine when they listened to people who knew what they were talking about, but that's been turned upside down. Now millions of people get their information from on-air performers posing as journalists. From entertainers pretending to understand science. The more complex the world is, the easier it is to lie. The easier it is to manipulate people."

Mac shook his head. "I knew that the America I grew up in wouldn't last forever, but I didn't think I'd be around to watch it fall apart. I guess I should've seen it coming. I remember when I saw that first photograph of the earth. The one taken a half-century ago from a space capsule above the surface of the moon. I thought that seeing how beautiful and vulnerable this planet is… I thought that people would change the way they think. But it hasn't made any difference."

I could hear the sadness in his voice. "Maybe people, most of them at least, are just too damn limited. The biggest thing the majority of people focus on is political theater. Or football or movie star gossip. Or pro wrestling."

Mac stopped talking. He glanced up at the angel again, and then he walked over and stood next to me. "I didn't mean to give you a sermon."

"That was pretty short for a sermon."

"Well, that was just the introduction."

'When do I get to hear the rest of it."

He smiled and gave me a little wink. "I don't know. But it shouldn't be much longer."

28

The rain held off and the ground dried out, and Mac called Millie Warwick in Woodbury. Back in the summer, she'd said to let her know if we wanted to look for the rock on Short Mountain. That she had a relative who could go with us.

But things had changed. "A couple of months back there were some bear sightings around the mountain. So Wilton went up there to look around. He was climbing up to a deer stand, but his foot slipped. He fell about twenty feet and broke his leg. He's the only one I'd trust to keep quiet about the cave. Now I don't mean to tell you your business, but you might not want to go by yourselves. When I was growing up, I knew people who lived up there. But now... Well, I don't think I know a soul."

Mac was in good shape for somebody who was seventy-two years old, but I wasn't sure he could make the climb. Then he showed me the topographical map he'd bought back in the summer. The terrain looked daunting in some areas, but he'd spent hours studying the map. He thought that Sugar and Jimmy's rock could only be in a handful of places. He'd already marked the route we'd take up the mountain. It was hard to visualize how steep the climb would be, but if we took our time, I thought he could probably make it.

The first Saturday morning in December, Pearl Harbor Day, was sunny and cool. Mac and I got off to a late start. If Carla knew we were doing anything out of the ordinary, she would've suspected that we were up to something. I just said we'd probably go out and do some hiking. She went shopping, and after she left, it took me almost an hour to find her camera. She'd had it since she was in college. There was something distinctive about the pictures it took.

We were on our way to Woodbury when I reached into my pocket for my phone. I'd left it on the kitchen counter back at Carla's. When I told Mac, he just shrugged and nodded at *his* phone, which was plugged into the charger. I spent most of the trip thinking about Cash and looking out the window. And I kept imagining Carla on Christmas morning, looking at a photograph of the rock.

After we went through Woodbury, Mac decided to get some gas. He stopped off at a little country market north of town. I went inside and bought a bottle of water. When I was on my way to the counter, the guy at the cash register was staring at me. He looked like a convict looking at porn. He had tattoos of crosses on his knuckles, and one of a teardrop beside his right eye. He kept staring at me while I was paying, but he never said anything.

The pump didn't take his credit card, and Mac got in line behind me to pay for his gas. He tried to be friendly and make conversation, but the guy at the counter didn't say anything to him either. We went back outside, and Mac pointed at Short Mountain. It had looked a lot more imposing when we saw it from the church cemetery during the summer. We got back in the car, and Mac's phone was gone.

He was irritated at first, but then he just shrugged. "I guess it doesn't really matter. I'm overdue for a new one anyway. I didn't have a bunch of pictures on there, and it's not like we'll have any cell service."

We got back on the highway, but it wasn't long before we turned onto a gravel road. It followed a creek into an area that was more and more remote. We finally came to a much smaller road. It led up into a hollow on the southwestern flank of Short Mountain. We went over a little bridge, and then we passed a few barns and a couple of houses. The terrain on both sides of the road kept getting steeper and steeper until it seemed like the mountain was swallowing us. After about a mile, the road came to an end.

Mac turned the car around and pulled off into the weeds. We were both wearing hiking boots, and we put on our coats. He took a flashlight from under his seat, and then he opened the trunk. Along with a backpack, he pulled out a walking stick he had carved from the branch of a hickory tree. I slipped the camera into the backpack, and he handed me the topo map.

He left the car unlocked. "Some folks see a locked car as a challenge, and there's nothing in here worth taking."

I walked ahead of him. It was a steep climb at first, but we took our time and did some traversing on our way up through the trees. I stopped a few times to keep him from pushing himself too hard. There wasn't much underbrush, and even though I knew how unlikely it was that we'd run into a bear, I kept thinking about it. I jumped a little the first couple of times I heard a squirrel scurrying through the leaves, but I finally got used to it.

The map showed a shelf of level land about 400 feet higher than where we left the car. The shelf got narrower as it extended to the east, and then it led north to a section of the mountain that looked rugged enough to conceal a cave. We stopped again when we got up to the shelf. I looked in the direction of Sugar Tree Knob. Even though the trees had lost most of their leaves, the knob was all but obscured.

A hawk called, and several deer ran down the slope in front of us. We started walking again, and after a few hundred feet, the shelf led us to the top of a deep draw that Mac had marked on the map.

I stared down into the gully. "This doesn't look too bad, but there's no reason for both of us to go down there. Just stay here and rest, and I'll check it out."

Mac shook his head. "Haven't you ever heard the phrase, age before beauty?"

Before he started picking his way down the draw, he reached into his coat pocket. "Here. I brought you a surprise. Remember last summer when I was telling you about Short Mountain? How it used to be connected to the Cumberland Plateau?"

I remembered.

"Well, a couple of nights ago I wrote a poem about it. Or at least it's what *I* call a poem."

There were poems scattered throughout his book, but I assumed he'd stopped writing poetry. Mac handed me a folded piece of paper, and then he started down the gully. He used his walking stick and held on to trees when he could. It wasn't long before he was out of sight, but for the next minute or two, I could hear him moving through the leaves. I kept picturing him below me, looking for the overhang that Urban Warwick had spotted back in the 1940s.

I unfolded the paper and read Mac's poem. I was glad he wasn't there. I wouldn't have known what to say.

The Mountain

Sculpted from the rock,
Looming in isolation,
The mountain sensed two lovers
Concealed in its shadows.
Then death…
Death tore one from the other,
And the mountain saw their journey end.
But when evil…
When evil tore an infant from her mother,
The mountain understood
That another journey was beginning.
Years before, the mountain had watched
Another journey,
Had seen a nation grow and prosper.
And then, after two centuries,
It watched the nation being torn away
From the best of what it had been.
And the mountain…
The mountain endures in silent isolation,
And understands.

I wasn't ready to analyze the poem. I made myself think about something else. I ended up wondering if I'd ever be alone in the woods with Cash.

Mac was breathing pretty hard when he got back. He didn't say anything about the poem. After he opened the backpack, he pulled out a thermos of water and offered me a drink.

I just looked at him. "Age before beauty, remember?"

We both had some water, but his breathing was still heavy. I wanted him to rest, and I pointed to a spot I'd found while he was gone. "If you stand right there, you can see a little of Sugartree Knob through the trees."

He knew I was keeping an eye on him, but he didn't mention it. When I walked over and sat down, so did he. The air was mostly still, but every now and then a breeze came through the branches, and we watched the knob disappear and reappear across the valley. I heard the hawk again, but when I looked up, I could only see limbs and branches and patches of sky.

Mac was gazing across the valley. "I've been thinking about when I showed you where my parents are buried. I was telling you how I saw the world, and you said it sounded like a sermon. This seems like a good place to pick it back up. I mean if you're ready to hear a little more."

I said I was more than ready, and he smiled and pointed across the valley. "When we were over there in the cemetery… When I was talking about how family history ties into history… I was also trying to tell you who I am. You already know a lot from reading my book. But I wrote it over forty years ago.

"What I believe hasn't changed all that much, but it wouldn't be the same book if I wrote it today. I can probably make things a little clearer at seventy-two than I did back then.

"For as long as I can remember, I've tried to understand who I'm supposed to be. My parents wanted me to be a good Christian, and I wanted them to be proud of me. I went to Sunday School and church every week. Back then… sometimes when I'd talk to Jesus, I felt this glow. Like there was a spirit of… *goodness* inside me. When I was eleven, after I went through confirmation class, there was a ceremony in the sanctuary. I said what I was told to say, and I joined the church.

"Things started changing when I was thirteen or fourteen. I wanted to believe what I was supposed to believe, but the older I got, stories like Adam and Eve and Noah's Ark – they didn't seem true anymore. They just seemed like stories. And I started noticing discrepancies in the Gospels. Then there was hell and the Book of Revelation. The idea that part of God's plan allowed souls to be tortured for an eternity… Well, that drained a lot of the goodness away from what I'd been taught to believe. I still accepted a lot of what I'd learned in church, but I wanted to see how much I could figure out for myself."

He closed his eyes and yawned. "Not long after I started high school, I read about a philosopher who said that life could just be a dream. But even if life is a dream, something was clear to me. The dream had to come from somewhere. Something had to do the dreaming.

"By the time I got out of high school, I'd figured out something else. If something existed, there were two possibilities. Either something had always existed, or something had come from nothing. Since I didn't see any way that something could come from nothing, it was obvious that something had always existed. I didn't realize it back then, but that's where things would eventually get interesting."

A crest of wind rippled through the trees.

"I did the best I could to grasp what it meant for something to have always existed. What it meant for something to be eternal. Last summer, when we were over there in the cemetery, I was talking about all the ancestors you had. Back to the Romans. Well, just keep going back from there. Before the Greeks and the Egyptians. Before there were civilizations. Back thousands and thousands of generations. Before humans emerged. Before there were organisms. Before the advent of chemical processes. Back to when there was just a dense mass of matter, ready to explode.

"Even though some other theories are being considered, that's the trail that's been accepted by science. It's a trail that goes back through time and stops at a wall. I'd already followed the trail that was mapped out in the Bible – the one that leads back past Adam and Eve to the Creation. The way I see it, science and religion go back to pretty much the same place. A wall. The Biblical account starts with, 'In the Beginning, God…' And the accepted scientific account might as well start with, 'In the Beginning, the Big Bang…'"

Before he said anything else, we heard a gunshot. It came from pretty far behind us. From back where we'd already been. Then there were three more gunshots in rapid succession. I looked at Mac, but I couldn't see his face. He was staring toward the area where the shots were fired. I tried to tell myself that people who lived out in the country hunted all the time, but the shots we heard sounded like a signal. I wondered if somebody was following us. Maybe some lone wolf psychopath had seen us driving up into the hollow. He could've found the car, then started looking for us in the woods.

I thought about the movie *Deliverance*, and the psycho cashier who stared at me when we stopped for gas. I imagined him studying the ground and trying to pick up our trail.

He saw that I was trying to read his face. "Whoever is behind us… he probably saw the car. He knows we're out here. Let's just stay where we are for a while. He'll either come this way, or he won't."

29

After a couple of minutes, we got moving. Mac was still steady on his feet, but he wasn't walking as fast as he had before. I was the one who went down the next draw. There weren't any gunshots during the twenty or so minutes while I was looking around, and I went down four more draws after that. I understood why we stopped taking turns. The further down the mountain I was, the further away I was from where the gun was fired. And from whoever fired it.

Every time I went down a gully, I held on to as many trees as I could. When I got to where the slope started leveling out, I moved to the left, which was in the general direction of the car. I'd walk several hundred feet, and if I didn't see anything that looked like an overhang, I turned around and went back the other way – further up into the hollow. All I found was a couple of rotted-out barrels beside a little stream. It was probably the remains of an old still.

It was a slow process. I looked at the sky when I came up out of the fifth draw. There was plenty of daylight left, and I thought we had enough time to check out one or two more draws. Mac had heard me coming through the leaves. He angled his walking stick between the ground and a tree, and he used it to get to his feet.

He was staring at me. There was a grim look on his face, and he kept his voice low. "A few minutes ago, I heard a couple of guys calling to each other. They weren't too far behind us. We need to get moving."

I tried to be pragmatic. Whoever it was either knew we were there, or they didn't. If they knew we were there, they were either dangerous or they weren't. All we could do was keep moving and stay quiet. And keep our eyes open. From then on, I felt like we were being watched.

The map was on the ground beside Mac. I picked it up and handed it to him, and he pointed to where we were. "Instead of going back the way we came, we can go down to the bottom of the hollow. Then we can follow the branch to the car. We wouldn't have to come up any more draws. What do you think?"

I said what he hadn't let himself say. "You're right. Somebody could be waiting for us to retrace our steps."

He just nodded and looked over at the gully that led to the bottom of the hollow. We started down, and after a few minutes we were standing beside a little branch. It was only a foot or two wide, and it was flowing in the general direction of Mac's car. I kept listening for voices, but all I heard was the pecking of a woodpecker, and the calling of some other birds off in the distance.

Even though the slope wasn't too severe, there were places on either side of the branch where the terrain was too steep to climb. We kept crossing and recrossing the stream, and the land to our right finally started to flatten out. Mac was behind me when we came to a big slab of limestone. It was several feet thick, and it was right at the edge of the water. If it hadn't ended up on its side, it would've dammed up the stream.

After we went around it, he stopped. "Hey Ches, hold on."

He was looking up to our left. He stepped across the branch and pointed. All he said was, "There it is."

I went over and stood beside him. At least a hundred feet up the mountain, there was a pile of rock beneath an overhanging ledge. Urban Warwick couldn't have gotten there by climbing the wall of rock on that side of the branch. It was way too steep. I was trying to figure out the way he went, but then Mac turned around and started staring behind us. I thought he might have heard something.

He finally looked at me. "Maybe it's my imagination, but I can't shake the feeling that somebody is back there. We'd be easy enough to follow."

I glanced down at the boot prints we'd left on the bedrock.

He looked at the ground on the other side of the branch. "We can talk about this later on, but if somebody *is* back there, maybe we can get them off our trail. Just do what I do."

We moved to the right across the stream bed, and I followed him up the bank and into the weeds and brush. After we got to a fallen tree about three hundred feet away, we turned around and went a different way back to the branch. I didn't know if it would buy us enough time to get to the car, but if somebody was following us, it was worth a try.

The branch ran south, and the overhang we'd seen was to the east. Our boot prints made it look like we'd gone west. The bottoms of our boots were still wet, and we sat down and took them off. We carried them back across the stream before we dried them off on our pants. We didn't put our boots back on until we got to the next draw on the overhang side of the stream.

I thought we might be going to the car, but I followed Mack up into the draw. I wasn't sure what he was thinking. We did what we could not to leave a trail. After we'd gone about fifty yards, we went to the left – up the side of the draw. The ground was as steep as anywhere we'd been. We made it up to a shelf about thirty feet above us, and then we found a narrow lip of rock that led up to the next shelf. Mac was breathing hard, and he used his walking stick to steady himself. After a couple of minutes, we reached a narrow gap and walked out onto a fairly flat surface of stone.

I looked up and saw where a mass of rock had broken away from the ledge. Mac moved behind a boulder, and he started watching to see if anybody was coming down the hollow. Unless we stood up and started waving, there wasn't much chance of either one of us being spotted. I got the backpack, and while he kept watch, I went back to look for the cave. It was right where Urban Warwick said it was – beneath the overhang. But it wasn't the way I'd pictured it. It was just a narrow, jagged opening at the base of a bluff, and it was less than seven feet across.

I was afraid that the rock we'd come to see wouldn't be there, and I made myself turn around and look. About forty feet away, beside a small cedar tree, there was a limestone slab. It was leaning against a much larger shelf of detached rock. It was partly covered with moss, and there was a deep crack running along the surface. It could've been where it was for less than a century, or it could've been there for a hundred thousand years.

At first, I wasn't sure if I'd found what I was looking for. But after I moved a small branch and brushed away some debris, I saw where Sugar and Jimmy had gouged their names into the rock. The letters were shaped differently, but they were legible. And from the way the numbers were shaped, it looked like Jimmy was the one who cut in the year, 1937. He must have brought along a chisel.

It was the most inaccessible place I'd ever been. I wondered why they'd gone up there. I got the camera out of the pack, and I took ten or twelve pictures. Then I went back down to where Mac was standing.

He was still watching the bottom of the hollow. He kept his voice low, but he wasn't whispering. "Did you find the rock?"

I spoke as softly as I could. "Yeah. And the cave. I think I got some pretty good images."

He didn't say anything. He was thinking about something else.

30

Mac looked into my eyes. "I can't explain it, but something told me not to go to the car. I felt like somebody was down there waiting for us. Maybe I'm… I could be overreacting to this. To this… situation. You and I should be back there looking at the rock. And shining the flashlight into that cave. But I've got to think worst-case scenario."

"Which is what?"

He glanced at me, and then he went back to staring down into the hollow. "When I heard those voices – men's voices – there could've been two guys, or there could've been more. It seemed like they were coming in my direction. If they'd gotten any closer, I would've gone down the draw and found you, but I didn't hear anything after that.

"This is what's worrying me. If they catch up with us… If we were a couple of old men, they'd just move on. But an old man and a young woman? If they're bad guys… I'm sure you can take it from there. And if they're *really* bad guys… Maybe neither one of us makes it back home."

I wasn't sure why, but I was a little calmer after I heard Mac say what he was afraid of. I was afraid of the same thing. Then he asked me a question.

"Have you ever fired a pistol, Ches?"

"Yep. One of the guys I dated was really into shooting."

He was still watching the hollow. "Have you ever fired a .45?"

"Sure have. But I wasn't too wild about the recoil. Should I assume there's one in your backpack?"

He nodded. "I brought it along in case we ran into a bear. Or a mountain lion. Can you hit what you're shooting at?"

"Yeah. I'm pretty accurate." I didn't tell him that I ended up being a lot better shot than my boyfriend.

He pulled open the front of his coat. The .45 that had been in the backpack was in a holster. "At least we aren't defenseless. We're fine where we are, at least for now. Once we figure out who we're dealing with – if there's anybody back there – then we can decide what to do next. Unless they have a bloodhound, I don't think they can find us. But like I said, I don't want to go straight back to the car.

He was staring at the place where we'd left our false trail. "I haven't given you a chance to say anything. I just…"

"Not a problem. There hasn't been much time to talk."

Mac nodded. "Well, one of us needs to be the lookout, and one of us needs to study the map."

I watched the hollow. I hadn't asked him why he wanted to know if I could shoot. He was probably just going through his options. But if that's what it came down to, I was pretty sure I could pull the trigger.

A hawk called and its shadow slid across the rock in front of me. When I looked up, I saw it gliding above the trees. It called again, and a rabbit shot out from under some brush down by the branch. It might've been scared by the hawk, but I wasn't sure. I put the tip of my tongue against the roof of my mouth, and I made a light, clicking sound.

Mac came over beside me. Less than a minute later, a bearded man dressed in camouflage came into view. He was wearing a backpack and he was carrying an assault rifle. There was a black beret on his head, and he was smoking. He was looking down at the stream bed. He stopped when he got to our false trail. He turned around and motioned to whoever was behind him, and two men with bushy beards came up to look at our tracks. They were carrying assault rifles, too. They were in all camouflage, and they both had black stocking caps on their heads.

Even though he was smoking, the lead guy looked fit. The other two were pretty overweight. We couldn't hear their voices. As soon as the guy in the beret finished his cigarette, they all followed the trail we'd made. They went up the bank on the far side of the branch, and disappeared into the woods.

Mac glanced over at me. "Have you figured out who they are?"

I thought I had. "They look like locals pretending to be soldiers. Now what?"

He crossed his arms and took a deep breath. "I have a couple of ideas, but what are you thinking?"

I was thinking that I might get raped, but that isn't what I said. "First off, we don't know what they're up to. Maybe they're just out here playing war games. Maybe tracking us is a game. They might just want to see if they can find us. And there could be more of them around. Like you said, they're either bad guys or they're not. They might be fine, upstanding citizens, but those three look like trouble."

I kept talking. "If they're bad guys, there's a pretty good chance you're right. Somebody is staking out the car. Even if most of them get tired and go home, some psycho could stick around and wait for us to walk out of this hollow. Crossing our fingers and hoping for the best isn't an option. We have to assume they're as dangerous as they look. I think we should stay here – at least until dark."

Mac was still staring down at the place where we'd seen the men. "Okay. Then what?"

"It'll be a while before we can go back to the car. I don't know if it's something you want to try, but… I think we should try to hike out of here. We could go up the mountain. At least most of the way. The map shows a fire tower at the very top. They could have somebody up there, too."

I picked up the map. I pointed to where we were, and then to a narrow shelf not too far uphill from the cave. "Once we get up to where it flattens out, we could swing over to this draw. It's about a quarter of a mile straight uphill, but it isn't any steeper than the ones we've already been up. There isn't much of a slope after that. We could stay below the summit, and after we work our way to the north, we could swing around to the west. From there it's less than a mile to a road, and it's all downhill. We could play it by ear after that."

Mac reached for the map, and I started watching the hollow.

After a few seconds, he glanced up at the sky. "We couldn't use the flashlight, but we're only a few days from a full moon. If the clouds don't get too thick, we should be able to see well enough. We'd just have to stay quiet and take our time."

He looked down into the hollow. "I'm not too worried about the two fat guys. But the one doing the tracking… The way he moved… He looks like he's had some training. If anybody stays up all night looking for us, it'll be him."

31

We kept watching from behind the rocks. It wasn't long before the men who were tracking us came back to the branch. They stood around for a couple of minutes, and then they moved on down the hollow.

Mac stayed where he was. His voice was just above a whisper. "They sure didn't take long to figure out what we did. They know we didn't go back up the hollow. That means we either went east, higher up the mountain, or we're on our way down to the car.

"By now the lead guy is probably… he's getting to the draw we just came up. He'll be looking for a trail. Even though it's rocky, and even though we were careful, if he's good enough, he might be able to see where we went. If he doesn't notice anything right off, they'll probably go down to check on the car. Maybe they won't come back. But we have to be ready in case they do."

Then Mac told me his plan. I didn't like it, but I couldn't come up with anything better. I would take the backpack and the gun and the flashlight, and hide in the cave. He would sit where he could watch the hollow, and where I could see him. If they showed up, he would pretend to be having chest pains. He'd say he was having a heart attack, and that I had gone to get help.

If they believed him, they'd take him to Woodbury. Or at least to his car. When he got to town, he'd find the sheriff and I would be rescued sometime after dark. But if they didn't believe him, they'd start looking around. They'd find the cave. When they started to go inside, I'd have to decide what to do. That's why he'd asked me if I could shoot.

He walked with me toward the cave. I thought he'd look at the inscription that Sugar and Jimmy had made on the rock, but he didn't. When we got up to the entrance, we took turns shining the flashlight into the darkness. It looked like the floor sloped down for fifty or sixty feet to a pile of rocks. That was as far as we could see.

Mac put the gun and the camera into the backpack. After I got my legs into the entrance of the cave, I backed into the darkness. The temperature was close to what it was outside, but the air smelled different. It was stagnant and lifeless. I'd been in caves a few times before. I knew about stalagmites and stalactites, and that piles of rock that fell from ceilings were called breakdowns. And that was about it.

Mac's face was framed by the outside light. "Are you okay, Ches?"

"Yeah. I'm good."

He reached into the opening and handed me the flashlight and the backpack. "If they don't come before dark, that probably means they don't know we're here. If that's the way it goes, just sit tight until I come to get you. If I leave with them, wait until help shows up. But…"

I cut him off. "I know. If it goes the other way, I'll be okay. Just stay where I can see you."

I had a plan, too. Or at least part of one. If they tried to hurt Mac, I'd start yelling. They wouldn't know that I had a gun. The lead guy would come to the entrance. As soon as he was close enough, I'd blow off his head. I wouldn't miss. And if the two fat guys were close enough, I could probably take one of them out, too. I turned on the flashlight. Mac must have put in fresh batteries.

I stared out at him, and after a while I started thinking about the black and white Springer Spaniel we had back when I was in school. Carla had named her Miss America, but we called her Missy. She had a gentle, loving spirit. She was family. One summer I was home from college, and I was walking her in a park near our house. I heard something behind us, and I turned around just in time to see a big male pit bull running toward us.

He'd picked up Missy's scent, and he went straight for her. I got in front of her, but the pit bull ran into my leg and almost knocked me down. Then he attacked her. He had his mouth around the top of Missy's shoulders, just below her neck. There wasn't anything she could do.

The dog was shaking her, and I started hitting him with my fists. It didn't do any good. Missy was gasping, and I got her leash unhooked. I wrapped it around the pit bull's neck as fast as I could, and I started pulling. I got down on the ground and put my knees against the back of his neck, but he barely even choked. He started shaking her again, and when Missy was almost limp, he put her down and walked away. I thought she was dead, but she took a breath and then she whimpered. It took me a while to carry her back home. She died three days later.

I wasn't the same after that. I despised my helplessness. For the next couple of years – nearly every day when I was in town – I went back to the park. I always had a dog treat in my right pocket and a Taser in my left pocket. And a serrated knife in my back pocket. I fantasized about killing the pit bull, but I never saw him again.

I thought about what happened every day. It was several months before my anger finally started losing its edge. Before my headaches went away. Before sleeping through the night got easier.

I sat on a rock and looked out at Mac. When I thought about him getting hurt, I felt the same rage I'd felt about Missy. I visualized the guy in the black beret. He would be confident when he walked up to the opening. I would be kneeling in the dark. He'd hear me begging not to be hurt. He would move closer and reassure me. I would keep my breathing steady. I would be aiming at the middle of his face when I squeezed the trigger. If anybody was with him, the second shot wouldn't be that easy.

I couldn't stay that amped up for long. I started taking long, deep breaths, and after a few minutes, I settled down. I kept thinking about the men hunting us, but I also tried to think about Cash. After an hour and a half, I was pretty sure they weren't coming for us. It was a little before sunset when Mac walked back to the cave.

He brought his face up to the opening. He kept his voice low. "I think we should change our plan – at least some."

"All right."

"Since the car is still there, they know we didn't go south. They've already checked across the branch, so they also know we didn't go west. And we wouldn't have gone north – back up hollow. That means the only way we would've gone is the way we went. East. Up the draw. Up the mountain. Unless they went home, they're down there staking out the car. There's a good chance they'll come back and start sniffing around up here. It might not matter, but there's something else we can try."

32

Mac handed me his walking stick, and I helped him get through the entrance. As soon as he caught his breath, we crouched down and he followed me back to the pile of rocks we'd seen through the opening. We made our first discovery as soon as we went around the breakdown. If Sugar and Jimmy ever came into the cave, they weren't the first ones who'd been there.

On the far side of the breakdown, we found a circle of rocks surrounding a mound of ashes and a few mostly burned-up logs. And near the remains of the fire was what was left of an old pair of boots and a couple of broken jugs. Then I swept the ceiling with the beam of the flashlight. Several names looked like they'd been written with the flame of a candle.

Mac let out a whistle. "Good Lord. Hand me the flashlight."

He started reading the names on the ceiling. "Ike Gleason. E J Hawkins. Jack Neely. I don't know who they were, but I sure know who this guy was. I read about him when we were at the Library and Archives."

He used his stick and pointed at the only name he hadn't said out loud. "Pomp Kersey. He was a Confederate soldier for a while. He wasn't much past twenty. After he deserted, he was the leader of a guerilla unit – here in Cannon County. He was a local celebrity. Kersey and his band killed their share of Union soldiers. And they went after private citizens, too. Even some Confederate families.

"Union patrols hunted them for months. One night Pomp and his gang showed up at a party. They killed one or two Union sympathizers, then they headed for Short Mountain. Maybe they were trying to get to this cave. Wherever they were going, they didn't make it. They were killed not too far from here."

It didn't take long for Mac's excitement to fade. "Well, we better keep moving. We need to see if this cave goes anywhere."

He handed me the flashlight, and I led the way. The chamber we were in kept getting narrower. I finally took off the backpack. I had to turn sideways to squeeze through the passageway, but then it widened into a room that was about fifty feet across. Mac came up beside me, and the beam of the flashlight lit up a thirty-foot-high wall of broken rock and slabs in front of us. A thick layer of the ceiling had fallen, and the breakdown reached from one wall to the other. I handed the flashlight to Mac. He started moving the light along the gap between the rock and the ceiling.

He was shaking his head. "I don't know about crawling up those rocks. If one of us slipped and got hurt..."

I felt the same way. I turned around to go back, but Mac stayed where he was.

He still had the flashlight and he kept shining it along the top of the wall. "Do you notice anything different, Ches? I... I mean between here and back where we found those names?"

I didn't know what he meant. "You mean the rockfalls?"

"No. The way the air smells. It doesn't... doesn't smell the same."

I could hear how cold he was getting. I heard it every time he stopped talking in the middle of a sentence. I wasn't sure if the air smelled different, but it felt like it was getting even colder. It took us a while to get back to the opening, and I sat down on the same rock where I'd been sitting before. A sliver of light was coming in from outside, and I could still see Mac after he turned off the flashlight. I wondered if I was as cold as he was.

I didn't like the silence. "You might be right about the air. Back where we turned around… it didn't smell quite as… as old."

"That's what I thought."

Mac had put down his walking stick, and he was trying to stretch out his back. He stretched a little more, and then he was still. "We should probably stay… stay in here for a couple of hours after it gets dark. We might as well get… some rest. The floor of the cave is pretty smooth. Why don't… don't you lie down? You can use the backpack for a pillow. It could… be a long night."

"It'll be a long night for both of us. I don't… mind going first, but you should rest, too."

I should've known what he'd say. "If I lie down, it might… be morning before I can get back up."

I slid my feet across the cave floor. I only felt one rock. After I put the backpack where I wanted it, I lay down.

Mac wanted to take my mind off of the situation we were in. "You know what you could… use right now? A bedtime story. How… about *Hansel and Gretel*?"

He still had his sense of humor. "Really? Two children leave a… a trail through the forest? And they get captured by an evil witch who… wants to kill them? Nice."

I heard him shiver. "I can see how… how that might hit too close to home. Then what about *Little… Red Riding Hood*?"

It was my turn to shiver. "Yeah, I… remember that one. A wolf stalks a little… girl who's walking through the woods. He wants… to *devour* her. Something about that seems so… familiar. Maybe you could get back to… to your sermon. You know, back to what you were telling me before we… heard those gunshots."

"Well if hearing me talk about… about God and metaphysics doesn't… put you to sleep, nothing will. I'm game if you are, but the… the next part of the sermon might… remind you of *Through the Looking Glass*."

There wasn't much light outside, and Mac was staring out through the opening. "When we… heard those shots, I was saying that religion and science… They both go back to a wall. That religion might as well… have a wall with *The Beginning* written on it. And science… it should have a wall that says, *The Big Bang*. But I think they're… both wrong. There should be a… a mirror on the wall, and the trail… the trail should go right through the mirror.

"I'm not sure why the… preachers and the scientists don't see it. Scientists don't say much about… what exploded in the Big Bang. What set it off? Had… had it always been there? And why don't preachers talk about where God was… back before the heavens and the earth were created? Did God suddenly… wake up from an eternal coma… and just start creating?

"I'm pretty sure there's something… on the other side of the wall, Ches. If we went through the… through the looking glass, I'm pretty sure we'd… find an earlier universe. Back when I first thought about… an earlier universe, I just pictured matter. Atoms… and particles. I wasn't thinking about… awareness."

It was such a bizarre situation. While armed men were outside trying to hunt us down, I was hiding in a cave, listening to Mac shiver and talk about metaphysics. And it was strange that I could take in what he was saying.

"Science is... pretty clear about awareness. About... how it came to be. It says that... billions of years after the Big Bang, awareness... arose from matter. But I... eventually figured something out. If matter really *is* eternal... If there was another universe before... before this one, then... science might be wrong about the source of awareness.

"Why wouldn't the... chemical makeup of an earlier universe be... the same as it is in this universe? If matter generated awareness in... in this universe, wouldn't matter have generated... awareness in *that* universe, too? And if... there was one previous universe, there have probably been... been an infinite succession of universes. If... if that's true, couldn't awareness have... been generated an *infinite* number of times?"

I was still keeping up. Barely.

"Science... science is limited. To what can be observed. Most scientists... they've decided that matter only... exploded into existence one time. Exploded and... and formed a single universe. That was it. But what if... both matter and awareness have... existed in an infinite succession of universes? How would it... be possible to prove which one... gave rise to the other?

I could hear a smile in his voice. "That's my favorite... part. Why is it any more likely that matter... gave rise to awareness, than that awareness gave... rise to matter? And there's... there's something else. Why couldn't matter and awareness... why couldn't they both... have always existed independently? If that's the way it is, if... if there has always been... an eternal awareness, that... well, that sounds like God to me."

Not long after that, we both heard voices.

33

Mac eased off the rock and looked through the opening. There was still enough light to see who was outside. He spoke just above a whisper. "It's the guy with… the beret. I can't see who he's talking to. If he knew about the… cave, he'd already be back here. But it… won't be long before he finds it. When he does, he and… whoever he's with, they'll… come inside. We need to get going."

"You mean further back in the cave?"

"Yeah. They won't… be sure if we're in here. If we can get on top of… the rockfall in that… that other room, they might not be curious enough to… to keep looking."

I didn't know how Mac could make it up the rocks. "Are you sure they'll come in here? Maybe they don't have flashlights."

"It's almost dark, and… they're country boys. They have flashlights. They might even… have lanterns."

I knew what Mac would say about killing the leader. We didn't know how many other men there were. And there was a chance that they weren't planning to do us any harm. After I got up and put on the backpack, he handed me the flashlight and we took off. I checked everywhere we'd been between the entrance and the breakdown.

Except for the fire and what Pomp Kersey and his gang had left behind, there was no sign that anybody had ever been in the cave.

It helped a little to be on the move, but not much. I was still shivering.

We got to the second chamber, and we passed the flashlight back and forth while we were trying to find a way to get to the top of the rockfall. One route was near the wall to our right. While Mac pulled himself up onto a four-foot-wide slab, I pushed him from behind. I handed him the flashlight and his walking stick, and when he was pulling me onto the slab, I felt how cold his hands were.

I tried to focus on finding the next rock we had to climb, but I was listening for voices behind us. My anger was boiling up again. I pictured Mac and I being cornered in the rocks. The man with the beret holding his light – moving closer and closer to where we were hiding. I would be looking into his eyes when I pulled the trigger.

After the flash, I'd shoot toward the sounds of scrambling bodies, but it wouldn't be long before I heard movement all around me. Men moving closer in the darkness. A fist crashing into the side of my head. Then being pulled from the rockfall. Lying on the floor of the cave. Boots kicking away my breath. Being led through the passageway by my hair. Dragged through the opening. The rock scraping skin from my nose and mouth. The taste of blood.

Lights in my eyes. Bearded, ignorant faces. Mouths spewing contempt. Lowered pants. A hairy, flaccid belly. Heavy breathing. Tearing. Grunting. The stench of sweat and lust. Rancid breath. Searing pain. Numbness. Then the next man. And the next. Mac on his knees – forced to watch. Then a gunshot to the back of his head. His blood and his brains hitting me in the face. Another flash and then nothing.

Mac kept shining the flashlight along an expanse of rocks that rose ten or twelve feet above where we'd climbed. He ended up training the beam near the middle of the rockfall.

He moved to the base of a boulder. "This rock… is almost straight up, but there are… a couple of good-sized cracks, if we… can get up that high. You might make it okay, but I'd… need some help."

I put down the backpack. After Mac positioned the flashlight where it would shine on the upper part of the boulder, he got down on his hands and knees. I put my left hand against the rock to steady myself, and I stood on his back. He was trying not to move, but his arms and legs were shaking. I reached up and got a handhold, and I brought my right foot high enough to slide the front of my boot into a crack.

I managed to go up another couple of feet before I stopped. "I can't get to the… next crack. We need to find a… another way."

I was about five feet up the boulder. I told Mac what I was about to do, and then I jumped.

I didn't see how we could get to the top of the rockfall, but I followed Mac. He was picking his way toward a second slab that had broken away from the rest of the ceiling. Its lower end was wedged against the left wall of the cave, and it slanted in at a steep angle. When Mac got there, he handed me the walking stick and leaned into the space between the wall and the base of the slab.

He moved the beam of light along the surface of the rock. "Look at the… part that fell. It stays close… to the contour of the cave wall for… most of the way up. It's steep, but I… think I can make it. You better… take the flashlight. If… if I fall, you'll need it."

It was the only chance we had. I took the flashlight, and gave Mac as much light as I could. He steadied himself and moved into the space along the side of the cave. Before he braced his feet against the cave wall, he leaned back against the slab. I handed him his walking stick, and he put it between his teeth. Then he used his legs and his hands, and started working his way to the top. When he was high enough, I moved underneath him. I was ready to break his fall, but he made it all the way up without slipping.

I left the flashlight on when I put it in the backpack. It was shining out of the top. A little light was better than no light at all. I put my arms through the straps of the backpack, but I had to wear it in front of my body. After I leaned back and put my feet against the wall, I started moving up the slab.

I kept listening for voices, but I didn't hear anything. The beam of the flashlight made it look like the cave was moving, and I closed my eyes. My heart was racing, and I tried to focus on my breathing. When I was close to the top, Mac got his hand under one of my arms and helped me the rest of the way up. "Are… you okay, Ches? You're breathing… breathing pretty hard."

At least I felt a little warmer. "Just a little… panic attack. I'll… be fine." I took off the pack and got the flashlight. We were close to the top of the breakdown, but we still had to get over the tops of several slanting slabs that were leaning against each other. I held the flashlight, and Mac stepped out onto the jagged surface. He grasped his stick with one hand, and he kept his other hand on the rocks. It only took him a minute or so to get past the slabs and reach the crest of the breakdown.

I put on the backpack and started across. I had the flashlight in one hand and I was steadying myself with my free hand. When I was about halfway to Mac, I had to step across a wide gap. I lost my balance when one of my feet slipped. My hand hit a rock and I dropped the flashlight. It bounced off my foot and fell into the gap between the rocks. It was gone.

34

The darkness swallowed me and I froze. Disbelief. Anger. Fear. Guilt.

I held onto the rock. "Mac?"

"Right here."

"I'm so…"

"I know, Ches."

He sounded far away. "What you need to… to do now is… get over here. Just follow the… sound of my voice."

I started feeling for the next rock. I was trying not to shut down.

Mac tried not to sound worried. "You want to hear… hear something funny?"

I was too upset to think. "Okay."

"Well if I… think of anything funny, I'll… I'll let you know. But this… This is a long way from hopeless."

I didn't have far to go. He didn't stop talking, and I felt my way across the rocks. I kept moving toward the sound of his voice until I finally found his hand. He led me to what felt like a horizontal slab, and we sat down.

He didn't give me time to apologize. "I've been trying to… tell myself that they… won't hurt us. But with the way they… they've been tracking us… How relentless they are… Their weapons. We can't shoot… shoot our way out of here. If we pull the… the trigger, we won't get back alive.

"By now they… might be more interested in this… this cave, than… in us. When they get back here and see… all this rock, they might just turn… turn around and leave. We could… wait a while, and if we can get off this break… breakdown in one piece, making it… back to the entrance shouldn't… be a problem. They could be… gone by then."

I stared into the darkness. I imagined light building up in the passageway before they came into view. I pictured them walking along the edge of the breakdown, the light moving across the rocks. Talking. Arguing. Then walking away. If that's the way it went, we'd still have a treacherous journey back to the entrance.

We'd have to pick our way across the top of the rockfall, and make it back down the other slab. Bracing ourselves with our feet. Keeping our backs and our palms flat against the rock. Inching through the blackness. Then we'd feel along the wall, and after we passed the old fire, we'd move around the front breakdown to the entrance.

If that's what it came to, we could get out of the cave. As long as hypothermia didn't shut us down before we got there. As long as we didn't fall in the rocks and get hurt. And they could be waiting right outside the cave. That wasn't a chance I could take.

Mac took a deep breath. "Or we can just stay where we are. Stay here and hope that Elinor… Elinor and Carla don't take too long to… to report that we're missing. All Elinor knows is that we're some… somewhere outside of Woodbury. When… when we don't show up, they'll… get in touch with the Cannon County sheriff and the… the Tennessee Bureau of… Investigation. I have a friend… he's worked at the TBI for years. It won't take Carla long to… post a reward. She knows how loud… money can talk. And in a place like this, it… it screams.

"But the longer we stay where we are, the… the colder we'll get. And we'll get weak… weaker. I don't know how… long we can last."

Mac was right about not being able to stay where we were. I was colder than I'd ever been in my life.

He said it before I did. "I think we should… see what's on the back side of these… these rocks."

But I dreaded going deeper into the cave. Deeper into what seemed like a tomb. Closer to where Mac and I could spend our last hours. Getting weaker and weaker. Holding each other in the blackness. Trembling in the cold until one of us, and then the other, slipped away. Searchers finding the cave too late. Or not at all. Carla in her final days. Never knowing what happened. Cash growing old without answers. Our remains not being found for decades. Or centuries.

Mac stayed focused. "There's something I… keep thinking about. This was one of… of Pomp Kersey's hideouts. He was hunted… for months without getting caught. It makes… makes sense that he'd want a place with… another way out. Maybe that's why the air… why it smells different back here. If they come… up here to look around, we won't… have time to get away. We can't just… wait for them to show up."

I followed him over the rocks to the back side of the breakdown. He was tapping with his walking stick like a blind man. Before long the tapping stopped, but I could still hear him breathing. He was only three or four feet away.

"There's a… drop off. It's right in front of me. I need a few… a few rocks."

I was beside a boulder. I kept sliding my feet until I located a few small pieces of broken stone. Then I found Mac's hand and gave him one of the rocks. His fingers were colder than mine were.

He sounded like he knew what he was doing. "I'm going to… to say 'A B C *drop*.' As soon as… When I say, 'drop, I'll start count… counting up from one… As fast as I can. Listen for… the number I'm on when… when you hear it hit. Are… are you ready, Ches?"

"Yeah."

"Okay. A B C *drop*, onetwothreefourfivesixseven… Did you get… get it?"

"Yeah, the rock… It hit around three. Then it took a couple of… bounces to the left."

Mac heard it the same way. He moved to the left and dropped the next rock.

"A B C *drop*, onetwothreefourfivesixseveneightnine."

It didn't hit until four or five. Mac had the rock hitting at five or six before it bounced away in the same direction as the first rock. Then he went several steps to the right and dropped another rock. It hit at two.

We were above a slab that slanted down to our left. We moved a little to our right, and Mac found it with the end of his walking stick. We kept moving until it was only a foot below where we were standing. I took Mac's arm and helped him onto the slab. I could feel him shivering. After he sat down, he probed to the right with his stick. He couldn't find an edge.

It didn't take us long to make it to the floor of the cave. Before we went any further, a faint fringe of light appeared above the crest of the breakdown. It looked like the moon was about to rise. Then we heard indistinct voices. I kept listening and staring up at the light, but when Mac touched my arm, we went deeper into the cave. We moved along a wall to our left, and after twenty or thirty feet, the room narrowed into a low passageway.

Mac was in front of me, tapping as lightly as he could with his walking stick. We had to stoop down for a few feet, but then the passage got high enough for us to stand up. That's when I was sure I smelled air from outside the cave. Mac smelled it, too, and we both stopped. Then I heard the scratch of his walking stick as he started moving its tip across the floor, and then along the ceiling.

He found my hand and gave me his stick. His voice was just above a whisper. "Take this. See if you… can find… find where the air is coming in. Make a sound when you want to… know where I am."

I kept sweeping the stick in front of me and above me as I moved along the cave wall. It gradually curved up into the ceiling. It wasn't long before I put my tongue against the roof of my mouth, and signaled Mac with a click. He clicked back. He was behind me at first, but after a few more signals he was directly to my right. The room we were in was smaller than I thought.

I was still scared. Even if we found where the air was coming in, we might not make it outside. It wasn't long before I located a lateral opening with the tip of the stick. It was along the base of the wall, just above the floor of the cave. I got down on my knees and moved my fingers around the rough edges of the crevice. It was about four feet wide, and not more than a couple of feet high. The air was flowing in from outside. I clicked three times with my tongue.

Mac kept his voice down. "Did… did you find it?"

"I think so."

He felt his way along the wall until he got to me. Then he went down on one knee and felt the fissure. "Either this stays big… big enough for us to make it out, or… or it doesn't."

He crawled into the opening. I waited before I followed him in. I'd already taken off the backpack. I started pushing it, and the walking stick, ahead of me. The crawlway got a little wider after a few feet. Hope was pushing away the fear, but then Mac stopped moving.

"Ches, do you… hear that?"

"Not unless you're talking… about the silence."

"Keep… listening."

35

I heard an owl calling in the distance. A barred owl. Like the one I'd heard a few years earlier, when I was on the field trip with the girls in my class. It still sounded like it was saying, '*Who looks for youuuu?*'

Mac started crawling again. He was breathing harder and I could hear him grunting. The crawlway got narrower the further in I went. I kept moving the backpack and the walking stick ahead of me. Then I couldn't hear Mac anymore. The ceiling of the crevice was pressing against my back. I closed my eyes and turned my head sideways. It got harder and harder to move.

But when I pushed again, the cave seemed to relax. I opened my eyes, and there was a swath of illumination a few feet ahead of me. I kept moving until I crawled out into the night from underneath a small protrusion of rock. The moon was behind the clouds, but I could see trees against the sky.

Mac came over and helped me stand up. His voice was almost a whisper. He sounded like he was freezing. "We're not that far from… from the front of the cave. There probably isn't any… anybody back here, but… but we need to act like they are. I've mem… memorized the map. If we bear north and… head uphill, we should run into… that hollow."

The longer I was in the cave, the more I felt like I was in another dimension. Being outside was like being in a trance. The clouds were sliding in front of the moon. I watched Mac start to move up the slope with his walking stick. And then I was watching myself. Watched myself as I followed him. As I stopped to listen for pursuers. As I exulted in the light when the moon emerged from the clouds. I inhaled the darkness. I didn't hear myself walking through the leaves. I was a ghost.

The calling of the owl. More trees appearing when the clouds slid away from the moon. Branches moving with each breath, then still. Moving and still. Moving and still. Mac breathing and sighing. The night breathing. And sighing.

Gliding higher and higher up the mountain. Dreaming that Cash was beside me. The breeze stronger. The sighs deeper. The night colder. The fatigue heavier. And finally floating up out of the draw – the crest of the mountain just above us. Moving north across the sloping terrain, then angling west before we began our long descent. Down through the rising and falling breeze. Down through the breaths and the sighs. Down and down and down. Wiping away cold tears. Feeling myself shudder. Trying not to break.

We finally saw the headlights of a lone vehicle moving slowly along the road below us. We stopped walking, but we didn't sit down. Mac came up beside me. We were both shivering. When the wind came, the night was twice as cold. We went over and stood behind a massive tree. We put our arms around each other, but we couldn't keep back the cold. Then we were walking again. I tried to think about Cash. I couldn't stop shaking. Couldn't lose focus. Couldn't let myself fall. We stopped just before we got to the road.

We were behind a fallen tree. The cold flowed over us like water. We were less than a mile from the little country church on Sugartree Knob. Where we'd stood, looking across at Short Mountain. Where I read tombstone inscriptions in the warmth of a summer afternoon.

Mac's voice sounded like it could blow away. "Maybe I'm… missing something. But I… I think I know what to do."

He hadn't missed anything. Once we got on the road, if we walked fast enough, we might not be as cold. If we saw a house, we would avoid it. If a car came, we would hide. When we got to the church, we would wait. It was Sunday, and the preacher, or whoever had the key, would be there early and open the door. Mac said that one of the men who was hunting us, or some family member, could be in the congregation, but most of the people who showed up to worship would be decent people.

I went back to thinking about Cash. Being thankful for him. Thankful that he wasn't with me. Thankful that his fate wouldn't be in the hands of a few white strangers in a country church. Thankful that whoever was trying to catch us wouldn't find a black man if we got cornered.

We would stay out of sight and wait. Wait until we saw somebody who would help us. Somebody who would take us to Woodbury. We'd find Miss Warwick, and tell her what happened. If she couldn't help us, she would know who could. One way or another, we'd get to Mac's car. Then we'd head back to Nashville.

The road was empty. After we went a few hundred yards, we heard a dog barking ahead of us. After we went a little further, we saw two houses that were right across from each other. We got off the road, and stayed in the woods until we got to the back edge of the cemetery. Then we walked up to the little cinder block church. We stood where the church deflected some of the wind sliding across

Sugar Tree Knob. Mac leaned his walking stick against the building. We were both shivering. I had my back to the wall, and we put our arms around each other again.

I needed to hear his voice. “Are you… still worried?”

“Not like I was. We just can’t… can’t let them find us. Or… or let the cold get us.”

36

We were quiet for a couple of minutes. It was colder when we weren't talking. I needed to break the silence. "When I was in the cave… When you were still outside… The guy in the beret… I wanted him to… to find us. So I could kill him. I still want to kill him. If… if I say it, maybe I'll… stop thinking about it."

Mac was quiet at first. "Is it… working?"

It wasn't.

Even though he was shivering, he tried to turn on his backwoods accent. "Know what… what *I'm* thinkin' about? It's… all that Cannon County blood you… wuz born with. I believe it's… turned you downright *vengeful*. Too bad all that vengeance… don't make you no warmer."

Our faces were almost touching. I didn't want him to stop talking. Every time he said something, I could feel the warmth of his breath. "I wouldn't mind hearing… more of your sermon. What better time to… learn about the meaning of life? Than… when we're freezing to death in… the middle of the night."

He held me a little tighter. "Even though it ain't… no warmer on the… other side of the looking glass, I doubt it's any… colder."

He dropped the accent. "Back when we… were in the cave. I was talking about awareness… how it might be eternal. How that could… open another door to God."

The moon came out from behind a cloud. Mac leaned back and tried to look at me. "There's something I want you to… understand. Believing in God… It isn't illogical. The path to God… It doesn't have to… come from holy scriptures. Or preachers. It… can come from reason. From… intuition. I've… I've always sensed *a spirit*. I've sensed God… from as far back as I can remember.

"Learning about Jesus. Loving… my neighbor. Doing unto others. Trying to be… kind. Those teachings… they got inside me. Fed my spirit. Later on, when… when I was older, I'd see some… act of grace. And I… could feel the spirit glowing."

The sky lightened up a little, but the night was just as cold.

"Back when I was in college, it… it looked like the Apollo 13 astronauts wouldn't… get back to Earth. All these scientists… stayed up all night… working at their desks. It was on TV. They'd dedicated their lives… to the jobs they were doing. When the capsule finally splashed down… when the astronauts were safe… All those scientists. They… they were crying when they stood up. Then they… started cheering."

The wind pushed across the church, and I could hear the barred owl calling from across the valley.

"And it was like that whenever I… watched a symphony orchestra. The musicians… dedicated their lives to music. The beauty of what they created… always got to me.

"I felt the same spirit when… I was coaching. Acts of courage. All the time. Kids… being heroic. The ones who… overcame fear. The ones… who pushed themselves. That was beautiful, too.

"The kids. The… the musicians. The scientists. It was…

inspirational. It was like… like they were part of something bigger… than themselves. They helped me understand… that we're all part of a journey. And when I understood that, I… felt the spirit even more. The longer I thought about it, the… the more I saw the journey as *sacred*."

There was another gap in the clouds, and the moon cast the shadows of trees across the cemetery.

"Humanity keeps… learning about itself. Keeps learning… about the universe. We were hunting… and gathering. Scavenging. Barely… surviving. A few thousand years later, we're… unraveling the human genome. Discovering… how the universe works. The journey we're on… It has a direction. Like there's something… *behind* it. We move away… from ignorance. We eventually understand… what we wonder about.

"You should… look past the villains. Past the people who… bring darkness to humanity. Watch people… who bring light to the journey. People who shine. Find people who… make the world better. Through their kindness. Through… their *grace*."

The breeze faded and picked up again.

"The journey of humanity should… unify humanity. Orthodox believers… they say they believe that God created humanity. They should understand… that God also created the journey. And the teachings of Jesus… they bring light to the journey. Believers should understand that… the human journey is sacred. How can they… see destroying the journey that God created as… as serving God?

"And those who… don't believe in God, should understand… the *meaning* in the journey. They… should know they're part of something… larger than themselves. Part of something… *magnificent*. But if… the human journey… comes to an end, wouldn't that… make their lives meaningless?

"We're part of... the fabric of the universe. We're... made up of the same molecules. Same atoms. Same particles.

"How is a discovery about the universe... How is that different... from the universe understanding itself? We're part... part of the universe. Isn't the human journey... part of the universe becoming aware... of itself? Of... of understanding *itself*? Isn't awareness woven into... the fabric of the universe? The same way... that matter is? Couldn't awareness... be part of God?

The dogs we heard earlier started barking again, and Mac stopped talking. Their barking got louder and more intense. Then they were suddenly quiet. A few seconds later, we heard the sound of gravel being crunched by tires. Mac touched my arm, and we slipped into the woods behind the church.

37

An old pickup truck was coming up the road with its lights off. It pulled in and stopped in front of the church. We watched the beam of a spotlight move along the wall where we had been standing, and then sweep across the cemetery.

I could barely hear Mac's whisper. "That… That could be an off-duty… deputy sheriff. Or it might… be whoever is after us."

I imagined the sound of the truck door opening, and the guy in the beret coming toward us. I would take a deep breath and aim at his pelvis. The gun would flash and recoil, and he would crumple to the ground. But nobody got out of the truck. A couple of minutes later, whoever it was drove away.

The breeze was stronger, and after we walked back up beside the church, we put our arms around each other again. Mac leaned against the wall, and I felt him take in a deep breath. "You're thinking if… if that was one of them in… the truck, we could've… could've killed whoever it was. We… could've taken the truck and… gotten out of here."

I held Mac closer. His breath didn't feel as warm as it was before.

"But people… maybe they know that a couple of … hikers are

missing. Whoever was in the truck could've… been trying to help us. Or maybe it… was just some hunter. Out spotlighting deer."

It felt like the wind was blowing through the church. And blowing right through me. "I'm ready for… more of your sermon."

He reached behind him and slid the palm of his left hand across the wall of the church. "Well, I'm almost done."

He was quiet while he gathered his thoughts. "The human journey it… it should guide *everything*. Including… politics. There's so much darkness… in campaigns. In elections. Lies. Greed and… racism. Hatred. Cruelty. But there needs… to be light. Truth and… knowledge. Tolerance. Love and… grace. That's what sustains the journey.

"I learned so… much about the journey from… my friend, Palani."

I'd read about Palani in Mac's book.

"One night we were… out on a pier. Looking at the ocean. Palani… He said we were given brains so… we can know God. He said when… when Galileo used the brain God gave him, he discovered that the Sun… didn't revolve around the Earth."

The barred owl called again from the direction of Short Mountain. The call was answered by another owl closer to the church.

"But Galileo… what he discovered went against church… church doctrine. He was tried and… and convicted. Palani said that the truth… leads to God. And religion should always… be in search of truth. That we can begin to *understand* God… through what God has created. That God speaks to us through… the beauty and elegance of nature. From atoms and particles to… stars and galaxies.

"Ches, the journey… the human journey… can help us find God. That might be… the purpose of the journey."

The breeze gathered up into a gust of wind that disappeared almost as soon as it came. Mac was still between me and the side of the church. The front of my body was cold, but my back was almost numb. My spine was ice. When he felt me shudder, we changed positions. I touched the concrete wall with the palm of my hand. There was still a trace of warmth where his back had been.

He started rubbing my arms. "We should've… swapped places sooner."

"Didn't want to… to interrupt your sermon."

I needed Mac to keep talking. "What about the people… who come to this church? What… would they think about your sermon?"

"A few might want to… take me out and stone me. But most of them… they'd clench their teeth. Try… to be polite. When people… Once they get a story in their head, they… don't want to hear anything they don't already believe."

Another wave of wind came through the trees and blew across the church. He held me a little closer. "When we… when I took you where… where my parents are buried. You said… that you wouldn't bring a child into… such a troubled world.

"Last summer, back here in… this graveyard, I was telling you about… your ancestors. But I didn't talk about… their lives. How most of them… lived in poverty. What they… survived. Wars. Plagues and famines. All kinds of… of misery. But they… they all had children. Every… one of them. They passed along… as much love… As much light as they could.

"The world has… has always been broken, Ches. But your ancestors… everybody's ancestors… They kept going, and they're… they're all still part of the journey.

"Maybe you'll… never have children. If you don't, you've… you've already brought more than your share of… light to the journey. You brought light to… to those girls you taught. To Sam and... John Armstrong. To Cash. To Carla. To... to me. And to people I don't... know anything about.

"But there's something I see as... clearly as I've ever seen anything. If you... ever do have a child, you'll... pass along all the goodness and grace... that was passed along to you. And through that child, the... light you inherited will... keep illuminating the journey."

Then he paused for effect. "Or... not."

I couldn't see his face, but I knew he was smiling.

38

When it started getting light, we walked back to the edge of the woods. The breeze was picking up a little. We got behind a large beech tree, and held each other again. A car with squeaking brakes pulled in and parked about a half-hour after the sun came up. A couple got out and went inside the church. They were probably in their mid-sixties. The man was wearing a blue suit, and the woman was wearing a brown coat over a purple dress with white polka dots. A few minutes later, another couple showed up in an older-model pickup truck. They must have been in their eighties.

We'd planned to wait for more of the congregation to show up, but Mac picked up his walking stick. We had to get out of the cold. We walked out of the woods and went around to the front of the church. As soon as we opened the door, the four people inside stopped talking.

The younger of the two women came over to us. When I looked into her eyes, I didn't see any warmth. "You folks look chilled to the bone."

Mac spoke up. "All the way down to… our toes. We've been out all night. My name is… is Mac Allen, and this is my daughter. We drove… drove over from Nashville yesterday."

I wondered how much he was going to tell her.

"We got turned around when… we were out in the woods. Then it got dark. Her mother has family from… from out in this part of the county. We came to… take a look around."

The woman introduced herself. "I'm Hattie May Bogle. Pleased to meet you, Mr. Allen."

The other three came over and spoke, and Mrs. Bogle turned toward me. "Now, who are your people, Hon?"

"Well until a… few months ago, I didn't… know that I had family from here. My grandmother was Susan… Susan Pearcy. She was a… was a Cunningham before she got married, and people called her…"

The older man, whose name was Mr. Cook, had straightened up a little. "You're grandmother was Sugar?"

"Yes sir."

He was studying my face. "Sugar married Jimmy Pearcy. He was a cousin of mine. I wasn't but nine or ten when he died. He'd take me fishin' every now and again. My mother – she and Sugar grew up together. I believe Jimmy and Sugar had a couple of girls. Let's see. I think one was Ruth Lynn, but… I don't recollect the name of the other one."

"My mother's name was Lucy May."

Mr. Cook, who must've been a big man when he was younger, had a serious look on his face. "J.A. Buford takin' her away from Sugar like he did…"

Mrs. Bogle touched his arm, and he caught himself. "Well, we're in church, so I'll jus' say that some folks reap what they sow."

I smiled at him, and he smiled back. I could see the kindness in his eyes. Before he said anything else, Mrs. Bogle put her hand on his arm again.

She had a stern expression on her face. "Pardon me, Miss, but I need to borrow Mr. Cook."

The people who I assumed were Mrs. Bogle's husband and Mr. Cook's wife had moved down near the front of the sanctuary, and they were joined by their spouses. There hadn't been time for the building to get warm, but at least we were out of the wind.

I moved a little closer to Mac. "Are… we okay?"

"I think so. But there's… Something's going on."

The sanctuary was small. It had a low ceiling, concrete walls, and a linoleum floor. At first we could only hear pieces of what was being said, but then their voices got louder.

Mrs. Bogle was staring at Mr. Cook. "I can go down and call him from Flossie's. It won't take five minutes. He's kin. We can't jes…"

Mr. Cook was shaking his head. "Yes we *can*. As soon as Donnie Lee finds out, he'll head straight up here. Then what? Jus' let him take 'em off? Jus' leave it up to *him*? *No mam*. That girl is kin, too. And even if she wadn't… I won't lie for Donnie Lee, and that's what I'd end up havin' to do."

Mrs. Bogle was about to say something else, but the door opened and a man and a woman came inside with their two children. Mrs. Bogle turned her back on Mr. Cook. Then she went over and sat down in a pew by herself.

Mr. Cook walked back to where Mac and I were standing. "I believe I should take you where you need to go. If we leave right now, I can prob'ly make it back before the preacher gets started. My truck… well it's old, but it's got a *mighty* fine heater."

We walked out and got in the truck. It was still warm. I sat between Mac and Mr. Cook. My hands started shaking a little, but I slid them under my legs. My fear had gone to my hands. I wondered where my anger was. I mostly felt numb. I wasn't struggling anymore. I was letting go. I was starting to drift downstream. It was like watching a movie.

When Mac told him that we'd left the car in Young Hollow, Mr. Cook just nodded. I noticed his hands when we were pulling away from the church. Even at his age, they were thick and powerful. I could smell chewing tobacco, but I didn't see any. We were going in the opposite direction from our car, but Mac didn't say anything.

Mr. Cook finally spoke up. "Last night we was over at the school to see our great-granddaughter. Her class was havin' a little Christmas play. There was talk about somebody bein' lost on the mountain. I reckon that was you. And I reckon you woulda made it back before dark if you was the only ones up there."

Mac understood what Mr. Cook was asking him. "Yessir, that was us. Somebody got on our trail. We didn't… didn't know what would happen if they caught up with us. It took some doing, but… well here we are. I guess we kind of bumped into a wasp nest."

Mr. Cook was quiet for a few seconds. "Wasn't your fault."

Mac spoke slowly. "We appreciate you helping us out. Maybe there's something we can do to… to ease the situation. Maybe we can… you know, keep things to ourselves for a little while."

Mr. Cook glanced over at him. "Givin' things time to smooth out would… Well, we'd be much obliged."

Mac reached across me, and they shook hands. The truck was getting warmer.

Mr. Cook's eyes were fixed on the road. "We're goin' to your car, but I'm takin' the long way around. About them boys that was trackin' you. They started callin' themselves the Copperheads, and they ain't worth a damn. Not a one of 'em. It's the drugs and the liquor and everything else. It's poisoned their lives. There's a few that's been to prison, and a couple that's still on parole. They ain't supposed to have no guns, but they run around up there like it's about to be World War Three.

"Their ringleader is Donnie Lee Buford. Well, Donnie Lee's about half-crazy and he's full-on mean. If the law finds out he's been messin' around with guns, he'll go straight back to jail. You know, fer breakin' his parole. He got off light the last time, considerin' what he done. Like I said, he's half-crazy. And even though he's also half-stupid, he does know the woods. Always had a nose fer trackin'. My son's house is down this road a bit. When we show up at your car, we might want to have some company along. That sound okay?"

It was like Mac was talking about the weather. "Sounds fine. And like I said before, we can keep things to ourselves for a little while. But unless somebody straightens those boys out..."

Mr. Cook was slowly nodding his head, but all he said was, "Yep."

Mr. Cook's middle-aged son, Jesse, had two adult sons of his own, and they followed him outside. They all had thick shoulders and big arms. Three grim-faced, rough-looking farmers in overalls. They got into a battered truck that had rifles on a gun rack. They drove ahead of us. After a few minutes, when I was pretty sure my hands wouldn't shake, I put them in my lap.

Mac's car was right where we'd left it. It hadn't been vandalized. I wondered if I was about to see Donnie Lee. I wasn't angry, but he needed to die. Mac gave his keys to Mr. Cook's son. He walked to the car and looked around for a few seconds. Then he stretched and yawned. His voice was deep and strong. "Hey Donnie Lee? It's Jesse Cook. These folks ain't aimin' to cause no trouble. So you can jus' leave 'em be."

He waited for a response, but there wasn't one. "Well alright then. I guess I'll be seein' you around."

And that was it. Jesse got back in his truck with one of his sons. His other son got in Mr. Cook's truck, and Mr. Cook rode with Mac and me. We followed the pickups back toward Woodbury.

We hadn't gone far before Mr. Cook looked over at Mac. "Did you see anybody, you know, where we was just at?"

Mac was staring out the window. "Just the one over in the brush pile."

Mr. Cook looked over at me. "How about you, Miss?"

"I didn't see anybody."

Mr. Cook was tapping his fingers against one of his knees. "Me neither. Not till we was leavin'. He was over in the sinkhole. My eyes ain't what they was, but I believe it was Donnie Lee."

We followed Jesse to the home of one of his cousins. Mac called Elinor and I called Carla. They had been talking to an investigator at the Tennessee Bureau of Investigation. After dark, when she hadn't heard from me, Carla called Elinor. They were both worried, but they waited a couple of hours before they called the TBI. A little after sunrise, they got a call from Mac's friend at the Bureau. Mac's stolen cell phone had been tracked. It was still in Cannon County.

Carla must have been beyond tired. "I have two questions. What in *God's name* were you and Mac doing way over there? And why in *the hell* didn't you call us?"

"It's a long story. I'll tell you all about it after we've both gotten some sleep."

We thanked Mr. Cook and his cousin, and before we left Woodbury, I looked over at Mac. "Are you okay to drive?"

He shrugged. "Okay enough. I've been in training. Thanks to my prostate, I've been sleep-deprived ever since I turned seventy."

There was a question I had to ask. "About what you told Mr. Cook… When are we going to tell somebody what happened?"

He didn't say anything at first. "I'm not sure. We can't just go over and tell the Cannon County sheriff. What if one of his deputies is involved? My friend at the TBI will want to know what's going on up here. They might want to infiltrate Donnie Lee Buford's band of criminals. It's probably better to just keep everything quiet for a while."

When we were on our way out of town, my hands started shaking again. I closed my eyes, and before long I was floating above Sugar Tree Knob. I woke up when I heard Mac crying. I didn't let him know I was awake. My anger flowed back from wherever it had been, and I started thinking about killing Donnie Lee again.

We got to Carla's, and Elinor was waiting for him. When I hugged Mac goodbye, I had to make myself let go.

39

I was exhausted when I went to bed. I fell asleep, but after a few minutes, I woke up. My heart was racing. I was cold. I dozed off again, and the next time I woke up, I was angry and I was sweating. I kicked off the covers. My anger was turning into a headache. When I fell back to sleep, I was imagining that I was killing Donnie Lee Buford. Killing him when he came up to the entrance to the cave. Killing him when he got to the rockfall. Shooting him in the pelvis up on Sugartree Knob, then taking off my belt and choking him from behind until he stopped struggling. Until he was still.

I stayed in bed until the next morning. I didn't get up until I heard Carla in the kitchen. She made breakfast, but I barely ate.

She started her interrogation before I sat down at the table. "My *darling* daughter. Out *all* Saturday night with her father. Slept from Sunday afternoon until Monday morning. What set of circumstances could *possibly* account for such an *unusual* state of affairs?"

She looked out the window and rubbed her fingertips together. "This is Carla trying to come up with an answer. If only her daughter would give her aging – and yet *still beautiful* mother – a clue."

I imitated her, rubbing *my* fingertips together. "My still-beautiful mother needs to show just a *little* more patience. All of her questions will be answered, but first I need to check with Mac."

Carla eyed me. "Ah yes. It's always wise to get your stories straight."

I'd planned to wait until Christmas morning to tell her about her Cannon County family, but there was no way I could hold her off for that long. Mac said he wasn't feeling too bad, and we decided that he'd come to Carla's the next afternoon.

I started to call Cash six or eight different times, but I never finished dialing his number. I was too messed up to talk to him. He would hear the darkness in my voice. He'd think it was because of the way I felt about him. And I was afraid I'd hear indifference in his voice. I was afraid he might tell me he was moving on with his life.

I tried to focus on what Mac and I were going to tell Carla. It was happening fifteen days early, but I wanted Tuesday afternoon to be like Christmas morning. Along with her attempts to embarrass me, Carla had a knack for coming up with the perfect gift. And it was usually something I didn't know I wanted. No matter how hard I tried, I'd never given her anything that came close to what she gave me. That was about to change.

Mac showed up late the next afternoon. I still felt like I was watching myself in a movie. I wanted to be all the way in the moment, but I wasn't. He knew I was struggling. All he could do was kiss me and give me a hug. We followed Carla into the living room. Logs were burning in the fireplace.

After she sat down on the sofa, she looked at Mac and then at me. "Well, here we are. Let the revelation begin."

Mac was carrying a binder. He sat down, and I went over and stood by the fire. I started by telling her about Sherry Smith. Then I played the recording of what she said about Sugar and Jimmy. Carla stared at the floor while she was listening to what happened to her when she was a baby.

She didn't say a word until she asked me to play the recording again. There was a look on her face I'd never seen before. She finally held up her hand and took a deep breath.

She glanced over at the binder in Mac's lap. "And there appears to be more."

Mac was studying her expression. "Do you want to take a break? We don't have to do this all at once."

Carla shook her head. "No, no. I... I might as well hear everything right now."

After Mac told her a little about what Cannon County was like when she was born, I played her the recording of what Miss Warwick had told us. Carla heard more about Sugar, and about her dark-skinned great-grandmother, Eula Cunningham. And along with everything else Miss Warwick said, Carla heard what happened to J.A. Buford, the man who had taken her away from her mother.

She looked at me when the recording was over. She was struggling to keep herself together. "I'm not sure how much more..."

I tried to reassure her. "Well, that was the last recording."

Carla just nodded. "I thought I might need an intermission, but maybe I don't."

Mac didn't say anything. He just handed her the poem about Short Mountain. She read it in silence. After she finished, she put it beside her on the sofa.

Mac opened up his binder. "And this is some family history I put together."

He handed her the binder, and she seemed to relax while she was reading about the Pearcys and the Cunninghams, and about the other families Mac had researched. Then, after she asked a few questions,

I started telling her about going to Short Mountain to look for the rock.

I went through just about everything that happened, but I didn't tell her what we'd found. Or how much I wanted to kill Donnie Lee Buford. Carla was staring into the fire. She heard about the cave. And about our escape. And about freezing outside the church. The longer I talked, the colder I got. My hands were shaking a little, but I kept them behind me, closer to the fire. When I was finished – after I told her about Mr. Cook and his son and his grandsons helping us – she looked up at me.

I squeezed my right hand into a fist to keep it still. Elinor had taken the film from Carla's camera, and had it developed. There was one especially good photograph of the rock. It had been enlarged and framed. I went over and reached behind the sofa. I handed her the photograph, and when she saw Sugar's name and Jimmy's name, she finally broke down.

It was the first time I had ever seen my mother cry.

40

I went back to Woodbury two days later. I made myself go. I didn't tell Mac or Carla what I was doing. Miss Warwick was where she'd been before. Upstairs in the courthouse, looking through old documents. I told her that Mac and I had found the rock and the cave. And after I told her about the names that were written on the ceiling, I told her about being hunted. I told her how it wouldn't have happened if we'd taken her advice. If we hadn't gone to Short Mountain by ourselves.

She got out of her chair and went over to a window. "I have a great deal to tell you, but I'm not sure where I should start."

She talked about Pomp Kersey, but it was mostly what Mac had already told me. Then she talked about Sugar Tree Knob and about Mr. Cook. She had known him for over eighty years. She'd always heard that his father was one of the men who killed J.A. Buford. Even though they were cousins.

She stared out the window, and then she looked at me. "You were told that Donnie Lee Buford was one of the men who was tracking you. I'm sure that's right. I had a niece who taught Donnie Lee in school. He has always been troubled. His family was troubled. J.A.

Buford was Donnie Lee's great-grandfather. J.A. had been dead for more than forty years when Donnie Lee was born, but when the apple fell from the Buford family tree, it might as well have dropped straight down and buried itself in the dirt."

J.A. Buford's granddaughter had gotten pregnant with Donnie Lee when she was fourteen. J.A.'s daughter, Pearl, had raised Donnie Lee. He was in and out of jail when he was in school, but he didn't go to prison until he was in his twenties. He had almost beaten a woman to death in the western part of the county, and before his trial, he raped a woman who lived in Woodbury. He was convicted of both crimes, but he only served five or six years of his sentence.

Miss Warwick talked about his drug abuse, and said that he and a few other men had organized a small local militia. Donnie Lee lived alone in a trailer north of Woodbury. When Mac and I were on our way to Young Hollow, we must have driven right by it. He did odd jobs around town, and he cut grass in the summer.

But there was one thing about Donnie Lee Buford that people admired. He had been devoted to his grandmother. Pearl died back when Donnie Lee was a teenager, but unless he was in jail, he visited her grave every Sunday afternoon.

Miss Warwick said the cemetery was four miles outside of Woodbury. I wanted to see it before I went back to Nashville. I hadn't planned to stop, but I changed my mind when I got there. It was right beside the road, between a cornfield and a patch of woods. Except for an old barn at the far end of the field and a farmhouse a quarter-mile or so away, the area looked uninhabited. Somebody – probably Donnie Lee – had kept the cemetery from getting overgrown. It had about sixty gravestones.

It wasn't Sunday, but there was an outside chance that Donnie Lee would show up while I was there. I wasn't afraid. I got out of the car, and some crows started cawing from the lower end of the cornfield. I felt like I was being watched. I looked over at the woods, and a small hawk was staring at me from the lower branch of a tree. I was pretty sure it was a male. Back when I'd gone bird watching, one of the girls had told me that male hawks were usually smaller than the females.

I finally found Pearl Buford's grave at the far edge of the cemetery. The hawk watched me the whole time I was there. By the time I left, I knew what I had to do.

The situation couldn't stay like it was. I had to start sleeping again. I had to get myself under control. I felt like I was surrounded by thorns. Poisonous thorns. It wouldn't be long before I'd need to see a shrink, or check myself into a psych unit. There was blood in just about every thought I had. Donnie Lee Buford would keep staining my life until I did something about it.

That night, lying awake in my bed, the only thing that calmed me down was planning how I would kill him. It wouldn't be hard. He had no idea who I was. He didn't know that I wanted him dead, and I knew where he lived. It would be dark when I went by his trailer. I'd make sure he was alone. Right before I knocked on his door, I'd think about Mac crying in the car.

Donnie Lee would want to know who was there. I'd say I was lost and that I needed directions. When he heard a woman's voice, he would relax. He would open his door, and then it would be over. He wouldn't stalk anybody else. He wouldn't hurt anybody else. He wouldn't rape anybody else. It would probably be like stepping on a roach.

But by the next morning, when it was getting light, I had imagined Donnie Lee as a child. A child who was crying. Who Donnie Lee became was probably inevitable. He would stain my life whether I killed him or not.

I was back in the cemetery three days later. Early on a cloudy Sunday morning. I guessed that Donnie Lee went out drinking on Saturday nights. He was probably still in bed. It wasn't that cold and I still didn't feel afraid, but there were times when I shivered. There were times when I had to open and close my fingers to keep my hands from shaking. The crows were calling from across the cornfield. I walked to Pearl's headstone, and I put an arrangement of flowers – amaryllis and baby's breath – on her grave. Then I left. No trucks or cars went by while I was there. I didn't see any people. I didn't see the hawk until I started to drive away. He was perched across the road in an oak tree.

I went back the next Sunday morning, three days before Christmas. There was a little sun, but the clouds were starting to build up. I was exhausted. The crows were across the field, and they cawed from time to time. The flowers I'd left the week before were in the dirt, about fifty feet from Pearl's marker. I put a bouquet of roses and lilies in the same place I'd left the amaryllis and baby's breath. Donnie Lee would've been puzzled the first time he found flowers. When he came back and found a fresh arrangement, his curiosity would turn into anger. Just before I got to my car, I heard the hawk. He was flying a couple of hundred feet above the cemetery.

On the last Sunday of the year, I made another trip to Cannon County. It was fairly warm, but it was raining. I hadn't gone to bed the night before. My fatigue was as deep as a grave. I felt like a ghost when I was walking toward Pearl's headstone. Crows were grazing at the far end of the field. If the hawk was watching, I couldn't see him. If Donnie Lee wasn't still asleep in his trailer, maybe he was hiding across the road. Or watching from the woods.

The stems of the flowers from the week before were twisted and mangled. Withered rose petals and the dried-up remains of lilies were all over the ground. It looked like Donnie Lee had picked up the bouquet and beaten it against a tombstone. Then he must've torn at the stems and thrown them down. I put a fresh bouquet of narcissus and carnations where I'd left the other flowers. I stood in front of the headstone for a couple of minutes in case he was watching. There was thunder in the distance.

I decided that if Donnie Lee didn't show up the next week, he probably wasn't coming after me. If he didn't come after me, he might not attack anybody else. I told myself that even if he drove up in a truck or came out of the woods, as long as he kept his distance, I wouldn't kill him. But if he came toward me – if he got too close – I was ready.

When I visited the cemetery the next Sunday, the sun was out. I was carrying a box of pansies I'd bought a couple of days earlier. It wasn't cold, but I was wearing my heavy coat. It had big pockets. The old bouquet was right where I left it, but it had been burned. All that was left were blackened stems and scorched petals.

I saw a wisp of cigarette smoke at the edge of the woods. Donnie Lee was watching. He wanted me to know he was there. I had a pistol in my right coat pocket. Abused child or not. Troubled child or not. It wouldn't matter. I wondered if killing him in self-defense would make me feel any less guilty.

I turned my back to the woods. The air was still. I'd hear him if he was coming. I put down the box of pansies and pulled a trowel out of my left pocket. I kneeled beside the charred petals and stems. The ground was soft. Then the crows started cawing all at once. I looked behind me, but Donnie Lee wasn't coming.

I watched the crows fly off toward the ridge beyond the field. They lit in a big tree. Their cawing got louder, and the hawk finally swooped out into the open. The crows darted and dove at him while he was flying over the field. They were still harassing him by the time he flew out of sight.

After I finished planting the pansies, I scraped the dirt off the trowel. The flowers looked better than I thought they would. I put the trowel and the plastic containers into the box from the nursery. I wanted Donnie Lee to know I was leaving. But before I left, I stood up and put my left hand on Pearl's tombstone. And I said a prayer I hadn't planned to say.

When I looked over at the edge of the woods, the cloud of cigarette smoke was still hanging in the air. I made sure he could hear me. "Donnie Lee? I just said a prayer for you. Maybe it's not too late to make your grandmother proud. From what I've heard about Pearl, she deserves that."

I made sure that I waited a little longer than Jesse Cook had waited. "All right then. Now I'll be going."

I wasn't coming back. It had been long enough for the militia to be infiltrated, or at least be under surveillance. Donnie Lee was the law's problem. If he hurt somebody else, it was on them.

A couple of days later, while Carla was taking a nap, Mac and I were packing up some of her Christmas tree decorations. He was sitting on the sofa next to a box of ornaments. That's when I told him that I'd heard him crying when we were on our way home from Short Mountain. That I'd driven back to Woodbury to see Miss Warwick. That I'd been going to the cemetery. I didn't leave anything out. He didn't ask any questions. He just kept staring into the fireplace – and digging his fingers into the sofa.

He was trying to decide what to say. "I'm having a hard time thinking about you being out there. Being alone. If I'd known what you were up to… I thought you were seeing a therapist. Or maybe you were off somewhere meditating."

He was studying me. "I should've told you what I've been doing. I've had a couple of meetings with the TBI. I told them as much as I could about what happened. An informant should be in place pretty soon, but I think he's still trying to work his way inside."

He wrapped an ornament in tissue paper and put it in the box. "I was never sure if… you would've killed Donnie Lee. I mean if that's what it came down to. Now I know. When you were in that cemetery… The position you put yourself in… You didn't give yourself a choice. Thank God it didn't come to that. Killing Donnie Lee… That could've killed who you are.

"I know we'll talk more about this later on, but there's something I'll go ahead and tell you. It was something I kept saying to myself when we were in the cave. And later on, when that truck rolled up to the church with its lights off. It's from a writer named William Saroyan. I don't remember exactly how it goes, but it's pretty close to this. 'If the time comes in your life to kill, then kill… and have no regret.'"

41

Cash hadn't heard from me in over two months. I'd given up on calling him, but I finally finished the letter I'd been trying to write. Instead of mailing it, I decided to give it to him in person. I wanted to be looking into his eyes when he saw me. I was ready, or as ready as I'd ever be, to find out if we were going to be together.

I hadn't been online since Mac and I went to Short Mountain, and I checked to see if John had a wrestling match. He was supposed to start off in small-market venues, but he was scheduled to wrestle in St. Louis that Saturday night. It was a tag team match. *The Iowa Farm Boy* and *the Haitian* against *Splitter* and *the Borneo Beast.* But it was the main event – *Calcutta Ice* against *Brando* – that would bring in the fans.

I left the day before the match. The trip from Nashville was four hours of inner voices and out-of-focus images. Images of all the different ways Cash might respond when he saw me. Images of Sam and John joking with each other and laughing. Sam wasting away. John turning hard. Dominoes falling forward and backward in slow motion. *Brando* and Donnie Lee lurking in the shadows like pit bulls. Lurking like death.

I drove straight to the arena. I said I was a reporter covering *The Iowa Farm Boy*. I asked for directions to the gym where the wrestlers worked out. It was only ten minutes away. John wasn't there. But *Brando* was. I didn't see him at first. He was doing bench presses with so much weight that the steel bar was sagging. When he sat up, he looked right at me. He kept staring at me, and after a couple of seconds, he opened his mouth and ran his tongue along his half-open lips.

Before I left, I got directions to three other gyms in the vicinity. John was in the first one I checked. I looked through a window before I went inside. Cash wasn't around. John was across the room, cooling down from his workout. He saw me before I had a chance to sneak up on him.

He didn't seem surprised. "Hey, Ches. It's been a while."

"I know. There were some… I've been working through some things. Where's Cash?"

John had gotten more muscular, but he wasn't nearly as big as *Brando* was.

"He was in New York yesterday. You know, for the TV deal he's been working on. He went to sign some contracts. He's busted his butt to get everything done. I could see how much he missed you, but he's had plenty to keep him busy. He's supposed to meet me here tomorrow morning.

John leaned back and stretched his shoulder. "I might as well bring you up to speed. He's worried that I'm pulling the trigger too soon, but… Well, this seems like the right time. *Brando* has really sped things up. Every time he hurts somebody, I move up the ladder. That's how come I'm wrestling tomorrow night. But it's just a popcorn match. I'll almost pin *Splitter*, and after the second near-fall, *the Borneo Beast* will knock me down from behind. Then he'll take me out with a slingshot suplex. Will you be there?"

"I wouldn't miss it."

The tone in John's voice changed a little. "Cash says *Brando* is only one step away from the big time. We're on the same card, but he doesn't know I exist. It needs to stay that way until I get my shot. I'm doing everything I can to get ready. Gymnastics. Mixed martial arts. All of it. And I've been watching him. Studying him. I'm seeing how to push his buttons. It doesn't take much to make him mad. Not with all the roids he takes."

He looked at the clock on the gym wall. "I've got to get moving, Ches."

Before he left, I told him I wanted to surprise Cash. He promised he wouldn't say anything.

I didn't sleep much that night. I wanted to be waiting when Cash got to the gym. If I was looking into his eyes when he first saw me, I'd know how he felt. About me. About us. I wouldn't blame him if he pushed me away. If that's what happened, I'd have to do the best I could. It would be on me.

The next morning, I made it to the gym before Cash showed up. I stood just inside the front door of the gym and waited. He drove up twenty minutes later and parked across the street. I was only three feet away when he pushed open the door. Then his arms were around me. I didn't need to see the look in his eyes, or give him the letter I'd written. We didn't want to let each other go.

We were still in front of the door, and I didn't say anything until somebody needed to get past us. I already knew the answer, but I went ahead and asked the question. "So we're good?"

He let me go and smiled. "I don't know. Maybe."

"Maybe?"

He pretended to play hard to get. "Yeah, maybe. I don't hear from you for *two months*? But *maybe* there's a way to make it up to me. I guess we'll just have to figure something out."

John got there right after that, and I stayed with them while they had their meeting. The TV deal had been signed, and the first check had been deposited. It was for six hundred and fifty thousand dollars.

But Cash had a concern. "If this coronavirus thing ends up spreading everywhere, it could stop us in our tracks. I've been asking around. It could turn into an epidemic. If it does, a lot of the country – wrestling venues included – might shut down for a while. All we can do for now is keep on moving. And hope for the best. I was afraid the network would start playing wait-and-see, but they didn't. Whatever might be coming… I guess it isn't on their radar yet."

After John talked him through the moves he would use in his tag team match, Cash told me about *Brando*. He'd gotten a contract with a management company. Things had gone okay at first, but *Brando* was a loose cannon. They didn't mind him being crazy, but he was too crazy.

They wanted him to connect with the TV audience. He'd started walking around with a microphone before his matches, talking to people in the crowd. And *Brando's* agent had come up with the signature move he was using to end his matches. It was called the Falling Angel. The other wrestler would be lying near a corner of the ring. He'd pretend to either be semiconscious or out cold. *Brando* would climb up and balance on the turnbuckle. He'd close his eyes and look up like he was praying. Then after he spread out his arms like they were wings, he leaned forward and fell on top of his opponent.

But they were having a hard time controlling *Brando*. He had a really short fuse, and if something set him off, he punished whoever he was wrestling. His agent took him to see a therapist, but he only went once. The management company would've probably dropped him, but he was drawing bigger and bigger crowds.

John had an appointment with a chiropractor, and Cash and I went to a little diner down the block. We showed up between breakfast and lunch, and we got a booth in the corner. We were looking at each other when I reached across the table and took his hand. I didn't know where to start.

He spoke up before I said anything. "Ches, I wasn't sure what I was supposed to do. I thought I'd hear from you after a couple of weeks. After a month, when I hadn't heard anything… I almost called you a hundred different times. The little voices in my head kept reminding me about the women who walked away from me. The ones I told you about. The voices kept saying I should've known that… that you and I wouldn't end up together.

"But every time I pictured you… When I thought about the way it is when we're together… That kept me hoping. And there were other voices. They said that something could've happened to you. That you might be in trouble. If you needed me and I wasn't there I… I couldn't live with that. If I wasn't talking myself out of calling, I was talking myself out of flying to Nashville. But you said you needed some space, so I ended up leaving you alone."

I started to say something, but he held up his forefinger. "I've been kicking myself for the last two months. I should've already told you this. Whether we ever touch each other again or not. Whether we end up living together, or getting married, or not… If you don't want children… I still want you in my life. And I want to be in *your* life. For the rest of our lives, no matter what."

There were tears in his eyes, but he kept himself together. So did I. Barely. I usually cried when I was that happy, but I couldn't let myself lose it. Not until I told Cash why I pulled back. Not until I told him what happened. Not until he knew how much I'd wanted him there. Not until he understood how glad I was that he *wasn't* there. Not until he knew what Short Mountain had done to me. He stayed quiet while I was talking, but I watched the anger building up in his eyes.

He didn't say anything until I was finished. "I've been thinking that there's too much to say. But… maybe there isn't as much to say as I thought. When I think about you in that cemetery… If… If I'd known what happened on that mountain, there would've been one less worthless cracker in the world. You wouldn't have ever gone to that cemetery. But then… Then you couldn't have done what you did. I guess I was right to stay away. You… really didn't need me."

I shook my head. "You're wrong. I've *always* needed you. Needed *you.* It would've been different if you were there. It just turned out that you weren't. I got lucky. Mac and I got *lucky.*"

I'd told him about the rage I felt, but I hadn't told him everything. He didn't know that I wasn't afraid when I was in the cemetery waiting to see whether Donnie Lee would come for me. That I wasn't afraid of the future anymore. Maybe I was just numb. Maybe the fear would come back. Maybe it wouldn't. I quit thinking about it.

Cash was busy, and we ended up having a late dinner. And we spent the night together. I'd never let myself be that primal before. I was somebody else. I didn't think about that either.

And I wasn't worried about the match John was about to have. It was pretty much scripted out. He was prepared for what he had to do. John and I had lunch the next day. A few hours before he would be wrestling in front of the biggest audience he'd ever seen. But he was pretty laid back. I asked him if he was as relaxed as he looked.

He just shrugged. "Yeah, I'm okay. As long as I stay focused, I should be fine. I'm teamed up with *the Haitian*. He's been around for nine or ten years. He's a nice guy, and we get along really well. The other team, *the Borneo Beast* and *Splitter*, are friends of his. We've all worked out together a few times, and they've been teaching me some techniques. The stuff we'll be doing is pretty routine."

He was eating pasta, and the bowl was still half-full when he put down his fork. "*The Haitian* – his real name is Phil… He said to eat a light lunch with plenty of carbs."

He shook his head. "Phil has told me a lot about *Brando*. Guess what his real name is. Albert Wald. Most of the wrestlers stay away from him, but he has *a lot* of fans. A few weeks ago, right after a match, he groped a woman when she tried to keep him from hitting her husband.

"And right after that, guess what the management company did? They signed him to a big contract. Then they hired a consultant to market him. To build up his brand. But once *Brando* gets in the ring, he likes to freelance. He likes to hurt people."

I remembered wanting to talk John out of going after *Brando*. But that was before Donnie Lee Buford came along. John wouldn't be able to move on with his life until he dealt with *Brando*.

"And you think you're ready?"

"I better be."

42

Cash had a meeting and some calls to make. He left me a ticket. He said if he didn't see me before things got rolling, he'd find me after John's match. I thought about taking a nap, but I ended up going to the arena. I was there an hour and a half before the opening match. My seat was on the second row, about thirty feet from the ring.

A few fans had already started to trickle in. They looked pretty much like the people I'd seen in Des Moines. I thought about Big Momma. If she wasn't on her way to see a match somewhere, she was probably home in a recliner, getting ready to yell at her television.

I was watching the wrestling fans when I heard some murmuring and a little scattered applause. *Brando* had walked out onto the floor of the arena. He was wearing jeans and a tight T-shirt, and he went to the opposite side of the ring. A few fans gathered around him, and he started signing autographs. But when more people converged on him, he climbed up into the ring. He began examining the ropes, but he was just getting away from the fans.

He moved around the perimeter of the ring, and the people who wanted an autograph moved with him. The closer he came to me, the more I slumped down in my seat. My section was still mostly empty, and there wasn't anybody to hide behind.

Brando was looking down at the fans who had crowded into the area between the seats and the ring. Then he glanced up. Our eyes met the same way they'd met the day before, when he was working out. He winked at me, and after he hustled across the ring, he slipped between the ropes. He was gone before his fans could cut him off.

The seats around me gradually filled up. I was surrounded by a few VIPs and a lot of hardcore wrestling fans. The husband and wife sitting in front of me were both wearing red, white, and blue T-shirts and matching red baseball caps. *Brando's* face was on the front of the T-shirts, and on the back was *Let's Go Brando*. WWBD, which stood for *What Would Brando Do* was on the caps.

After I sat through three lackluster one-on-one matches, the lights went down and the music got loud. The next event was a women's tag team match. The announcer sounded like he was introducing the most consequential females on the planet. Along with being athletic, all four wrestlers were fairly attractive, which was probably what it took to make it all the way to the top. Their match went on for about fifteen minutes. The crowd was paying attention, but they weren't yelling and screaming.

Two more matches came and went, and then it was time for John to wrestle. The lights went down again, the music got loud again, and two spotlights illuminated John and the *Haitian* as they made their way toward the ring. The couple in front of me – the *Brando* fans – didn't seem very interested until *The Iowa Farm Boy* took off his overalls. That got their attention. The husband seemed to admire John's physique as much as his wife did. It looked like the crowd felt the same way. He was the handsome, All-American boy. With a great body.

The match started, and there seemed to be more cheering when John was in the ring. Toward the end of the match, when he bounced off the ropes and turned a flip on top of *Splitter*, there was a cheer from some of the crowd. He took a few hard falls and got a cut on his chin, but he seemed to be okay. It was pretty clear that the fans liked him.

After one other somewhat entertaining match, part of the crowd – including the couple in front of me – started chanting "*Brando. Brando.*" The lights finally went off, and after ten or twenty seconds, a laser show exploded and deafening music filled the arena. There were some cheers when *Brando's* opponent, *Calcutta Ice*, was introduced. He got into the ring, and the emcee asked him a few questions. *Calcutta Ice* was big and muscular, but he was shy and he seemed like he was in over his head. John had told me that *Ice* was an ex-Marine from Hawaii, and that his real name was Reuben Kahale.

Then *Brando* made his grand entrance. Light glimmered from the sequined American flags that decorated his robe, but there were boos mixed in with the cheering. He jumped up onto the apron, and then he grabbed the top rope and vaulted into the ring. The emcee started to ask him a question, but *Brando* took the microphone. He looked down at the section next to the one where I was sitting.

After he scanned the audience for a few seconds, he pointed at a Hispanic couple sitting three or four rows from the ring. "Hola. Buenas noches."

A guy with another microphone was standing near the couple. He walked over to them, and they both stood up.

Brando grinned at the woman, who was smiling and looking at herself on the jumbotron. "Do you speak any English?"

She took the microphone and nodded. "Yes. Of course."

Brando looked at the crowd. "And she doesn't even have an accent. Okay, I have a question."

"All right."

"What's your husband's name? Is it Pedro?"

She shook her head.

"Then it must be Juan. Or Manuel."

She shook her head again. She was still smiling, but not as much as before.

Brando looked puzzled. "Well, I'm pretty sure his name isn't Jesus. Your hombre sure doesn't look like the son of God to me. He looks more like a drug smuggler. Or a rapist. Or maybe a murderer."

There were some boos, but they were quickly drowned out by cheering. The woman wasn't smiling when she sat down.

His next victim was a young man sitting near the Hispanic couple.

Brando eyed him for a few seconds. "And what do we have here? Let's see. I'm guessing you're from… Man, it's hard to tell. Somewhere in the Middle East?"

The guy stood up and took the microphone. "I was born in Iraq, but I came to America when I was five."

Brando stared at him. "Well, at least you aren't wearing a suicide vest. I sure hope nobody lets you on an airplane."

There were more boos, and the cheering got louder again.

Brando looked out at the audience. He seemed frustrated. "You know what would be nice? It would *really* be nice to talk to an actual *American*."

Then he turned in my direction and pointed at me. "What about you, sweetness? Are you an American?"

I stood up, and the man came over and handed me the microphone.

One of my suitemates in college was Ukrainian. I'd always been taken by her accent. "I am begging your pardon?"

That took *Brando* by surprise, but he kept talking. "I asked if you're an American. But it sounds like that's a *huge no*. So here's a different question. Is there... Do you have a man in your life?"

There was some laughter from the crowd. The couple in front of me turned around and looked at me. They both had big smiles on their faces.

"A mon? No. I have no mon."

"Do you want one?"

"Why are you ask? Are you knowing one?

There were some whistles from the crowd.

Brando was trying to figure out if I had insulted him on purpose. "Yeah, I am *knowing* one. You're *looking* at one."

I leaned forward and stared at him. "And you... you can satisfy woman?"

He licked his lips and leered at me. "I know how you can find out."

There was laughter from the *Brando* fans in the audience, including the two in front of me.

I pretended to be thinking. "Then I have question."

"What's your question, sweetness?"

I stared into his eyes. "You have much the beeg muscles. My cousin in Ukraine, he also have the beeg muscles. But for him to have the beeg muscles, he must take the steeroid. And soon his... How do you say... his *bollocks* – they shrivel up like prunes. And with the women, he is no longer a mon, he is like... like *leetle boy*."

Brando glared at me, and the laughs and the boos and the cheers got louder and louder. I handed back the microphone and sat down. The people in front of me were confused. They turned around and looked at *Brando*.

He was glaring at me. I stared back at him and yawned. He finally bellowed at the crowd. "This Ukrainian *dike* doesn't know a man when she sees one. How about you? Do you know what a *man* looks like?"

The crowd started chanting, *Let's go, Brando. Let's go Brando,* and he bellowed even louder. "Do you want to see a *real* man?"

The crowd erupted and he walked to the middle of the ring. But before he handed the microphone back to the emcee, his eyes swept the arena.

"Well if you want to see a man, an *American* man – get ready. You're about to see one."

Then I got a text from Cash. All it said was, "As soon as the light show starts, get out of there. Leave through the main entrance. We'll be out front in a car. I'll flash the lights."

I wasn't worried about some *Brando* fan bothering me, but Cash was. Right before the match, there was a brief laser display, and the chant built up again. I stood up and walked outside, but I took my time. I understood why Cash, or John, couldn't come to get me. Whenever they had their match, *Brando* had to think that John was just another wrestler.

When I got in the car, Cash was laughing. John was smiling and shaking his head. They both gave me fist bumps. The match had just started, and they were watching it on Cash's tablet.

Cash could barely talk. "Bollucks like a little boy? *Damn*, Ches. You sure didn't do *Ice* any favors. If he was smart, which he isn't, he'd say he has a stomach virus, and run back to the locker room. *Brando* is flat-out angry. He's fixing to dish out some *serious* pain."

We sat in the car and watched *Calcutta Ice* try to survive *Brando's* fury. *Brando* knew the match had to last long enough to satisfy the fans. He let *Calcutta* perform the moves they'd scripted, and he made sure that *Calcutta* could keep wrestling. But after fifteen minutes or so, he had waited long enough. He lifted *Calcutta* over his head, and slammed him down onto the canvas. *Calcutta* was still conscious, but he was dazed. When *Calcutta's* manager jumped into the ring and tried to stop the match, *Brando* threw him through the ropes.

Then John looked over at me. "And here comes the Falling Angel."

Brando climbed up and balanced on top of the turnbuckle. The crowd was chanting *Let's go Brando*, and the camera zoomed in. He looked up, and his face filled the jumbotron. He closed his eyes, and as the camera was zooming out, he pretended to pray and then he spread his arms apart. His eyes stayed closed when he started falling forward, and he landed on top of *Calcutta* with all of his weight.

The chant filled the arena, but instead of pinning *Calcutta* right away, he got up and walked around the ring. I thought he would glance over to see if I was still in my seat, but he just kept walking. He finally stopped and looked down at *Calcutta*, who was trying to get up. Then he raised his arms and let out a roar, and after he dove on top of *Calcutta* again, he pinned him.

Brando stood up and went to where the emcee was sitting, then he reached through the ropes and grabbed the microphone. He stared at *Calcutta*. All he said was, "Welcome to America. Now get the hell out of my country. Go back to wherever in the hell you came from. And don't ever come back."

There were boos from the crowd, but the cheers got louder until they drowned them out.

43

Cash and I didn't talk much after we got back to the hotel. Not about the children he wanted, or about anything else. We chose lust over talking. We wanted to move in together. But on my way back to Nashville, I had too much time to think. I wanted to focus on how good life would be with Cash, but questions rolled in like a series of squalls. If I didn't have kids, would he resent me? And if I went ahead and had children, wouldn't I resent *him*?

I should've been happier. I had Cash in my life, and I still had Carla. I had Mac and Elinor, and three half-brothers and a half-sister I was getting to know. I told myself that I could do whatever I wanted with my life. Make documentaries. Dig into family history. Whatever. But how would life be after Carla was gone? How many more years would I have with Mac?

I still didn't want to bring children into the world, but something had changed. Ever since I got back from Short Mountain, I hadn't been as afraid of the world that was coming.

I wasn't intimidated by the future, but I still dreaded it. I saw it closing in every time I turned on the news. The coronavirus was rushing in like a tidal wave. America was crumbling. And I hated what human stupidity was doing to the planet. The world was falling apart, but if I ended up having children with Cash, I told myself that I'd face what I had to face. We both would.

And something else was on my mind when I was on my way back to Nashville. I wondered if I was turning into a psychopath. There was a coldness inside me that hadn't been there before. I'd felt cold when I was waiting to see if I'd have to kill Donnie Lee. I felt the same kind of cold when *Brando* stared at me in the gym. And when I was staring back at him before his match with *Calcutta Ice*.

I didn't see any way that John could beat *Brando*. John's strategy was to provoke him, and I saw what happened to *Calcutta Ice* after I embarrassed *Brando*. I saw what happened when he got mad. I didn't want to spend the next few weeks looking for a way to kill *Brando*. Or figuring out how to hurt him so much that he wouldn't be able to wrestle. But if that was the only way to keep him from destroying John, I'd do what I had to do.

I got back to Nashville in the middle of the afternoon. I'd been thinking about the coronavirus, and how to keep Carla from getting infected.

As soon as I mentioned it, she gave me a facetious smile. "Oh *my*. Were you listening to one of those *demonic* liberal radio stations on your way home? Pandemic, pandemic, pandemic. It's just another way to attack our wonderful and *brilliant* president. He says not to worry. He's promised that as soon as the weather gets warmer, the coronavirus will *miraculously* disappear. He keeps saying that he's a genius. That means he *must* know what he's talking about, so *Hallelujah!*"

I was reluctant to tell her about the situation with John and *Brando*, but she'd be suspicious if I didn't say something about where I'd been and what I'd been doing. It was hard to tell her anything without telling her everything. And *everything* included how much I'd wanted to kill Donnie Lee. After I told her about my trips to the cemetery, she just stared at me.

I saw the worry in her eyes. She was trying to figure out what she should say. Or do. She wanted to buy some time, and she shook her head and smiled. "Ches. The love of my life. I changed your diapers. Told you bedtime stories. Taught you how to ride a bicycle, and to drive a car. Now you're all grown up, and look at you. My *darling* little girl has become an aspiring *murderess.*"

I should've known that she'd turn to humor. When I told her what I said to *Brando*, it took her a while to stop laughing. But that wasn't the end of it.

She pulled herself together and tried to look serious. "I may have a solution to your *Brando* problem. What if I go to his next match, and I arrive a day or two *early*? I could *seduce* him. I would just need to get him alone. And find a witness who could testify that we were alone *together*. After I killed him, I could claim that he had raped me. *No wait.* I could claim that he had *seduced* me, and then discarded me in some *scurrilous* manner."

She put the back of her hand against her forehead. "Yes, your honor, I went to him – a grief-stricken, *abandoned* woman. Then he shamed me. Of course, I had to shoot him."

Carla broke into a big smile. "I can see the headlines now. 'Heroic Woman Murders Wrestler.' 'Romance-Gone-Wrong Ends in Tragedy.' Or how about this? 'Wrestler Killed by Jilted Femme-Fatale.' The possibilities are *endless.*"

She stood up and walked across the room. "I could have such *fun* with the detectives. Think about the expressions on their faces when I described, *in pornographic detail*, what was done to me. If one of the detectives was sufficiently handsome, I suppose that I'd have to submit to *any* additional interrogation he had in mind. And when I finally disclosed my *dire* medical condition, I would be released."

After Carla finished her performance, she asked more questions about John and *Brando* and Cash. The more I told her, the more curious she was. I made dinner, and by the time she went to bed, there wasn't much that she didn't know.

Even though I needed to be open with Mac, I didn't want him to be involved. If he *did* get involved, there was a chance that I'd have to protect him. The situation was too complicated already, but after what we'd been through together, I couldn't just shut him out.

A couple of days later, I picked him up and we drove to Woodmont Park. We'd already driven past some of the places I'd read about in his book, but I wanted to take a walk with him around his old neighborhood.

As soon as Mac got out of the car, I thought he'd start showing me where things happened and where things used to be. But he just glanced at me and smiled. "So, what's on your mind?"

"How do you know there's something on my mind?"

"Because something always is."

He was right. "Well, I actually have *two* things to tell you."

While we were walking through what was left of the place where he grew up, I gave Mac a pretty good explanation of how things stood with Cash. I thought he'd want to talk about it, but he was waiting to hear what else I had to say. Then I went through the whole situation with John. When I told him what I said to *Brando*, he almost stopped walking.

All he said was, "Good Lord."

We were approaching three big houses. He said they'd been built on the field where he played football and baseball when he was a boy. They were right across the street from where he'd learned to play basketball. But the backyard court had been destroyed, and a house was there.

Mac slowed down and looked at me. "How worried are you about *Brando*?"

"Very. He's twisted. He's a… beast. I might need to protect John."

I could see how concerned he was. "Are you thinking about killing him? Like you thought about killing Robbie Lee?"

I made sure he saw me smile. "Yeah, but just when I'm trying to relax."

Mac was breathing harder than usual, but we kept walking. I finally got around to asking him how he felt about what happened to us on Short Mountain. I should've asked him sooner.

He took a while to answer. "Well, I've got a couple of things going on. I've wanted to tell you everything, but… I don't want things to sound any worse than they are."

I touched his arm. "Well now that I'm worried, why don't you give it to me straight up?

"Straight up? Okay, how should I say this? For me, the last month has been a lot like… like the way things were forty-three years ago."

Back in the mid-seventies, there was a period when Mac was in danger. When he didn't think he would survive.

"I can fall asleep okay, but I wake up after a couple of hours. And I wake up worried. About a lot of things. About what's happening to my body. About what's happening to the country. About everything."

I thought he might be telling me he was sick. "What's *happening* to your body? Are you…"

"I just mean I'm starting to feel like an old man. Five months ago,

I turned seventy-two. You know what I did? I went out and ran six miles. But now, after what happened, my legs are getting weaker. I can feel it. And my balance is off. I keep thinking I'll get stronger, but I'm not. And time seems different. It's flying by. I'm starting to realize something, Ches. The faster I seem to be falling, the closer I am to hitting the ground."

I didn't know what to say.

"I understand that I'll end up as a broken-down geezer. I mean if I live long enough. You should've seen the guys at my last high school reunion. Maybe it's finally my turn. Maybe this is just the way it is. And there's everything else. I used to think that most of the people I know saw the world pretty much the same way I do. I was wrong. I know plenty of people, people I've known most of my life, who see something totally different.

"There's a presidential election coming up, and the issues are complex. But people I care about, people I *love*... All they want are simple explanations. But the world *isn't* simple.

"Some even want to argue about evolution. It's a lot easier for them to believe that a divine being up in the sky created everything just the way it is. That *the great being in the sky* only created heterosexual males and females, and that everybody else is a sinful deviant. They're sure that all the teachings they grew up believing are true, and that science is some sort of vast, evil plot against their religion and their political beliefs. And it's not just that they're wrong. They're *sure* they're right. They believe that one plus one equals three, and it's turning this country upside down.

"So here's the way things are, *straight up*. I wake up in the middle of the night, and I worry. America is breaking down even faster than I am. And if America, with all the advantages we have... If we turn into a nation ruled by half-baked ideas and ignorance and superstition, how much of a chance does the rest of the world have?

"I was born right after World War II. I came to believe that America had saved the world from becoming a global dictatorship. I came to believe that America, when it is at its best, is the guardian angel of democracy. And that democracy is a guardian angel of the human journey. If America comes crashing down… It'll be like dominoes."

He took a deep breath. "I try to remind myself that the United States was in trouble way before we went to Short Mountain. But after that… That's when I really started to feel it. If half of the people in this country can't distinguish propaganda from reality, maybe that means that democracy has taken us as far as it can. Maybe the only hope is for an enlightened oligarchy to take over. So I lie in the dark, and I think about how things will be for you and the rest of my family, and for the kids I used to coach.

"Fewer species will be around and the planet will be hotter, but I tell myself that humanity will survive whatever is coming. Billions of people will be dead, but after a few generations, we'll end up on our feet. Then people will go back to believing that one plus one is two. But then what? Won't some other demagogue come along and get people to believe whatever they're told all over again?"

He stopped walking. "Maybe I should've kept all that to myself, but you probably knew it already."

44

Three weeks later I got a call from Cash. In ten days there would be a big wrestling event in Cincinnati. John was finally getting his shot at *Brando.* One on one. It was the main event. *Brando* had been scheduled to face a veteran wrestler called *The Great Johann,* and after *Johann* claimed to be injured, two or three others had declined. I didn't think that John would get his match that soon. Neither did Cash.

I could hear the tension in his voice. "I kept hoping that *Brando* would get banned, or get hurt. Or get killed. But here we are. And there's no way to talk John out of it. He's on a mission. I guess my job is to stick to the plan. Just make sure everything gets captured on video."

I went ahead and told Carla and Mac about the match. They'd know about it soon enough anyway. I decided that all I could do was be ready if John needed help. I would only intervene as a last resort. John couldn't keep carrying around his vengeance. He needed to get it over with.

I checked with Cash every day. The coronavirus outbreak was spreading, but the Cincinnati matches were still on. Cash told me that he and John would understand if I didn't want to expose myself to getting sick, but he knew I'd be there.

It wasn't very far from Nashville to Cincinnati, and I got there the day before the match. But romance wasn't in the picture. When Cash wasn't preoccupied with all the preparations he was making, he was worrying. We ate with John in the hotel restaurant. He was quiet and focused, but as far as I could tell, Cash and I were more worried than John was. Cash got a call toward the end of the meal.

When he went outside to talk, John looked across the table at me. "It means a lot that you're here, Ches. I just wish I could keep you from worrying."

"Is it that obvious?"

He broke into a smile. "The expression on your face... You look like you're on your way to a hanging. I know what you think you're about to see. It's true that I'll spend a few minutes getting my butt kicked. I'd tell you to close your eyes for the first five or ten minutes, but you wouldn't do it. But whatever you see, it won't be as bad as it looks."

I rolled my eyes. "So it won't be real blood?"

He was still smiling and he shook his head. "Oh, it'll be real blood all right. *My* real blood. And if you hear me yell... Well however much pain there is, I'll mostly be mad. I can take a punch. I'll look like I'm out of it, but I won't be. It's all part of the plan. You'll see."

John put his napkin on the table. "Have you ever seen *Butch Cassidy and the Sundance Kid*?"

"Only seven of eight times."

"Then you know the scene where Butch is about to fight that giant, Harvey Logan."

I nodded. "Yep."

John leaned back in his seat. "And you remember the dialogue?"

I remembered.

He did a pretty good job of delivering Butch's line. "Listen, I hate to be a sore loser. But if I'm dead when it's done, kill him."

My line was much shorter. "Love to."

He looked at me and started laughing. "But don't get the wrong idea. I'm not going to kick *Brando* in… in the *bollocks*."

Cash came back to the table. John and I thought he was talking to one of the camera operators he hired, but he'd been on the phone with a sound engineer. There would be microphones in each corner of the ring. Everything that happened during the match, and just about everything that was said, would be recorded.

After John finished his meal, he went up to his room. But Cash wasn't ready to turn in. He ordered a bottle of wine, and we stayed at the table.

We lifted our glasses, but I couldn't think of a toast.

Cash finally clinked his glass against mine. "Here's to survival."

I was restless all night. I wasn't sure I slept at all, but when I got up the next morning, Cash had already taken a shower and left. The hotel had a decent exercise area, and I had a good workout. I didn't want any breakfast. I tried to watch a couple of movies in my room, and then I went out for a run. I couldn't stop thinking about what *Brando* would do to John. In the middle of the afternoon, I talked to Cash. He said it wouldn't be a good idea to get to the arena too early.

I showed up twenty minutes before John wrestled. I felt like I was going to the execution of somebody I loved. But the execution wouldn't be at a prison. It would be at a circus.

I was wearing the same coat I'd worn when I left the flowers at the grave of Donnie Lee's grandmother. Even though I hadn't eaten anything, I felt like I might throw up. It was hot and I took off my coat. Underneath I was wearing a T-shirt with an American flag on the front. Just like the girl in the bar had been wearing when Brando terrorized her in Sioux City. None of the *Brando* fans seemed to notice the flag.

I felt like I was sleepwalking. My seat was on the third row of the VIP section. Cash was about sixty feet away. He was standing beside the ring, talking to a woman with a camera on her shoulder. When the match before the main event was over, the crowd started chanting *Let's Go Brando*. There was an answering chorus of boos. I wanted to put my hands over my ears, but I closed my eyes instead.

Then the lights went down. *Eye of the Tiger* started playing, and lasers and spotlights swept across the crowd. When John was introduced, the announcer didn't sound like he was heralding the arrival of a last-minute sacrificial lamb. His voice got deeper, and he proclaimed the arrival of *The Iowa Farm Boy*. The spotlight focused on John as he walked to the ring and climbed through the ropes. He was wearing a straw hat and plain blue overalls, and underneath the overalls, he had on black and gray tights. The amplified music compensated for the muted response of the crowd.

But when *I'm Proud to be An American* started throbbing through the arena, the crowd roared. *Brando* was introduced, and the crowd started chanting again. It sounded like John was up against everybody in the arena, but he looked relaxed. He just stood in his corner and waited. He looked like he could've been standing under the big tree in his front yard.

The red, white, and blue sequins on *Brando's* robe sparkled with reflected light. Then he took off his robe. He was wearing red tights, and his arms and thighs and upper body looked even more massive than usual. He glowered at John when they met in the center of the ring. *Brando* was half a head taller than John, and he must've outweighed him by at least 100 pounds. John smiled and reached out to shake hands, but *Brando* shoved his hand away and grabbed the microphone. He looked out at the crowd and started walking around the ring. The spotlight was on him. I was pretty sure he couldn't see who was in the audience.

He held up his hand, and the chanting stopped. "We got any Americans in here tonight?"

The crowd roared.

Brando looked unimpressed. "*I said*, have we got any *Americans* in here?"

The roar got louder.

"Well, I guess we do."

He stared at John. "How about you, boy? Are you an American?"

John kept smiling. "Yes sir. I'm from out in northwest Iowa."

Brando was unimpressed. "Northwest Iowa? I've heard there's a lot of queers out there. And *liberals*. Is that right?"

They'd probably rehearsed that part, but John went off-script. He acted like he wasn't sure what to say. "There must be some, but… Well, I'm not sure just how many."

Brando clenched his jaw. He was probably trying to figure out why John had forgotten his lines. He leaned in and said something to John. When John said something back, *Brando* got angry. John was still smiling, and he tried to shake hands again. When *Brando* dropped the microphone and stormed away, John looked surprised. Then he picked up the microphone and looked over at *Brando*. "Well, good luck, sir."

45

The match started, and *Brando* stayed with the script. At first. But it wasn't long before he started getting rougher. His punches got harder, and he finally slammed John onto the mat so violently that most of the crowd stood up. John didn't conceal the pain, and after he stood up, *Brando* went entirely off-script.

John had staggered over to a corner, trying to recover from the body slam, and his back was half-turned to *Brando*. *Brando* moved in and took a vicious swing at John's head, but John ducked at the last second, and it was a glancing blow.

Brando was off balance, and John got out to the middle of the ring. *Brando* was snarling, but before he could charge, John shot in low and quick. He executed a move that I'd seen him practice with Sam. At the same time he drove into *Brando's* shins with his shoulders, he grabbed *Brando's* heels and pulled them toward him. *Brando* fell over backward onto the canvas.

John was up before *Brando* could grab him, and he got into his college wrestling crouch. Shoulders low, arms poised, and hands open. *Brando* charged as soon as he got up, but John sidestepped him and circled to the center of the ring. *Brando* turned to make another charge, but John shot in and grabbed his heels again, and executed another takedown.

At that point, *Brando* went berserk. He moved in and took a couple of wild swings at John. The crowd understood that *Brando* wasn't wrestling. He was fighting. John dodged and spun and kept moving, but he couldn't escape for long. *Brando* finally cornered him, and when he had John in his grasp, all John could do was try to cover his face with his forearms.

Brando wedged him into the corner, but John was able to get his head outside the lowest strand of rope. *Brando* threw punch after punch, and even though the ropes deflected most of the blows, blood was running from John's head and his face. There were boos from the crowd, but the boos were answered by *Let's Go Brando*.

The referee had been trying to intervene, and *Brando* finally got up and grabbed him. After he threw the referee out of the ring, he went back to beating John, who kept using the ropes for protection. Three or four guys working security came up, but the promoter waved them away. *Brando* still had John in the corner, and I reached into the pocket of my coat and got my Taser.

After I went through the ropes, I planned to come up behind *Brando.* As soon as I was close enough, I'd shoot a charge of electricity into the base of his skull. Then I'd do it again. I stood up and started toward the ring. The guys from security didn't notice me. They were all standing together watching Brando. Before I slid through the ropes, I glanced over at Cash. He was staring at me and shaking his head. Then he tilted his head toward the ring and gave me the okay sign.

I didn't understand. I stayed where I was for a few seconds, and then I went back to my seat. The crowd kept chanting until *Brando* finally stopped beating John. Then he stood up and went over to the announcer. As soon as *Brando* got a microphone, he started walking around the ring. He was breathing hard and his body was covered with sweat.

He looked down at Cash. "In a minute you can pick up what's left of your *farm boy,* and take him back to Iowa. And after that, you can head on back to Kenya, or Nigeria, or wherever you came from."

The crowd cheered, but there were a few boos.

Then *Brando* looked at the crowd. "It's gettin' late. I guess it's time for me to finish this up. Anybody ever heard of the Falling Angel?"

The crowd roared and he threw down the microphone. John was lying on his stomach. He looked like he was barely conscious. *Brando* grabbed John by his feet and started dragging him around the ring. He went from corner to corner, and Cash just kept watching. *Brando* ended up a few feet from where he started. After he turned John onto his back, he positioned him sideways, six or eight feet in front of the turnbuckle. While he was climbing up the ropes, "*Let's Go Brando. Let's Go Brando.*" echoed through the arena.

By the time *Brando* stood up on the top rope, John had stopped moving. The chants kept getting louder, and as *Brando* balanced himself, a camera zoomed in. After he looked up and closed his eyes, he put his hands together and pretended to pray. When he spread out his arms and leaned forward, his head was up and his eyes were still closed. *Brando* didn't see John quickly reposition himself. He didn't see him raise his knees and brace his feet. He didn't see him cross his arms in front of his face.

When *Brando* fell on John's knees with all of his weight, he let loose a guttural groan. I heard it over the cheers of his fans. He rolled off to one side, and ended up on his back. His hands were just below his chest. He was gasping. John crawled over to the turnbuckle and pulled himself up. He was unsteady at first, but he held on to one of the ropes. He started wiping the blood away from his eyes. Most of the crowd had fallen silent. They expected John to go over and start beating *Brando*, and end the match with a pin. But he walked to the opposite side of the ring. Then he just stood there and waited.

Somebody sitting a few rows behind me finally yelled out, "Let's go *Brando*."

The chant started to build, and there was a roar when *Brando* sat up. When he saw John leaning against the ropes and stretching his back and his neck, he pulled himself up and let out a scream. Then he started toward John.

John was in a crouch. He faked like he was going for another takedown, but at the last second, he raised up and hit *Brando* in the base of his chest with a devastating punch. He hit him in the exact spot where he'd already been hurt. *Brando* staggered back and put his hands against his ribcage – just below his sternum. He roared at John.

John crouched down again, and *Brando* charged. As soon as he was close enough, John made a quick move and drove the heel of his palm up into the base of *Brando's* nose. *Brando* stumbled back against a turnbuckle, and blood started gushing from his nostrils. Then John moved in again and hit him with a straight punch to the throat.

The crowd stopped chanting. *Brando* was still on his feet, but he looked frozen. Along with the blood he was losing, his eyes were overflowing. He didn't see John moving in. It was like watching a matador approach a wounded bull. When he was a couple of feet away from *Brando*, he stopped.

There was a closeup of John on the jumbotron. After he looked up, he closed his eyes and put his hands together in prayer. It was five or ten seconds before he spread out his arms. He finally opened his eyes again and looked at *Brando,* and then, using all the force he had – he slammed his open hands against *Brando's* ears. The arena had gotten quiet enough for the crowd to hear *Brando* scream. He put his hands against his ears, and collapsed onto the canvas.

After John went over to the announcer and got the microphone, he started walking slowly around the ring. He glanced at *Brando*, who was writhing in the corner and holding his ears. When John looked at the crowd, there were a few catcalls.

"My name is John Armstrong. I really was raised on a farm in Iowa. My mother still lives there. My father and my brother… they're both buried not far from our house. A few minutes ago, I couldn't fight back. I was getting hurt. But I could hear all that chanting. Now it's *Brando* who can't fight back. I've seen your… your red caps and your red T-shirts. I have a question. *What would Brando do*? Should I go over and beat on him for a while?"

The arena was mostly quiet. "But beating a man when he's down… when he isn't fighting back. Or hitting him from behind, the way *Brando* tried to hit me… I wasn't raised that way. Is that how you people were raised? Is that the kind of families you come from?"

There were more catcalls. John shielded his eyes from the lights, and tried to see who was yelling. "I guess you're mad because you came to see *Brando* hurt somebody. But you got your money's worth. You didn't just see a couple of guys pretending to wrestle, you got to see a *real* fight. Is that the problem? Did that remind you that the rest of this is fake?"

He started talking a little louder. "That's right, it's *all* fake. You know *Brando*'s real name? It's Albert Wald. He's from Wisconsin, but his parents were born in Poland. Albert likes to hurt people. And you love seeing him do it, don't you? All he had to do was put on that fancy robe. And have some lasers and some music. And some politics and some anger. Then all of a sudden he was your hero.

"But there's more to it than that. Right? He's powerful. Does that make you feel powerful, too? Can't you see that what he does is evil? Can't you hear that what he says is *evil*? Do you know where he gets his power? He gets it from from *you*. If you stopped worshipping him, he'd be nothing. Just another bully. But you people… you just pretend that you don't see any evil, or hear any evil. And by not speaking out against evil, you become *part* of the evil. And you keep cheering him on. You keep telling yourselves what good Americans you are."

He walked over to *Brando*. He was in a fetal position, holding his ears. John bent down and held the microphone next to *Brando's* mouth. The crowd could hear him groaning.

"Hey Albert, you got anything to say to your worshippers? Aren't you going to tell them what they should do?"

John waited for several seconds. When he finally stood up, he looked around at the crowd. "I guess he's having a hard time talking. Or hearing. Or seeing. You know what? I'd say that your big, bad hero… he's pretty much done."

46

Cash and John went back to the locker room. I stayed in my seat while the crowd was leaving the arena. The security guards helped *Brando* to his feet, and then they moved him through the ropes and got him down from the ring. I stood up and started to walk in his direction. I wanted him to see the T-shirt I was wearing. I wanted him to remember the girl he had terrorized in the bar. I wanted him to know how pathetic he was.

But I forgot about *Brando* when I heard Carla's voice behind me. "Mac took me to breakfast this morning, and we realized something. Neither one of us has *ever* seen Cincinnati in March. And what's a trip to Cincinnati without watching some professional wrestling?"

Mac was beside her. He was smiling at me. "Elinor would've come, but she's in Arkansas visiting her sister. I thought you might need somebody to bail you out of jail."

Two men were standing a few feet behind him. It was obvious that he'd brought them along, but he didn't introduce them. They looked dangerous. It was a different kind of dangerous than the way Jesse Cook's sons had looked.

Carla was clearly enjoying herself. "I hoped that there might be enough time for me to work my wiles on that *brute*. Perhaps *drain* him of some of his energy. But there was so much traffic on the interstate. It's probably just as well that I got here late. *Brando* struck me as one of those slam-bang-thank-you-mam types."

Mac came over and gave me a hug. "We needed to be here, Ches."

I held him closer. "I know. Just in case."

Carla, Mac, and I went to dinner. Cash took John to a walk-in clinic to get checked out. His hands and forearms were swollen, and along with some cuts, he was diagnosed with a slight-to-moderate concussion. They got to the restaurant about an hour after we did. I had a lot of questions. The first thing I wanted to know was what he said to *Brando* right before the match. He was reluctant to repeat it in front of Carla, but she coaxed it out of him.

He started grinning. "I just said, '*Are your bollucks really shree-viled up… like a lee-tle boy?*' I guess I touched a nerve when I said that."

Mac asked Cash if he'd been worried about the fight getting stopped.

"Not after the promoter told security to stay back. After that, there were only two things to worry about. One was John. But after he got his head under the ropes, all I had to worry about was Ches. It would've messed up our film if she killed *Brando*. But if I'd known that all she had was a Taser… Well, that might've made some pretty good footage."

He hadn't noticed the canister of bear spray in my back pocket.

I asked John what he was thinking about before he closed his eyes. When he was about to rupture *Brando's* eardrums.

"Just that I needed to protect people from *Brando*. That I needed to end his career. I didn't plan on saying anything to the crowd, but they made me mad. I just said what Sammy would've said."

There was something else on his mind. He was only drinking water, but he lifted his glass. "So Sammy, here's to you. You were with me tonight. You've been with me the whole time. I don't know exactly where we're going, but we're going together."

The table was quiet until Mac stood up and held out his glass. "And here's to John. When Ches told me about you, I thought she was exaggerating. She didn't begin to do you justice."

Cash made the next toast. "I want to thank Carla, and Mac, for bringing Ches into the world." He was about to say something else, but he got emotional and he had to stop talking.

Carla decided to lighten things up. "I spent the first few weeks of my life in the shadow of a drunken *miscreant*. From there I went into the lap of luxury, which I found to be *highly* overrated. *Crushingly* sterile. *Numbingly* artificial. And now here I am. Once again *thrust* into a life of discord. Mac and our daughter, *hunted* by criminals. Coming here and watching a *bloody* brawl. A brawl arranged by my prospective son-in-law. So, I raise my glass to my next adventure, for which I can *scarcely* wait."

It was my turn. I kept it short. "This is to my parents. And to John and Sam. And to Cash."

After dinner, I went back to the hotel with Cash. He had the video of the match with *Brando*. We were tempted to watch John destroy *Brando* again, but it was a couple of days before we got around to it. In the end, he decided not to put the match on YouTube. Not with a pandemic on the way. Not without knowing when there would be more matches.

It was a good call. Covid swept in and submerged the wrestling league along with just about everything else. Early in the pandemic, John went back to Iowa to stay with his mother. By the time Cash came to Nashville and moved in with me at Carla's, I'd finished the second documentary about Sam and John. I wanted it to have heart, and it did. I called it *Brothers*. It concluded with the interview I had with John not long after Sam died. Even though watching it took a lot out of me, there would be another documentary. It would end with John's match with *Brando.* But it would be a while before I put it together.

The lockdown went from weeks into months. Carla refused to be isolated, but the rest of us were committed to keeping her well. The only time I didn't see her was when I came down with a mild case of coronavirus. Carla never got sick. Of course. More days than not, Mac and Elinor would come by to see us, or we'd go to their house in the woods. We did a lot of genealogy online, and Carla relished each discovery we made.

Her decline was gentle. And very slow. She had more good days than I expected. Her doctor put her into a couple of clinical trials, but the treatments didn't seem to have any effect.

She finally made an announcement. "I am no longer willing to serve as a guinea pig. It's time to have some *fun.* Except for my youthful *flirtations* with marijuana, I showed surprising restraint when it came to recreational drugs. But I am now fully prepared to *succumb* to temptation. I keep thinking about all the unused dopamine I have. I intend to use up every last *molecule.*"

I ordered Carla an assortment of cannabis gummies. Her favorite flavor was mango. Despite what she said about using up her dopamine, she didn't overindulge. I expected her to get sicker, but her health didn't seem to change. At least for a while. She arranged to meet Sugar's granddaughter, Sherry Smith, who had offered to drive down from Kentucky. Covid was still raging at the time, but after Carla ended her treatments, she stopped worrying about catching it.

Sherry wasn't worried either. She believed that the coronavirus was a hoax, and that vaccines were a government plot. I called Miss Warwick, who arranged for Carla and Sherry to meet at the Cannon County courthouse. Carla said that it was one more part of her farewell tour. She was determined to visit the Buford place, but she didn't like snakes – or ticks – any more than the rest of us. She decided to wait for a frost.

When a cold front moved through in the middle of October, Carla was delighted. "Even if it wasn't cold enough to drive all those *odious* little creatures into hiding, it must have discouraged them."

Carla was up at dawn on the morning of our trip to Cannon County. She couldn't wait to get on the road. The trees still had most of their leaves, and the countryside was glowing with color. When we got to the courthouse in Woodbury, Mac and I took her upstairs to meet Miss Warwick. And to finally meet Sherry, who insisted on calling her, Aunt Carla.

After we'd all gotten acquainted, Miss Warwick let us know that Donnie Lee Buford was back in prison. He and three other men from Cannon County had been arrested in North Carolina. They were planning to blow up an electrical substation, but an informant had alerted the FBI.

It wasn't long before we left to see the place where J.A. had taken Carla away from Sugar. Miss Warwick wasn't sure how long her strength would last, but she went along, too. She rode with Sherry, and we followed them out to the old Buford farm.

The house was still standing, but part of the roof had caved in. In a few years, there wouldn't be anything left. Mac brought along a walking stick for Carla. She said she didn't need it, but she took it anyway. Miss Warwick showed us the tree where J.A. had been killed, and then she went back and got in the car. She said her balance wasn't good enough to go inside the house.

Carla didn't seem to be getting tired. She could be stoic when she wanted to be, which was most of the time. We walked up onto the porch, and then into the house. The floor was sagging, but it hadn't rotted away. The air was heavy with the smell of deterioration.

We followed Sherry into the larger of the two back rooms. "Mama said she was in that little room across the hall. But this is where you were, Aunt Carla. In here with Sugar – and, you know, with J.A."

I imagined J.A. reaching down and ripping Carla away from the warmth and the softness and the nurturing she had known. But I kept my anger to myself.

When Sherry walked into the hall to look at her mother's room, Carla moved closer to me. She was smiling. "I know what you're thinking, Ches. You wish you could resurrect my *evil* stepfather, and then carve him into little pieces. But I think you should let all that go."

"Have you let it go?"

Carla was still smiling. "How's this for an answer? If I could go back all those years and be standing right here, I would have *wanted* J.A. Buford to take me. For you to be born, he *had* to do what he did. You were born out of pain. One way or another, we all are. And there's something else. If I'd been here later on, I might've tried to save J.A. when those men came to kill him. There's no telling what he went through when he was little."

After a few more minutes, Miss Warwick said she needed to get back home. We went outside, and she left with Sherry. But Carla wasn't ready to leave. She was staring off into the distance. "Is that Short Mountain over there?"

Mac was closer to her than I was. He could see where she was pointing. "Yep. That's it."

Carla didn't say anything. After a few minutes, she strolled back toward a ramshackle barn that wasn't far from the house. She went inside, and when she came back out she was carrying a length of old rope.

"I'll take finding this rope as a sign from God. All right, it's time for us to get going."

Mac shook his head. "Where are we going, *Aunt Carla*?"

"I'm *surprised* you have to ask. What would my farewell tour be without taking a look at the place where my parents expressed their *undying* love for each other?"

Mac and I exchanged glances. We didn't know if she could make it up to where the rock was, but we were about to find out.

47

We passed Donnie Lee's place on the way to Short Mountain. The door was wide open, and the trailer was lifeless and empty. We gradually made our way around to the one-lane road that led up into Young Hollow. Autumn foliage covered the mountain. Carla marveled at how beautiful it was. Then she said she was picturing her mother and her father. It was 1937 and they were riding a big gray horse. Sugar was behind Jimmy, and her arms were around him as they rode up into the hollow.

Mac parked where we parked the year before. He looked concerned. He was wondering how we could get Carla up to see the rock, and then back down to the car. The last time we were there, we started by traversing a fairly steep slope. We had circled around to a draw, and eventually made our way to the branch that ran down the hollow. Ten months later, we knew where we were going. We had a much shorter walk ahead of us.

Mac picked up his walking stick and led the way. I tried to take Carla's arm, but she pulled it away. She clutched her walking stick. She said that if she needed any help, she'd let me know. Then she handed me the rope she took out of the Buford barn. We moved up into the hollow, and it wasn't long before we came to the branch. It was barely running. We followed it upstream, and within a few minutes, we were looking up at the overhang.

Carla didn't take my arm until we headed up the draw that led to Sugar and Jimmy's rock. Mac was dreading the climb to the top of the bluff as much as I was. Carla leaned her stick against a boulder. Mac took one end of the rope, and I held on to the other end. He stayed in front, slowly picking his way along the lip of rock that led up the side of the bluff. I was behind Carla, keeping the rope tight enough to give her something to hold onto. She held on with her left hand, and kept her right hand against the bluff.

Mac stopped a couple of times to let Carla rest. She was breathing hard when we made it to the top, but she seemed to be okay. I expected her to go straight to the rock, but she kept her back to the mountain. Mac and I walked a little further away.

The warm October wind flowed up the hollow, and rushed against the leaves. I remembered the way the wind had sounded the year before. It had been frigid and lifeless when it moved through the skeletal trees of December.

Carla finally spoke up. "I've been trying to get myself in the right frame of mind. We won't be up here for long. I don't want to waste any time thinking about loss. I'm almost ready to talk to them."

I went over to her. "Do you want us to leave you alone?"

She put one arm around me, and then reached out and took Mac's hand. "No. I want you both with me."

Carla took a deep breath, and then she let go of me and let go of Mac. After she took a few steps, she saw the opening of the cave. Mac gave her his stick, and we followed her to Jimmy and Sugar's rock.

Carla leaned down and stared at the names of her mother and father. She handed me the walking stick, and slowly knelt down. Her hand moved across the surface of rock and moss, and she whispered as she caressed each name. I tried to hear what she was saying, but all I could make out was the love in her voice. Then she traced each inscription, letter by letter, with the tip of her index finger.

Another breath of wind floated up the mountain, and she started singing a lullaby. "Hush little baby, don't say a word, Momma's gonna buy you a mockingbird. And if that mockingbird don't sing, Momma's gonna buy you a diamond ring."

She took a deep breath. "I've been trying to imagine them. Being here. So young. Loving each other so much. Dreaming about the future. Not worried about what could come. Kneeling right here and cutting their names into this rock. Consecrating their secret place."

The wind came through again, and she moved her face down and kissed each name. Mac and I were waiting to help her get up, but she wasn't ready to leave.

She finally turned around and looked at me. "This is the place, Ches."

Then she pointed to the deep crack that ran down the surface of the slab. "This is the place. Right here."

Carla wouldn't have made it to the bottom without the rope. But after we got to the flat ground beside the branch, the rest of the walk was idyllic. The wind came up a little more, and red and yellow and orange leaves swept and sailed and tumbled all around us. Carla was exhilarated. She kept stopping to rest and look at the leaves. We took it slow, but she was worn out by the time we made it back to the car. She fell asleep before we got to Woodbury. She didn't wake up until we drove up to her house.

I tried to prepare myself for what was coming. I kept waiting for her to decline, but the next few months were as gentle as our leaf-carpeted walk down the hollow. Carla kept saying that everything was part of her farewell tour. Including when Cash and I married in April in Mac and Elinor's log house out in the country. John was our best man, and Elinor and Mac's children – my half-sister and my half-brothers – all came.

The ceremony was conducted by Cash's father, Reverend Caruthers. Mrs. Caruthers sat with Carla – and with Carla's fifteen-years-younger-than-she-was date. Just after we were married, I looked at Carla and Mac, and at Cash's parents. In a few years, they would all be gone. Unless I had children, everybody but Mac would disappear from the gene pool. And so would Sugar and Jimmy.

But that wasn't why I was more open to having a child, or children. Cash and I both loved kids, and we had kept talking about it. If it happened, we'd try to be good parents. We'd do the best we could to deal with what the world brought our way.

And what we thought the world would bring us – and everybody else – was an increasing degree of misery. There had been a presidential election two weeks after we took Carla to Short Mountain. Almost seventy-five million Americans had voted to return a demagogue to office. A psychologically unfit demagogue, who had displayed his lack of character, and his lack of intellect, throughout his entire time in office.

Tens of millions of Americans ended up believing precisely what they had been led to believe. Even after the Capitol was overrun at the urging of the leader they worshipped. Even with the emergence of absolute proof that he had conspired to overturn the results of a presidential election. Even after he was condemned by an unprecedented number of those who had served in his own administration. After all that, and with the scale of his malfeasance continuing to emerge, it was still one plus one equals three.

We didn't talk about it in front of Carla, but none of us – not Cash, not Mac, and not me – none of us saw how democracy could survive when tens of millions of Americans refused, without any proof of voting fraud, to accept the results of a national election.

I told Mac that what had happened to us might make a good book. That it could be a sequel to his other book. He said he had started a sequel years earlier, but that he hadn't worked on it for a while.

"I'm way too slow, Ches. I get sidetracked. Maybe you should give it a shot."

When I said I wasn't a writer, he looked at me and smiled. "Yeah, the idea of writing a book can be pretty *intimidating*. It takes a lot of determination. You'd probably just end up quitting."

I started writing the next week. I felt my way along at first. I liked the way Mac wrote, and I found myself emulating his style. After a few months, I was pretty much through. I could've put a lot more focus on my relationship with Cash, but I thought that might be a separate book someday. I wasn't sure if what I wrote was any good, but Mac and Carla and Cash seemed to like it. I told Mac that if I ever tried to publish it, I would probably use his last name. I felt more like an Allen than a Thompson.

Compared to what the country was experiencing, Carla's decline continued to be gradual. She slept more. Walked more slowly. Ate less. Had fewer good days. But she still laughed. She still enjoyed mango-flavored cannabis gummies. She even learned to talk like she'd spent her whole life in the wilds of Cannon County. Her favorite line was, "I'm hangin' on like a hair on a buddermilk biscuit."

Covid was finally losing its grip, but the world was deteriorating faster and faster. Russian troops threatened global stability by invading Ukraine and murdering civilians. More and more democracies were giving way to dictatorships. The planet was getting hotter. It had only taken eleven years for the population of the world to grow from seven billion people to eight billion. And, *of course*, that's when I got pregnant.

Carla not only lived to see the birth of her granddaughter, she lived long enough to see Little Carla smile. She lived long enough to feed her. To change her diaper. To bathe her. To play with her and make her laugh. To read to her and sing to her and watch her fall asleep in her arms. But in the early spring of 2023, not long before she turned eighty, a morning came when Carla didn't wake up.

Three days later, Mac and Cash and I, along with Little Carla, drove to Woodbury and then out to the west side of Short Mountain. Carla slept the whole way there. She didn't wake up when I took her out of her car seat, and she stayed asleep when Cash helped me slide her into the canvas baby carrier I wore in front of me. But as soon as we started up Young Hollow, she woke up. Right on cue.

It was as though she was hearing birds for the first time. The more she heard, the more she cooed and babbled and kicked her legs. Then a dove called from further up the hollow, and Carla got quiet and still. When she heard it again, she started looking around. Cash was quiet, too. He trusted me, but he was worried about taking her up the bluff. He knew we were in the place where Mac and I could've been killed. He didn't relax until we made it to the top.

After I nursed Carla, she became fascinated by the front of the T-shirt Mac had given me for Christmas. She kept trying to grab the blue and white image of the Earth that had been photographed above the surface of the moon in 1968. When I put her back in the baby carrier, I held the chrome cremation urn in front of her. She didn't notice her reflection at first, but as soon as she saw herself, her fleshy little legs started kicking again.

For a few seconds, Carla reached out and explored the urn with her palms and her fingertips. Then she tried to taste it. She stared at my hands as I unscrewed the top, and she was quiet while I poured her grandmother's ashes into the crack that ran down the length of the slab.

Then she was drawn to a thick patch of green moss growing on the rock. It was beside where Sugar and Jimmy had chiseled their names. I leaned down so Carla could feel the moss. As soon as she touched it, she let out a shriek and dug into it with her fingers.

When she finally turned away from the moss, I reached over and handed her to Cash. The birds were singing and she started cooing again. Mac was staring at me. His eyes were dancing and full of light. I breathed in all the life around me, and when I looked up past the mountain, Carla looked up, too. Clouds were moving in, but most of the sky was still clear. It was as blue and as beautiful as I'd ever seen it.